The Fox's Watch

M.A. SIMONETTI

ISBN: 1453613846
ISBN-13: 9781453613849

Library of Congress Control Number: 2010908256

To Marty, For making everything possible.

Acknowledgement

For all the love and support that I have received I would like to thank my very own 'A' list- Sister Ruth Delores for teaching me to read and then making me sit in the corner with a book to keep me quiet. To my mother, Marie, for taking me to the library three times a week while I was growing up. To G.M. Ford for teaching me the art of the first chapter. To Skye Moody for expecting me to finish a first draft. To Claudette Sutherland, editor extraordinaire, for her eagle eye and for understanding why Alana could not be a thirty-something. To my faithful readers- Jan Grazer, Helen Taylor, Gilbert Horst, Amanda Horst, Futsuki Downs and Claudia Campanile- for reading the story in its many stages. To Judy Weisman- for giving me the term 'Oh My Gods'. To Mort Weisman- for his valuable insights. To my writing group-Doris Schoenecker and Carol Busse-accountability is everything! To Julia Cameron-who I have never met- but her book 'The Artist's Way' changed my life. To Anthony Simonetti- my Darling Son- for his wicked sense of humor. And to my very own Patron of the Arts- my Wonderful Husband, Marty for loving me, believing in me and putting up with me all these years. Lo vi amo tutti!

Chapter One

My two o'clock appointment was losing her nerve.

Mia Kaplan sat hunched behind her steering wheel, eyes glued to the front door of Malibu's Lotus Day Spa. She was in serious danger of chewing off the tip of her thumb.

"Are you sure this is legal, Alana?" she whispered.

"Legal has nothing to do with it," I replied. "It's going to be an accident."

Across the parking lot, a red Maserati roared to a stop. Dimitri Greco, the director himself, emerged and sauntered into the spa for his weekly brow wax and nose hair trim.

"How can it be an accident if I wrote the note already?" Mia asked.

"Let me see the note."

She handed over a crumpled envelope. On the back she had written in fountain pen: *Apologies for scratching your lovely car. Please call 555-4210 so I may arrange for repairs. Mia Kaplan.*

"Excellent!" I said. "This is exactly the message we want to send. The envelope suggests you grabbed whatever was handy and the fountain pen suggests you are a woman of good breeding."

"Maybe this isn't such a good idea after all," Mia hedged.

Mia's innate sense of decorum is what led her to hire me in the first place. People contact me to help them establish new social connections. Some call me a matchmaker. Some call me a social coach. A few call me a pushy broad. Either way, I make a tidy little income by keeping society in order in Malibu. I know the local social circles and how they intertwine. I know the middle-aged bridge groups, the tight-knit golf buddies, the artsy nutcases, and the drinkers. If you are a single woman, I know the men. If you are married, I can get you and yours on the cocktail circuit. I can even find a nanny if you are unfortunate enough to need one. Suffice it to say, if you live in Malibu, have five thousand dollars in cash, and are willing to do exactly as I tell you, I'm your new best friend.

Normally the work is pretty straightforward. I meet with new clients, determine where they fit in and then introduce them around. Or send them away to a community with lower standards. Somewhere like Beverly Hills, for instance.

Mia's project required a little more creativity than usual. She had hired me to help her capture the attention of Hollywood's most elusive director. I do know Dimitri Greco, but sadly, he is not fond of me. Actually, his un-fondness falls just short of a restraining order. So, to put Mia face-to-face with the guy, I dreamt up a little incident that would force Dimitri to contact her. But she had to follow through for the plan to work.

"Dimitri Greco will be casting his film next week," I reminded her.

She concentrated on chewing her thumb.

"How long have you been trying to work with this guy?" I prompted.

"Five years," she replied, with her thumb firmly between her teeth.

"And how long have you hounded your agent to set up an interview for you?"

"Five years." Thumb slid out of her mouth.

"And you still haven't met him," I pointed out. "All you have to do now is put a little ding in his precious Maserati and Dimitri Greco will call you!"

She sat up straight.

I reeled her in with, "Or, you can spend the rest of your acting career cast as the grouchy mother-in-law!"

She turned on her ignition. "How hard should I hit it?"

"Just leave a scratch on the driver's side. Make it bigger than a dent but smaller than a gash. Call me when you hear from him."

I got out to leave as she put the car in gear.

It was best for Mia that there be no witness.

Chapter Two

My next appointment was meeting me at Coogie's restaurant in the Malibu Colony Plaza. I turned my car south on the Pacific Coast Highway (PCH). As usual, traffic slowed my progress.

The downside to living in this paradise is everyone else wants a part of it, too. Malibu's obvious charms—the glorious blue of the Pacific Ocean, the incessant sunshine, the wide sandy beaches and secluded, rugged coves accessible only by surfboard—are what draw people here in the first place. What keeps them here is the magic—the scent of purple sage mixed with salty air and how vast the ocean appears when viewed from atop a cliff; the turbulence of a winter storm barreling in from the west and the eerie warmth of the powerful Santa Ana winds. Once the magic is in their soul, they are willing to put up with Malibu's natural disasters—the real estate prices, the wildfires, the mudslides, and the paparazzi. So they stay, more and more of them every year. Thus, the traffic tie-ups on PCH.

I myself have been here over twenty years and fully intend to stick it out for the rest of my life. And then some. I've stipulated in my will that my ashes are to be spread on the lawn outside the Pepperdine University chapel. I realize that will take some doing. Fortunately, I know just the people to pull it off.

And because I know people was why I had my next appointment. Her name was Kymbyrlee Chapman. She had contacted me by phone and said her sister recommended me. I knew the sister well enough. Her name was Mallory Price and she lived in one of the McMansions up Corral Canyon. Mallory ran with a crowd of hard-partying gals too old to be called girls but too flighty to be called women. From time to time I would toss freshly divorced men into that crowd to sow their post-divorce wild oats. Then I would clean the men off, tend to their bruised egos, and find more stable women for them.

Kymbyrlee was evasive on the phone about what she wanted from me. She insisted on giving the details in person. I agreed to set aside a half hour for her because, frankly, I was curious what a sister of the man-eating Mallory Price looked like.

I pulled into the Colony Plaza's parking lot, searched for a parking space, and remarkably walked in the doors of Coogie's restaurant ten minutes early. I grabbed a booth at the back, ordered a black coffee and waited to see what walked in. I wasn't disappointed.

Kymbyrlee Chapman arrived dressed for an audience: white halter top, skinny jeans, red stilettos. Blonde highlights, almond shape to her eyes, flawless skin. Shoulders back, breasts set on high beams, she posed just inside the door. It was a wasted effort. The place was nearly deserted. She hefted a white leather hobo bag onto her bare shoulder. Impressive daytime jewelry gleamed in the sunlight: dime-sized diamond stud earrings, Cartier watch, diamond-dusted gold cuff bracelet. If the stuff was real, Kymbyrlee was running around in accessories worth about sixty grand.

She spotted me in a back booth, flung a smile my way, and moved forward in an impressive chest thrust/ hip sway intended to bring men to their knees. Another wasted effort. The only guy in the place sat at the bakery counter with his back to her. And he was gay.

When she got to me, she dimmed the smile a few watts and asked, "Are you Alana Fox?"

"I am." I rose to shake her hand.

I like to shake hands when meeting women in social settings. A female-to-female handshake will tell me if the other woman is a bitch, a babe, a broad, or a lady. It's all in the strength and time of the grasp. Not to mention if she looks you in the eye or not.

Kymbyrlee reached for my hand with confidence, shook with just the right amount of pressure, and looked me square in the eye. I felt my bullshit detector rise up. Kymbyrlee was barely thirty. No one in that generation shakes hands properly unless she is trying to get away with something.

We settled into position across from each other in the booth. She ordered Earl Grey tea and I consented to a refill on my black coffee.

"Thank you for agreeing to meet with me, Alana," Kymbyrlee began. "I have a great idea for a new business and Mallory said you were just the person to talk to."

Straight to the chase, I gave her credit for that. But I wasn't ready to discuss business. I have a set of questions I run by new clients on our first meeting. I like to know where people are from and who they know before taking them on. And then I double-check what they tell me against my own sources. Helps me weed out the riffraff before I invest too much time.

In Kymbyrlee's case, I knew she was related to Mallory. So that cleared up whom she knew. But where she came from was anybody's guess. I didn't recall Mallory mentioning a sibling. But then, looking at Kymbyrlee I figured Mallory would just as soon forget her sister. Kymbyrlee would be too much competition for the attention of fresh men.

I ignored Kymbyrlee's opening statement and cut to my own chase.

"How long have you been in Malibu?" I asked her.

"I've visited on and off for years," she replied. "I've just relocated recently."

"From where?"

"Stockton."

I suppressed a shudder. I recalled that Mallory and I had one thing in common—the dreaded childhood spent in the Central Valley. My upbringing had been even more dreadful than Mallory's in Stockton. I was raised in a tiny, one-doctor town in the middle of tomato country. My father was the doctor. My mother, a former Tomato Queen, reigned superior over the local community. My mother's sisters were her entourage and I was raised to follow in her footsteps. Right down to dating the son of a cattle rancher from one county over.

But a trip to Los Angeles to shop for my wardrobe for my very own Tomato Queen competition put an end to all that. I loved the noise, the activity, and the craziness of the city. And the blue of the Pacific Ocean mesmerized me. I stood on the Santa Monica Pier and vowed to spend the rest of my life gazing at it. I returned home to Tomatoville with an application to UCLA in hand. I landed a scholarship, gained ten pounds so the competition wardrobe no longer fit, and handed off the cowboy to my cousin.

And never looked back.

I was all of seventeen at the time. I asked Kymbyrlee what had taken her so long to leave.

She shrugged. "I wasted a lot of time on the wrong guy and then got caught up in some family obligations."

Fair enough. I knew from my own experience how much of life could get wasted on the wrong guy, having spent twenty years in a marriage that fell apart.

"Are you staying with Mallory?"

"Yes and no. She's on an extended holiday in Mexico. I'm house-sitting for her while she is away."

"Holiday." I found her choice of words interesting. Not "vacation," not "getaway," but the very European "holiday." Ms. Chapman had obviously wandered away from Stockton at some point in her life.

A waitress returned with Kymbyrlee's tea and a pot to refill my coffee. Kymbyrlee pushed the sugar packets away as if they harbored poisonous fumes. She glared at the tea bag the way an espresso drinker would consider a jar of instant coffee. Her nose wrinkled as she dunked the bag into the water in the teapot. Letting the tea steep, she added a generous portion of milk to the empty mug. Then, she wrapped the tea bag around a spoon, squeezing out every last drop of flavor. Finally, she poured the tea and leaned back, both hands cradling the steaming mug. I waited for her to take a sip but there she sat, apparently content to enjoy the tea's aroma.

My initial questions answered, I moved on to her reasons for meeting.

"What is this business idea you have?" I asked.

She cranked the up wattage on her smile, pushed the mug aside, and leaned forward just enough to give me a full-on view down her cleavage. She spent the next ten minutes explaining how between the wrong guy and the family obligations she had managed to travel extensively in Indonesia and Asia. She had contacts with artisans and craftspeople that lived outside of the usual tourist traps. Her idea was to lead tours of the artists' workshops for adventuresome art lovers. She needed my help to find potential clients.

I listened to the whole spiel.

She had the delivery down—all the way to supporting the dignity of Third World populations lest they fall even deeper into the clutches of poverty and ruin. It would play well among the wealthy, liberal bunch. Off the top of my head I could count a dozen women eager to tromp about the rainforest in search of the perfect Buddha for the mantle.

Kymbyrlee concluded her pitch with, "I think this tour business would appeal to women, and Mallory said that you know all the women in town. I'll pay your usual fee and all you have to do is introduce me around. What do you say?"

I took a minute before answering. She was right about one thing; I do know all the women in town. And some of the single ones were restless. A nice jaunt through the rainforest could be the perfect diversion until a few divorces came through.

But my bullshit detector was still up. The way Kymbyrlee steeped her tea suggested she was used to it being steeped and poured for her. And you just don't get that kind of service in Stockton, believe me. So where had she acquired her sophisticated manners? And why would a woman wearing a fortune in jewelry feel the need to lead a tour group around a jungle?

She wasn't telling me everything. But I didn't dismiss her right off the bat. If she was serious about the tour business there might be something in it for me. I have my ways of digging up secrets and I intended to consult them immediately. Meanwhile, I would keep Kymbyrlee in my sights until I knew just what to do with her. The last thing I needed was Ms. Chapman and her perky breasts and her flawless skin running loose around Malibu. The last time I had let that happen I lost a husband.

I bought some time by telling Kymbyrlee that I would think her business plan over and get back to her.

We made plans to meet the next day at Mallory's house. I made certain that she knew to pay my fee in cash and sent her on her way. I paid the bill for my coffee and her untouched tea, and joined the gay man sitting alone at the bakery counter.

"Hello, David." I greeted him with a kiss on both cheeks.

David Currie is the office manager for an outfit called Errands, Etc. For a price, his minions will pick up your dry cleaning, deliver your kids to soccer practice, or buy gifts for your spouse and/or lover. If you want to know who is doing what or whom in Malibu, David's your guy. He is also Stop One on my tour of checking references.

"I need some information from you," I said. "I have some to share, too."

"I don't know, darling. That last bit of information you shared was awfully tame. Everyone knows about George Ferguson's nasty temper. I think you still owe me."

"It's not much this time, either," I admitted. "But then, I'm not asking for much."

David sighed as if it hurt to part with the air. "What do you have and what do you want, then?"

"I have that Mallory Price is taking an extended vacation in Mexico."

"Really?" David's perfectly waxed eyebrows took off so fast, he had to sit up straighter just to keep them on his forehead. "Did she take that new boy toy she met in the desert?"

"I don't know who she went with."

David made an effort to look unimpressed. "And for this morsel you want what?"

"Do you know anything about Mallory's sister?"

"Her sister? Where have you *been*, darling?" David was shocked, just shocked. "You haven't heard about the brouhaha over the Stockton granny's will? Let me tell you..."

And he was off. Something about the granny dying after investing ages ago in almond orchards of all things, and who knew how much nuts could be worth, and Mallory inherited the whole lot of it which is how she could afford the house in the desert in the first place, and then the lawsuit absolutely split the family in two— well, three, if you count that second cousin...

I interrupted as soon as he stopped for a breath.

"Is it safe to say that Mallory wouldn't have her sister house-sit for her while she is in Mexico?"

"House-sit? Whatever for? That mausoleum she calls a house is nothing but glass and cactus. Her allergies are dreadful."

David paused for dramatic effect.

"Besides, haven't you been listening, Alana? Mallory detests her. The sister would only be there over Mallory's dead body."

Chapter Three

I left Coogie's feeling unsettled. My meeting with Kymbyrlee Chapman had raised more questions than it answered. Specifically, if she was on the outs with Mallory, how did she hear of me? How did she get my number? This is important to me because I work only from referrals. If just anyone knows how to track me down, my exclusiveness is diluted. And my reputation is built on my exclusive insider track on everything in Malibu. I needed a second opinion. From someone who appreciated the danger of becoming accessible to just anyone.

Fortunately, I knew just where to find the opinion. I went in search of my transportation.

In a sea of ubiquitous black Range Rovers, my car, a hot pink 1952 Porsche convertible, stood out in the parking lot like a Republican at a Streisand concert. I hopped in, literally—the top was down and the driver's door sticks—and off I went.

My second opinion lives on a bluff overlooking Malibu, in a place slightly smaller than a Wal-Mart. Her name is Jorjana York and she is my best friend, confidante, and the person whose name I enter on those forms requiring next of kin. She is also Stop Two on my tour of checking references.

The Porsche made quick work of the hairpin turns leading up to the York estate. I punched in the access code at the gate, whipped around the circular drive, and left the day chauffeur in charge of the parking details. I sailed through the front door, politely held open by the day butler. I crossed the foyer and walked past the double staircase, through the gallery, and out to the loggia. I found Jorjana on her usual perch—propped up on a chaise lounge with her back to the pool.

"Alana, look through these new lenses!" Jorjana greeted me with glee. "I can see the price on the cantaloupes outside Ralphs!"

With a perfectly tanned and manicured hand, she handed over a pair of military-looking binoculars. Five hundred feet below lay PCH and the scattering of strip malls that constitutes downtown Malibu. I peered as directed. Sure enough, the sign on Ralphs read ninety-eight cents per pound.

"That's amazing," I agreed. "Where did you get these?"

"Franklin brought them back from his last safari," she explained.

Franklin was her husband.

I took the chaise next to hers and settled in for a chat. She continued to gaze through the binoculars, informing me of who came and went from Ralphs. Her black hair, curly as a poodle's, was piled high on her head. A lime green visor shaded her eyes and matched her lime green bikini top. Her legs were covered with a light blanket and brightly colored wooden bracelets clattered happily as she illustrated her sightings with a free hand.

Eventually, she paused long enough to pluck a crystal bell from an assortment of tiny bells on the table next to her. Immediately, a Mexican maid appeared.

"Rosa, we'll have a pitcher of lemonade and some of your marvelous cookies, please," Jorjana instructed the woman.

"Yes, ma'am."

"And Rosa," Jorjana added, as if it were an afterthought, "I believe it is time for my medication as well. Please bring the bottle with the lemonade."

"No, ma'am! I cannot! Mr. York, he forbid it! He hide the bottle so you not fool me!" She bustled away, cursing in angry Mexican.

Jorjana pouted. "I was getting so clever about conniving that one!"

"Franklin is on to you," I told her, completely without sympathy. "You'd be better off following the doctor's orders instead of getting the help to smuggle drugs to you."

"Oh, hush!" Jorjana retorted. With an impatient grunt, she glared at the wheelchair parked at her side. After a moment, she picked up the binoculars and we fell into a companionable silence.

We sat in the sunshine at the top of Bella's Bluff—named for the daughter Jorjana and Franklin lost in a freak avalanche years before on a Canadian ski trip. That same avalanche put Jorjana in her wheelchair.

I met her shortly after the accident. The home that Jorjana, Franklin, and Bella had shared was built on four levels—not the best place to adjust to life in a wheelchair. Franklin and Jorjana moved into a rambling one-story ranch house and set about building the estate on Bella's Bluff. Call it fate or call it luck, but my then husband and I moved in next door. Five minutes after the movers left my house, the doorbell rang. I opened the door to find Jorjana perched in her chair, a plate of freshly baked cookies on her lap and a pitcher of martinis in her hand. She explained that she was covering all her bases. I told her to leave the cookies on the porch for the coyotes and bring the martinis in. We've been best friends ever since.

The maid returned, plopped a tray down next to me and scurried away. I poured the lemonade (freshly squeezed), divided up the Mexican wedding cookies (freshly baked), and fussed with the blanket at Jorjana's feet. Her skin was as cold to the touch as the lemonade.

"I had a meeting with a possible new client today," I began.

"Anyone interesting?" Jorjana's voice feigned indifference but she lay the binoculars down.

"Definitely interesting," I replied. I recounted the story of Kymbyrlee and her tales of woe over the guy and the family, and her plans for the travel business. I then highlighted David's gossip about the family woes.

Jorjana listened carefully. When I finished, she turned to me and asked, "Are you concerned with this girl's motivation?"

As always, Jorjana struck at the heart of the matter.

"Kymbyrlee gives the impression that she is used to being waited on," I said. "And you should have seen the jewelry she was wearing. Why would she want to start a business as a tour guide?"

"Perhaps she has fallen on difficult times," Jorjana pointed out. "Perhaps this wrong fellow is her ex-husband and the divorce settlement did not work in her favor. That has happened among our own, as you well know."

True enough. Half of my time is spent placing newly divorced women of suddenly reduced circumstances in suitable social circles.

"First, you must clear up the question of why she is compelled to pursue this venture," Jorjana continued. "Once that is settled to your satisfaction, take her under your wing with provisions. You would be well-advised to accompany her on the first trip."

"I was thinking that myself. But there is something else."

I told her about the Stockton granny and the will and the family uproar.

Jorjana brushed the story away like she was swatting a fly.

"She admitted to family obligations. It is likely she meant her grandmother's will. Perhaps this explains her current financial state."

"What about Mallory detesting her?"

"Our David has a tendency to exaggerate. You can address that issue when you meet with Kymbyrlee tomorrow. I think the true concern is whether she is an aspiring businesswoman with a novel idea or an interloper intending to prey on our own circle."

She was right. I could clear up the discrepancies at the next meeting.

I felt better. I leaned back on my chaise just as a turkey vulture sailed overhead. Why I didn't take this as a bad omen, I'll never know.

Chapter Four

A short time later, I left Jorjana's for home.

Home is a two-bedroom, two-and-a-half bath, mock-Tuscan villa-ette smack-dab on the sand on Malibu Beach Road. A one-car garage sits at street level and you access the house by climbing down a flight of steps and passing through a small courtyard. The place was a surprise fortieth birthday gift from my then husband. It was a surprise for both of us, actually. He surprised me by filing for divorce but offering the house as a consolation prize. I surprised him by accepting both and then hiring a nasty attorney to snag everything of his that was not nailed down.

I pulled the Porsche into the garage, collected the mail in the box at the top of the stairs, unlocked the gate and negotiated the stairs. The courtyard is tiled with Mexican pavers bordered by a stucco retaining wall six inches away from the place next door. The courtyard is filled with orange bougainvillea, yellow lantana, and dark green Mongo grasses. The purposely overgrown landscaping makes for a quiet, shady retreat. It is the only part of the property that I actually like.

I let myself in through an oversized stained glass door that realtors refer to as "regal." I dropped the car keys and the mail on the narrow table provided for that purpose and wandered into the "great room." Better described as "cozy," the great room contains a living area, a dining area, and the kitchen. Realtors make haste to point out that your eye is drawn away from the lack of square footage by the vast Pacific Ocean, which indeed lurks just outside. More Mexican pavers tile the outdoor patio, which ends in stairs leading to the beach.

The house felt stuffy so I opened the sliders to the patio and the window over the kitchen sink. Outside, the ocean swelled and retreated, seagulls screeched, and pelicans glided low across the waves. Endlessly, day and night, the noise of that surf never lets up. Constantly crashing in and grittily sliding back out, it's enough to drive you nuts.

I escaped to the study at the back of the house, closed the glass doors separating it from the great room, and opened the glass doors to the quiet courtyard. Settling in at the desk, I attended to business.

First, the question of my daily transportation.

Back in the days of my married life, my then husband and I shared a house high in the hills above Zuma Beach. Zuma Beach is a wide crescent of sand that frames a bucolic patch of the blue Pacific. And is spectacular when viewed from above. Just far enough away to appreciate the ocean's beauty—not close enough to come in for cocktails every night. It was the perfect spot to build a dream home. Particularly one with eight bedrooms, ten baths, and maid's quarters above the fourteen-car garage. The garage housed my then hus-band's collection of twelve vintage cars. His pride and joy.

The house was my pride and joy. I designed it, deco-rated it, and should have still been living in it. But my then husband (stupid, stupid man!) refused to give up my house in the divorce settlement. So, understandably, I took his cars.

Unfortunately, I now have room to house only one car at a time. So I keep the other eleven in storage in Calabasas. Above the storage warehouse is a studio apartment where I keep the guy who minds the cars. I called him to make the daily arrangements.

"Fred here." Fred, the minder of the cars, answered on the first ring.

"It's Alana. I want the forty-eight Jag tomorrow."

"Topless?" Fred installs or removes the tops on the convertibles as needed.

"Yes, please."

"The MG is due for some work."

Fred maintains the cars as well. And does a fine job, with the exception of the sticky door on the '52 Porsche. In Fred's defense, the car never has been the same since I insisted on having it repainted hot pink.

"How much?" I asked. Like I had a choice.

"Do you really want to know?"

"Is it more or less than the last time?"

"More."

"Fine." I sighed. "Send me the bill."

That completed, I went to the kitchen to make a drink. I pulled two bottles out of the freezer— one of gin, one of limoncello. I tossed some ice into a glass. I grabbed a can of diet ginger ale from the fridge. Poured some gin over the ice, added the ginger ale, and topped it off with a dash of limoncello. The perfect drink. The diet ginger ale settles my stomach without adding calories. The gin settles my mind. And the limoncello prevents scurvy.

I put everything away and returned to the office.

I checked my messages, retrieved the mail from the front hall, paid some bills.

And then the phone rang. The caller ID registered my ex-husband's home phone number. Stupid me, I answered.

"Alana? This is Tori."

It was Little Miss Tight Buns herself.

"Hello, Tor-ree." I always address her by slowly dragging out her name as if talking to a two-year-old. I do this because it annoys her.

"I want to talk to you."

I flipped on the gizmo that allows me to record phone conversations. A mechanical *click* told me it was working. "Go ahead."

"What is it with your phone? Every time I call you I hear static."

I let that one pass. "What do you want, Tor-ree?"

"I want to talk to you about the alimony."

"Oh, Tor-ree, Tor-ree."

"I want to renegotiate the amount with you."

Renegotiate? Big word. Little Miss Tight Buns must have consulted with a Big Girl's Attorney. A lousy one, too. My alimony was none of her business and any attorney worth his salt would have told her this.

"It's been five years, Alana, it's time you took responsibility for yourself. I'm willing to offer you a significant lump sum if you release Alan from his monthly payments. What do you say?"

I said nothing. I stared through the great room to the ocean beyond. The ocean, less than a hundred feet away with all those relentless, noisy waves. Tori, most likely, was making her call from my former study in my former house. The house with its vast views situated on five acres with no visible neighbors. And perfect silence. The house that I missed every damn day. The same house that Tori was systematically destroying with child-proofing devices and unsupervised tricycle riding. Not her tricycle—she had the nerve to have a kid after marrying my ex-husband.

And then there were my issues regarding the ex-husband. I had made Alan Fox who he was today. I had found him in a coffee shop I worked in to supplement my scholarship to UCLA. At the time he was just a confused graduate student at USC, but he had everything I had ever wanted in a guy—blue eyes and a trust fund. It was love at first sight.

I chased him until he caught me. Married him when I was twenty. Decided what to do with my brains and his money. I started him on a career in commercial real estate and spent my time meeting and entertaining all the right people. It worked like a charm. Two years into the marriage we bought our first home in Malibu.

I didn't stop there. Alan's line of work depended entirely on whom he knew. So I made sure he knew everybody. I worked as hard as he did to make the business successful. So I looked at the money he paid me more like residuals than alimony.

Like hell I was going to release him.

"No."

"You're not being reasonable, Alana!"

"I'm being very reasonable, Tor-ree. Alan and I were married nearly twenty years. There was no prenuppre-nup. He got the house. I get alimony. Seems fair to me."

"Fair? You're a single woman living in a house that's paid for. You have a business of your own! What do you need another one million, seven hundred and fifty thousand dollars a year for?"

"Tori, this has nothing to do with you. When Alan dissolved our marriage, he agreed to the alimony payments. Surely you remember that little agreement? You did have something to do with the fact that Alan divorced me in the first place."

Silence on the other end. I could just see her two little brain cells struggling over how to respond. They decided to play the pity card.

"I'm pregnant again."

"How lovely for you. I take it our discussion is over?"

"No, it's not! By the time this one is born, Chaucer will be in preschool and private schools are expensive. And I can't believe what the nanny is going to charge for two kids! The economy is a mess! The business made half of what it made last year! Alan can't afford to keep up your alimony and support a family!"

"Not my problem."

Although I did make a mental note to call Alan's board members and grill them on the business income. Which I had every right to do since I am one of the biggest investors in Alan's business.

Tori wasn't finished. Damn if she wasn't persistent.

"What would Alan do if I told him just what you charge your clients?"

That gave me pause. Apparently, Tori knew more about my business than I thought.

And the IRS didn't.

Initially, the IRS wasn't a problem. When I started helping people get their social footing in Malibu, I learned they paid more attention to my advice if they paid for the privilege. I took cash just to have some walking around money. At first, there was so little business (and so little cash) that it was too much trouble to report it on my income tax return. But before I knew it, I had quite a stash of cash lying around. And the awkward problem of informing the IRS that I had an extra thirty or forty grand to report.

From time to time, I had thought about making the business legit. But I never got around to it. Partly because it ticked me off how much I pay in taxes, anyway. What with property taxes, income tax, and the state tax that California just fritters away, $1.75 mil just doesn't go as far as you might think. God only knows what the IRS would grab out of my five-thousand-dollar fee. So, I just never bothered turning my service into a bona fide business.

But now, Tori, of all people, might give me the reason to get around to it. My worry was that she could influence Alan, who, unlike Tori, could spell IRS. Not to mention that if his business was really in trouble, Alan would look for every avenue to cut costs.

I needed to think this development through. First, I had to distract Tori. Fortunately, this was easy enough to do.

"I'll tell you what, Tori. I would consider a lump sum as opposed to the monthly payments," I lied.

"You would?"

Silly girl, she fell for it.

"Sure. Let's see. Alan pays me one million, seven hundred and fifty thousand dollars a year, and let's assume I will live for another forty-five years." I paused as if calculating an amount. "Yes, seventy-eight million, seven hundred and fifty thousand should do it. I'll take that in a cashier's check, if you don't mind."

Tori hung up. Raging pregnancy hormones, no doubt.

Tori's demands gave me pause. I needed a second opinion. Twice, in one day.

I dialed Jorjana. I used her most private number to avoid the house manager, the social secretary, or, God forbid, Franklin.

"Guess who's pregnant?" I asked her.

"Someone we love or someone we loathe?"

"Loathe."

"Not Tori?"

"None other. But get this: she wants me to give up my alimony."

Jorjana gasped. "Has she no shame? Your alimony is none of her business."

"I know. I told her that, not that she ever listens to me. She seems to think that since I make my own money, Alan doesn't have to pay the alimony. I may have to wave the divorce agreement under her nose to get her to back off."

"That might be the most prudent action," Jorjana replied carefully.

I detected a note of concern in her voice. "What do you mean?"

"I would hate to see you do something foolish again."

"Foolish? Me?" What was she talking about?

"Yes, Alana, you. Promise me you will not have another one of those beautiful cars repainted."

Jorjana was referring to the fact that I had the Porsche painted hot pink in protest to Tori reproducing. Of course, at the time I was convinced her brat was going to be a girl.

"Fred said the MG needed work. How do you think it would look with orange flames on its sides?"

"You cannot destroy a car every time Tori has a child!"

"Sure I can," I said with resolve. "Just watch me."

Chapter Five

The next day arrived with clear skies and full-on sunshine. No surprise there. I had just finished a breakfast of black coffee when the house intercom buzzed from the garage.

"I need the keys to the Porsche, Alana."

It was Fred, delivering the car of the day. On time. No surprise there, either.

My 1948 Jaguar XK120 convertible idled at a slow purr just outside the garage. Candy apple red with wide whitewalls and sporty black leather interior, the Jag is one of my "sunny days" favorites.

Hovering over it like a careful daddy was Fred. Six-plus feet, sixty-plus years of age, neither possessing nor desiring social skills, Fred spends his days in the Calabasas garage wiping fingerprints off the cars and anticipating their every need.

I tossed him the keys to the Porsche. He caught them one-handed.

"I'm going to start work on the MG today," he said.

"While you are at it, I'd like to have it painted orange, with red and yellow flames on the sides."

Fred glared at me with the look of a parent hearing criticism of a favorite child.

"Is Little Miss Tight Buns pregnant again?" he growled.

"Yes. So, what do you think about the MG?" I asked brightly.

"Leave the MG alone. It would look ridiculous with flames."

"Too much, then?"

"If you have to piss Alan off, paint it another shade of green. You'll ruin the car's value without making it look stupid."

Fair enough, I thought. The Porsche did look kind of silly in pink.

I agreed to take his advice under consideration.

He clambered over the stuck driver's side door of the Porsche and sped away.

I went back in the house, checked my calendar, gathered the stuff I needed for my day, locked up, and set the Jaguar in the direction of downtown Malibu.

The two strip malls of downtown Malibu harbor the usual grocery store, the usual drugstore, a great bookstore, and a wildly eclectic array of restaurants and boutiques. On the west side of PCH is the Colony Plaza, where I met Kymbyrlee Chapman in Coogie's. On the east side of PCH is the Malibu Country Mart, where the shops and restaurants surround a large courtyard featuring a sand-filled playground. My first errand took me to the Country Mart playground.

I left the Jag in the parking lot in the middle of the Mart. It blended in well with the obligatory sea of black Range Rovers and blue Priuses. Along with the usual collection of rusty buckets driven by the paparazzi.

It used to be that the only annoying creatures in Malibu were the aggressive seagulls that stole sandwiches out of your picnic basket. These days, the most aggressive creatures in town are the paparazzi. Unshaven, sloppily dressed, and as ubiquitous as the sunshine, the paps hang out in the Country Mart to snap photos of the hottest celebrities. Their telephoto lenses are the size of bazookas. They lurk in the shadows and wait for their famous prey to wander by. Then they jump out, shutters clicking like rapid-fire machine guns. Many an unsuspecting tourist has been flattened in the paparazzi charge.

As a local, I understand the dynamics at work. The paps are rude, loud, and exasperating. But they are also efficient. The photos they shoot at eleven a.m. show up on the Internet by noon. Which bodes well for any actor/celebrity/socialite needing a little publicity. So any actor/celebrity/socialite wishing privacy gets his or her morning espresso further north at the Broad Beach Starbucks.

"Who's on tap for today, guys?" I asked the gaggle of paps gathered at the entrance to the Coffee Bean and Tea Leaf.

"Britney."

"Demi."

"Matt."

One of the guys nodded in the direction of a rusty and battered Mercedes. "Jason is working on it."

Inside the car sat a guy with long stringy hair and a cigarette hanging from his mouth. He juggled a variety of cell phones while texting on a BlackBerry. He signaled the pap waiting for Demi. Money changed hands, and the pap hopped in a car and sped off. All in a day's work.

"Good luck, guys," I said, on my way into the CB&TL. I grabbed a black coffee, paid the bill, and then wandered outside to seat myself at a picnic table near the playground. Pulling out my cell phone, I pressed number six on the speed dial.

While the phone made the connection, I observed the melee in the playground. The sandlot positively crawled with screaming tots. I watched the frenzy in much the same way one regards a car wreck. That pretty well sums up my feeling about kids. I'll look at one if I happen upon one, but I sure as hell don't want one myself.

A safe distance from the swings, two twenty-something nannies knelt in the sand watching their charges dig holes. A little boy, a towhead around two, attacked the sand with a studied concentration. Occasionally, he stopped to compare his progress with his playmate, a little girl of Chinese descent. The nannies chatted happily until one of them dug into the pocket of her jeans for a ringing cell phone. Her face clouded as she read the number. I saw her mouth "I have to take this" to the other nanny, who apparently agreed to watch both kids.

I watched her step gingerly out of the sand and glance fearfully around.

"I can't talk very long, Alana," the girl said in a whisper. She moved away from the playground and settled on a grassy slope just outside the card shop. It was then that she spotted me. I could tell from the look on her face.

"This won't take long, Jessica," I said quietly. "When, exactly, were you going to tell me that Tori is pregnant?"

In the sandbox, little Chaucer Fox, Jessica's charge, stopped digging and noticed his nanny was gone. Jessica stood and waved at him, giving him a big thumbs-up and a super smile. Satisfied, Chaucer resumed digging.

"I just found out myself. I just got back from vacation." Jessica sat back down, hiding her mouth behind a hand.

"I am not paying you what I am paying you so I can get blindsided by Tori," I said evenly. "She called yesterday in a tizzy about money. What's going on?"

"Yeah, you wouldn't believe what she thinks she can pay me for two kids," Jessica said in disgust. "Two kids is twice the work. Twice the work means twice the pay and I told her that."

"Not my problem," I pointed out.

"Yeah, OK, right." She put a hand to her head in concentration.

In the sandbox, Chaucer and his little friend continued to dig to her homeland.

"OK, so Tori's mom was visiting just before I went on vacation, right?" Jessica began.

"Yes, I remember."

"Tori and Alan had this big fight just before her mother got there. He said he wasn't going to have them 'running all over Rodeo Drive this time.'"

Jessica cradled the phone against her shoulder and made quotation marks with her fingers.

"And?"

"Tori said he wasn't being fair, and then he said that they'd agreed on a budget and she wasn't sticking to it. And then—"

"How did the argument end?" I interrupted, for fear of "and then" going on all day.

"Well, I'm not sure because I had to run after Chaucer, but something weird was going on with Tori and her mom later on."

"And that was?"

"I brought Chaucer home early from the park 'cause he was way cranky, you know? And Tori and her mom had all Tori's jewelry laid out on the dining room table. Tori was doing something on a laptop and she acted real funny when she saw me."

"I'm listening."

"So I waited until everyone was asleep and then I checked Tori's e-mail on her computer, like you showed me."

"And?"

"And Tori's been getting a bunch of estimates on what her jewelry is worth."

Jessica paused. I waited to get my money's worth.

"You know, they've been arguing a lot. I was kinda surprised that she was pregnant."

She glanced over at Chaucer, who was looking around for her again.

"I've got to go, Alana."

"Just a second," I told her. "Keep an eye on her e-mail. And let me know what she gets in the U.S. mail."

"Isn't that illegal?"

"Only if you get caught."

Jessica snapped her phone shut and swooped in to snatch Chaucer from the sand. She said something to the other nanny while pointing in the direction of the Malibu Dog stand. Before you could say "beat a retreat," they were gone.

And there I sat, fighting off a terrible sense of dread.

Was there something to be worried about after all? Alan's business did depend on someone else's business having enough money to rent office space. And the economy was going to hell. This thought gave me pause. What if Alan really couldn't come up with my alimony/residuals? What if Tori's claim that the business had tanked was actually true? I mentally tallied up my expenses. After taxes, monthly bills, the upkeep on the cars, Fred's salary, and living costs, the remaining money was only chump change. If Alan really and truly could not cough up $1.75 mil, I was in some serious trouble. I made a mental note to place those phone calls to the board members.

But first I had an appointment with Kymbyrlee Chapman. Whose business idea was looking better by the minute.

Chapter Six

I left the playground and its incessant chaos. I passed the restaurant Tra di Noi on my way to the parking lot. The aroma of freshly chopped basil and sautéed garlic flooded the air. I exchanged quick pleasantries with the paparazzi sitting in the shade. As I headed to my car, my attention was diverted.

The Diversion stood at the far end of the parking area. His hair was dark and curled around the nape of his neck. He was tall, but not too tall. Old enough to be interesting, but young enough to have stamina. He wore a copper colored silk T-shirt stretched across a chest that was surely smooth and hard. His linen pants fell easily over a rear that was not too flat and not too fleshy. His tan was the kind you get when you sail bare-chested all summer off St. Tropez. His eyes were brown, and it would take an entire bottle of ice-cold Cristal just to get to the bottom of their depths. I know all this because I stood stock-still in the middle of the parking lot to nail down the details.

He chatted with some guy, a lesser being in every way. They said their good-byes. And the Diversion slid behind the wheel of an unremarkable rental car and drove away.

He was long out of sight before I started breathing again.

I drew a deep breath and let it out with a sigh.

I know all the women in town, but I also know the men. I know men who walk into a room and every guy wants to shake their hand and every woman wants to shake something else. I know men who think the world owes them something just because. I know men who send flowers to both their wives and mistresses but are thoughtful enough to send different arrangements to each woman. I know men who would sell their souls and the souls of their family members to land a deal, win an election, or get a starring role. Oddly enough, I even know men who are decent guys trying to get ahead and can't find a woman who appreciates that.

There are men and there are men. And the reason I always pass them on to my clients is that none of them has ever taken my breath away.

But I had business pending.

Namely, an appointment with Kymbyrlee Chapman. Followed by phone calls to Alan's board members.

I forced myself to start breathing, tossed my stuff into the Jag and roared out of the Country Mart.

All the while keeping an eye open for unremarkable rental cars.

Turned north on PCH. Traffic was light for once. I sailed past Pepperdine University, took the quick right turn at BeauRivage restaurant, and faced the steep switchbacks of Corral Canyon Road.

How anyone came to build a road on the impossible hill straddling Solstice Canyon and Corral Canyon
is beyond me. The climb up feels as if you are driving
straight up a sheer wall. Except the "up" consists of
series of sharp turns. And the road lacks sturdy guard-
rails. Which makes it hard to concentrate on the turns
when you are trying not to fall off the edge of the hill.
Suffice it to say, I don't venture up Corral Canyon often.
In spite of the difficult drive, I pulled up in front of
Mallory Price's "mausoleum" precisely on time.

The house balanced precariously on a steep lot with
breathtaking canyon views. That view includes a vulner-
ability to wildfires, a regular Malibu disaster courtesy of
a coastal desert environment, the Santa Ana winds, and
the stupidity of human nature.

David was right about Mallory's "mausoleum." The
house was constructed of glass and steel and sharp
angles. The front door was a stainless steel slab. Whoever
designed the place had a thing about oversized understatement—the doorbell, a round platter of steel, was
hidden among a mosaic of other round platters. I found
it by sheer luck. The bell sounded one deep tone—B
flat, I believe. After a reasonable time, the door swung
silently open. Just over the threshold stood Kymbyrlee
Chapman.

Kymbyrlee wore a black tube top pulled up high
enough to cover those damn breasts. Black-and-white
toile-printed capris, bare feet. No jewelry this time. She
stepped aside to let me in. Three large Louis Vuitton
suitcases stood guard just inside.

41

"Going somewhere?" I asked.

She smiled, a rueful adaptation of the full-wattage dazzle from Coogie's.

"I've found a place of my own. Come in, I'll explain."

She led the way into the living room—a soaring space of glass and steel that could hire out as an aviary. The furnishings were those black leather and aluminum contraptions so popular among masochists. In one corner, giant copper kettles held a forest of saguaro cactus. Just beyond the cactus lay a better-than-average view of the canyon and the Pacific Ocean beyond. Opposite the view stood a concrete slab harboring a fireplace. No mantle, no hearth, just a vertical rise of cold concrete with a hole in it. I could just hear the architect describing it as "a juxtaposition of cold and heat." My opinion differed slightly.

Kymbyrlee lowered herself onto one of the leather contraptions and curled her feet under her. She indicated that I was to sit. We exchanged niceties. She offered a drink. I declined. A pause ensued. Kymbyrlee spoke first.

"I haven't been entirely honest with you, Alana," she began, with earnestness splashed all over her face. "Mallory doesn't know I am here at all."

I arched an eyebrow to indicate that I was not entirely surprised.

"Our grandmother passed away and there was a disagreement over her will," she went on. "Things got ugly. Mallory and I have barely spoken in over a year."

I waited.

"I heard through the family grapevine that Mallory was out of town. So I moved in for a few days until I could find something of my own."

She paused there.

"How did you get in the house?"

"Oh, you know Mallory!" Kymbyrlee brushed away my question with a laugh. "Everyone knows where she hides a key!"

I remembered David's comment about Mallory allowing Kymbyrlee in over her dead body. For all I knew, that hidden key had been pried loose from Mallory's corpse.

"I did some asking around," I said to her. "I know all about your family feud. So we both know Mallory would be furious to know you are here. Why don't you start your story from the beginning, and this time give me the truth."

The mirth fell right off her face. Her lip actually trembled.

It was a nice performance. I refrained from applauding. In spite of my annoyance with her, I didn't get up and leave. Normally, I would have, as I don't tolerate deception from my clients. But I had two compelling reasons to get to the bottom of Kymbyrlee's story. The first was how she had heard of me, if not from Mallory. The second was the story from the nanny about the state of Alan and Tori's finances. If I had to start supporting myself, Kymbyrlee's tour business was as good a place as any.

Kymbyrlee lowered her feet to the floor. Concrete floor, by the way. She leaned forward, elbows on her knees, hands clasped. Her tube top slipped slightly. I could see a piece of paper tucked between her breasts.

"Before the mess with the will, Mallory and I did discuss starting a tour business. That part was all true. We were going to introduce her Malibu friends to my contacts in Indonesia. Now Mallory is more interested in decorating her new place in Palm Desert than in working with me."

She sat up and tugged at the tube top. She continued, her voice picking up bitterness with every word.

"I still think the business has merit so I decided to go ahead without her. I have a business plan. I have a place to live. Now all I need are the clients. Mallory talked about you a lot. She said you knew everyone in town. I thought you would be the perfect contact for me."

"How did you get my number?"

"She has your number in her Rolodex in her office." Kymbyrlee pointed to a hallway behind her.

"Convenient," I said dryly. That certainly cleared up how she had heard of me.

"I should have been up front with you, Alana," Kymbyrlee admitted. "But I was afraid you would turn me down if you knew Mallory and I were on the outs. Haven't you ever made a bad decision?"

Of course I had. Who hadn't?

"Alana, I understand that you must have reservations about this." Kymbyrlee looked me straight in the eye— woman to woman. "I'm sorry we got off on the wrong foot. I'll do whatever you ask to set things right. You can come on the first trip, or you can go with me when

I pitch the idea to the clients. Or you can just be a silent partner and tell me who to contact and I will leave your name out of it. You could be my consultant."

I knew her idea would take off faster than Botox among a certain group of women. And the fact that Kymbyrlee would be running around the Southern Hemisphere would prevent her from running around loose in Malibu. But it was the word "consultant" that sold me in the end. Alana Fox, consultant, might just make enough money to offset a possible decrease in alimony income. And becoming legit and filing taxes, I would not have to worry about the IRS anymore.

"I don't want to be a silent partner," I said. "I will accompany you to every introduction until I am satisfied that you are being up front with me."

As if I were the Queen of Ethical Behavior myself.

"Of course," Kymbyrlee agreed.

"I want to reserve the right to go on the first trip as well."

"Absolutely."

"How would you like to start, then?" I fully expected a discussion on the whys and whos and hows of Malibu Society to follow.

Kymbyrlee surprised me.

Again.

"I want to go to the Save the Bay Benefit on Saturday." Kymbyrlee said this with complete assurance. Like she was asking for a ticket to the high school car wash.

Save the Bay is no car wash. It is one of those hush-hush parties that is supposed to be oh-so-exclusive. The guest list is limited to two hundred of those willing to shell out ten thousand dollars for an afternoon of schmoozing under the auspices of saving marine life.

"I heard that you can get tickets," Kymbyrlee prodded.

That I could. The hostess was none other than CiCi DiCarlo, an actress of a certain age who puts on the shindig every year. And every year CiCi talks me into selling tickets to the new faces in town. I usually corral couples, but this year I sold one ticket to Mia Kaplan so I had an extra one. Kymbyrlee's request was perfect. It was the ideal place for her to troll for clients. And, more importantly, CiCi fully expects me to sell all my tickets or I have to pay for one of my own.

"I can get you in," I responded. "But I'll need a check made out to Save the Bay for ten thousand dollars."

Kymbyrlee resolved the mystery of the paper hiding between her breasts. Poking two fingers down the tube top, she plucked out a check.

"I know. Here's a check for that." She produced a cashier's check drawn from a bank in Stockton. So far, so good. She had done her research well.

I gave her the rundown on the festivities for Saturday and we made arrangements to drive there together. I was just about to broach the subject of my fee when she stood and pulled an envelope out of the back of her capris.

"And your fee. Five thousand dollars. Cash."

Where she hid 250 twenty-dollar bills in those tight pants was beyond me.

Chapter Seven

Back at home, I settled into my office to organize myself into a bona fide consultant. It wasn't as if I was a neophyte at running a business. I did make a fortune for Alan Fox, after all. But when I was busy turning my then husband into a success, I had a whole stable of people to handle details such as printing flyers, taking messages, tallying up income and expenditures, and yes, paying the taxes. Now I had just a Rolodex. But it seemed as good a place to start as any. I was spinning through the A's when the phone rang. It was Mia Kaplan.

"Alana! Dimitri Greco's assistant left a message for me! You said he would call me himself! Now what do we do?"

"Mia, everything is still going according to plan," I reassured her. "Which one of Dimitri's assistants called?"

"He has more than one?" Mia sounded aghast at such extravagance.

"He does. Which one left the message?"

"Jennifer."

"Perfect. She handles his personal life. Give me the number and I will take it from here."

"But—"

"No buts. Leave this to me. I have a plan."

I didn't, actually, but there was no reason Mia needed to know that.

"Your job right now is to look fabulous for Save the Bay on Saturday," I told her. "Remember, Dimitri will be there. This is part of the plan."

"Yes, but—"

"Good. I'll see you on Saturday at Save the Bay." I scribbled down the number she provided and hung up before she could protest further. Then I took a deep breath and tried to conjure up a plan. I have found that deep breathing exercises will help my creative process when I don't have a drink handy.

A plan surfaced. It lacked details, but it was better than nothing. I picked up the phone and dialed Dimitri's personal assistant.

"Greco residence. Jennifer speaking."

"Hello, Jennifer. This is Kathy Doyle," I lied. "I am Mia Kaplan's assistant. She asked me to make the arrangements to have Mr. Greco's car repaired."

"Thank you for getting back to me, Kathy," Jennifer replied, one lackey to another. "How would you like to handle this?"

"With as little inconvenience to Mr. Greco as possible, of course. Mia's insurance company can send out an adjuster on Friday to estimate the damages. Where will the car be?" I kept my voice coolly efficient, as if I had no idea who Dimitri Greco was or where he drove the car every day of his life.

"Friday is fine," Jennifer replied. "Are you familiar with Malibu?"

I pretended to take down the directions to Greco Productions, settled on a time for the adjuster to show up, and thanked Jennifer for Mr. Greco's understanding. After ringing off, I gleefully added his unlisted and impossible-to-bribe-from-his-people home number to my impossible-to-obtain-but-I-did-anyway list.

Another call put the new plan into action.

"First National Insurance. Todd Jacobs speaking."

Good ol' Todd is one of those decent guys just trying to get by. I keep him on my leash by trading services with him. I give him leads on single women I can't use in return for access to First National Insurance's database, which contains useful information like you wouldn't believe.

"Todd, Alana Fox here. I have a plan. I need your help." I outlined my plan, which was shaping up amazingly well, considering I was sober and all.

"Is this legal, Alana?" Todd asked warily.

"Legal has nothing to do with it," I answered. "Are you in, or should I just send you a bill for what you still owe me?"

"I'm in," Todd sighed. "But are we even after this one?"

"It depends on how well you do," I answered, and hung up.

I went back to the chore of setting up a business. I twirled through the Rolodex, making notes on resources I would need. People like accountants and bankers and printers for business cards. The business venture started to look like a lot of work. Enough work that I began to wonder if it was actually necessary. After all, I was basing this on Tori's hysterical claims of poverty. What if Alan's business wasn't going under?

What if Tori were mistaken? Gee, what were the odds of that? Cursing myself for ignoring the obvious, I spun the Rolodex again. This time noting the phone numbers of Alan's board members. Then, I wasted a good hour on the phone trying to track down just one of them. Left messages everywhere. I didn't bother trying to reach Alan himself. The man has an impenetrable wall of assistants—all of whom are paid entirely too much money to keep me at bay.

By the time I placed all my calls, I had no more information than when I started. This irritated me to no end. Thank God, it was nearly five o'clock and time to dive into the cocktail hour. I pulled Kymbyrlee's cash retainer from my purse and went to make the day's deposit. It was a quick trip because the bank is upstairs in my guest room closet.

One of the reasons I had need of a banker for a legitimate business is that I did not have a bank account for my cash enterprise. I just never got around to it once I had enough money to start stashing away. But my system in the guest room works rather well. You would be surprised just how much you can cram into a shoe box—one hundred and eighty thousand dollars, give or take, at my last count.

I kept out a few hundred for walking around money and filed the rest in a shoe box. On my way downstairs,

I tried to figure out how long it would take to launder all that cash into my new legitimate business. Then I wondered how much would be eaten up by taxes. All the wondering made me hungry. I went to the kitchen to hunt and gather dinner.

Another short trip. The fridge held diet ginger ale. The freezer held six bottles of gin, four bottles of limoncello, and ice.

A call from Jorjana saved me from one hell of a hangover.

"Franklin is out," she said. "Come dine with me."

The York dining hall seats one hundred. Ninety-eight upholstered chairs stand at attention around a gleaming table fashioned from one long slab of redwood. The west wall is an endless length of French doors leading to the pool—a concrete lagoon fed by a two-story waterfall. Just beyond the pool is the embankment overlooking PCH and the Pacific Ocean.

The view to the pool would take your breath away if you could ignore the décor of the other wall. There, Franklin York stores his trophies—mounted heads of the fruits of his safaris. Antelope, musk oxen, rhinos, and one unlucky moose protrude from a curtained wall like a long stable in a silent zoo. All those glass eyes staring emptily at the dining table so unnerved Jorjana that she outfitted each head with its own custom-made pair of Serengeti sunglasses.

Jorjana and Franklin preside over the hall from the north and south ends of the table. Franklin's chair is constructed entirely of elk antlers; a leopard-skin pillow saves him from impaling himself. Jorjana rests on a seventeenth century wooden throne decorated with the requisite Latin phrases and gilded everything else. Jorjana occupies the north end of the table, claiming it provides the best view of the pool. The best view, undoubtedly, but also the farthest spot from the kitchen. It is a testament to the skill of the York staff that Jorjana's dinners are not served ice-cold.

I arrived to find we would be a party of three. Seated with his back to the trophies was David Currie. I took the seat to Jorjana's right, unfolded a linen napkin slightly smaller than a bed sheet, and tried to ignore the moose peering over its sunglasses at me. The table was set exquisitely with Irish linen, Rosenthal crystal, and vintage Paragon china. Judging from the table setting, we looked forward to an appetizer, soup, salad, and an entrée requiring a steak knife. Three wineglasses, two white and one red.

Lucky for me I was able to rearrange my dinner plans on such short notice.

The three of us inquired after each other's health, commented on the lovely weather, and complimented each other on how well we all looked. Pleasantries out of the way, Jorjana plucked a gold bell from her collection of tiny bells. She jingled it twice, paused, and jingled it twice again. The service door at the far end of the hall flew open.

Dinner began.

Three waiters dressed in tuxedos made the trek to our end of the dining room. One carried a crystal pitcher of iced spring water laced with mint leaves. The second cradled a bottle of Cristal champagne. The third wielded a long brass wand. As the first two busied themselves with filling the water goblets and serving the bubbly, the third extended the wand (in reality a long lighter) and lit the candles of three chandeliers suspended from the beamed ceiling.

"Cheers!" Jorjana raised her champagne flute aloft as the waiters disappeared. David and I joined the toast, our flutes clinking like tiny gongs. I took a generous sip. It was perfect, of course, icy cold and playfully bubbly.

Jorjana jingled a brass bell. A waiter burst through the swinging doors at the far end of the dining hall. He held a serving tray high over his head and kept it up there until reaching a small table set behind Jorjana. There, he set the tray down carefully and began the business of serving our dinner. After topping off our flutes of Cristal, he presented an appetizer of smoked trout, chopped hard-boiled egg, red onion, and crème fraiche, with sourdough toast points. A second waiter discreetly deposited an antique glass saltcellar at Jorjana's elbow. The tiny bowl held a colorful array of pills, Jorjana's evening medication regiment. I suppressed a shudder.

"How was your day, Alana?" Jorjana asked, after downing four red pills with a swig of champagne.

"I met with Kymbyrlee Chapman today," I replied. I turned to David, intending to bring him up to speed.

"How *is* Mallory's little sister?" David asked smugly.

"I informed David of our conversation," Jorjana explained. "He assures me the difficulties between the sisters are real. Were you able to gain answers to the issues we discussed?"

"She came clean on the issue of the will and the fact that she and Mallory are on the outs," I said, building an egg, trout, and crème fraiche sandwich. "I think her business plan will work. I'm going to act as a consultant while she gets up and running."

I recounted the meeting, ending with Kymbyrlee's request to attend Save the Bay.

"La-di-da! Sounds like Mallory's little sister is something of a social climber," David exclaimed.

"Alana and I were concerned about that very possibility," Jorjana said, as she wiped up some loose egg from her plate with a toast point. "It sounds as though Alana has resolved her reservations regarding Kymbyrlee's motives. Is this not true, Alana?"

"She apologized for getting off on the wrong foot," I said. "I also got the impression she needs the work and is a little bitter that Mallory won't help her out."

"I told you that," David sniffed. He turned to me with an eager gleam in his eye. "So, darling. Who are you going to offer up as a sacrifice for the jungle trip?"

"Oh yes, Alana. Who is most suitable for an expedition of this sort?" Jorjana picked up a crystal bell and rang it once. As we discussed the possible clients for Kymbyrlee's new venture, a waiter appeared to clear our plates and champagne flutes. A second served a cup of mushroom soup as dark and fragrant as a forest floor. A nutty, crunchy roll and an ice-cold Pinot Grigio accompanied.

"Should we invite Kymbyrlee to Sunday Brunchbrunch?" Jorjana asked before she sipped her soup. "David and I spent the afternoon amending this Sunday's guest list."

Sunday Brunch is a weekly event that Jorjana and I host at the York estate. Two reasons. The most important reason is to bring the world to Jorjana, to save her the aggravation of conducting a social life in a world still poorly adapted to wheelchairs. The second reason is to allow me to mix people together in a kind of social laboratory to see how they do. Some people can pull off that upscale-casual-California-cool attitude and some people can't. I like to see who is who in a controlled climate before shepherding them out and about in Malibu. We limit the weekly invitations to a hundred or so and rotate friends and newcomers as we see fit.

Jorjana was right on target in suggesting Kymbyrlee attend Sunday Brunch. I did intend to add her name to list. But my bullshit detector went up. David and Jorjana spent an entire afternoon discussing the guest list for Sunday Brunch? That job takes all of ten minutes. Either someone is available or they are not. And Jorjana has a full-time social secretary to handle the details. So what had these two really been up to all day? And why did I have the sinking feeling that it had something to do with me?

"Inviting Kymbyrlee is a great idea," I told Jorjana, as carefully as possible. "Is Mitzi Lipman coming this Sunday? I think she would be a good prospect for Kymbyrlee."

"Oooh! Mitzi would jump at the chance to chase the cabana boys around the lagoon!" David actually clapped his hands in delight. "And the poor dear does need to furnish that new little condo of hers. I can't believe she sold all her furnishings after Gary left. I mean, really, in another decade or two the eighties will be in again!"

Jorjana giggled, downed a couple of white pills with a swig of Pinot Grigio, and chatted cattily with David about Mitzi Lipman's abominable taste in home furnishings. Giving me a moment to gather my wits.

Jorjana and David are voracious gossipers. David is catty and has access to people's secrets, not to mention keys to their houses. Jorjana is as nosy as an investigative journalist after a juicy scandal. Together, they impose an old-fashioned view of who belongs and who doesn't— views born of their backgrounds. Jorjana's from a childhood spent traipsing around after her father's diplomatic service and David's from his Ivy League education.

These two social enforcers are also my most ardent supporters. After my divorce, it was Jorjana and David who kept me in the social whirl. They supported me through the hurt, for which I am eternally grateful. And they helped me realize that my contacts were a priceless asset in establishing myself as a single woman. However, their friendship also gave them a sense of entitlement. Sadly for me, when gossip is slow, they tend to intrude on my life. Which is what had me worried. I had enough disruption in my life without having my friends decide I needed a new hairstyle or something.

My worrying and their gossiping took up the entire soup course. The next ring of a little bell produced crisp salads of baby spinach and nasturtium flowers dressed with orange-ginger vinaigrette. White wine number two proved to be a big, oaky Chardonnay, which Jorjana found useful in washing down her little blue pills. The dissection of Mitzi Lipman's decorating style ended and the conversation swung right back to me.

"Jorjana tells me that Little Miss is 'demanding' again, darling," David started. "What do you think she has stuck up her Tight Buns now?"

"Who knows?" I rolled my eyes and held my glass out for more wine. A waiter appeared out of nowhere. "She's pregnant again. Says Alan can't afford to support a family and continue my payments. She said the business had a tough year. So I have calls in to the board members. I may need to put more pressure on the nanny, too. Considering what I pay that girl, she should be a better source of info than she is."

Jorjana and David exchanged a look. Jorjana sat back and daintily dabbed her lips with a napkin. David looked at me like I was in need of sympathy.

"What?" I asked. Their reaction was strange. They couldn't be surprised by what I had just told them. They knew I kept a close eye on Tori. In fact, they fed me half of what I knew about her daily life. This was the part where we all gaily join in on discussing How Awful Tori Is.

"Is it not time to let go of your animosity toward Tori?" Jorjana asked.

She couldn't have surprised me more if she had said Tori was a darling girl.

"Let go?" I stared at her. "Are you kidding me?"
She wasn't.

"Alana, we are concerned for you." Jorjana reached over to squeeze my arm. "I agree that the alimony Alan pays you is none of her business. But once this is settled, you must put this vendetta against Tori behind you."

"What are you talking about?" I said. "That tramp stole my husband!"

"Tori married a man you had outgrown," Jorjana replied.

I winced at that. I put over twenty years into my marriage. I encouraged, guided, suggested, planned, and entertained until I was hoarse to get Alan Fox where he was. If it hadn't been for me, he would still be in a lousy studio apartment and living for USC game days. I built his career. I built our house. And, yeah, maybe I became a little distracted, but that didn't excuse Little Miss Tight Buns from bewitching my husband out from underneath me.

"It is time for you to move on, darling," David chimed in. "Why waste your time tormenting Tori?"

That was an easy question to answer. I tormented Tori because I could. When Tori married Alan and moved into my house, I had vowed she would never make a friend in Malibu. And I had succeeded. Tori had to lug Chaucer down to Westside for play dates. The closest hair salon that could ever fit her in was in Santa Monica. Restaurants in 90263 always lost her reservations. There wasn't a tennis club, preschool, yoga class, or happy hour in Malibu that would accommodate Tori Fox.

But, truth be told, I tormented Tori because I had to. Because my mother never stood up to the Other Woman who stole my father. Mother drew the drapes in our front room and lived on cigarettes, bulk wine, and Frank Sinatra albums playing endlessly on the turntable. And sent me out alone to face down the playground bullies and endure the smug looks from their mothers. My mother let the Other Woman get away with stealing my father. Come hell, high water, or mudslides (this being Malibu and all), Tori was not going to do the same to me.

David had the nerve to suggest I was wasting my time?

"Let me ask you two this," I replied, as calmly as possible. "What happened to our agreement to isolate Tori?"

David and Jorjana were my favorite teammates in my favorite sport—Tori Trashing. But now, they exchanged a look that made me think they were quitting the game.

David spoke first.

"That has been accomplished, darling. Now you are wasting entirely too much energy on Little Miss. If that girl had any brains at all she would move that cheating ex-husband of yours back to LA where he came from. They could prance around in matching USC outfits and live stupidly ever after. But they do insist on staying here, and since he is your ex-husband…"

Jorjana shot to the heart of the matter herself. "You must start dating."

It was worse than I thought. They didn't envision a new hairstyle for me. They envisioned a new life for me. A life with a man in it. Like I didn't have enough headaches already.

Fortunately, the entrée appeared. Individual Beef Wellingtons paired with a vintage Cabernet worth more than the car I drove up in. I directed the waiter to leave the bottle with me. I concentrated on the meal and pretended I hadn't heard Jorjana. It was a lovely course. Crisp pastry outside, a creamy pate and tender filet inside, nicely steamed green beans tossed in a little balsamic vinegar…

"ALANA!" David and Jorjana shouted in unison.

"What?" I asked innocently.

"Oh, for heaven's sake, Alana! Stop this foolishness!" This from Jorjana.

"Really, darling, don't you think it is time?" David added.

"You divorced over five years ago, Alana. Have you never once met a man you might consider dating?"

It took an act of will to force my thoughts away from the Diversion in the parking lot. The last thing I needed was for these two to learn that a man had caught my attention. The guy would be hunted down, hog-tied, and delivered to my bedroom before midnight. Fortunately, Jorjana was not tuned in to my thoughts.

Unfortunately, she had thoughts of her own.

"What about Donald Wesson? He seems smitten with you, I must say."

"Oh, Jorjana, please!" I pushed the Beef Wellington away in disgust.

Donald Wesson, Malibu's own gazillonaire, was the most unlikely of suitors. Yes, the man had more money than God, but he was a gangly as a teenager and had the attention span of a wasp.

David, remarkably, took my side.

"No! No, no, no, no, no!" David hid behind his napkin in mock horror. "The man has the social skills of a third grader! Really, Jorjana, Alana is better off alone and miserable."

"I am not miserable!" I protested. "Do you think I am miserable, Jorjana?"

Too late. One of Jorjana's pills had worked its magic. She sat slumped in her chair, snoring.

I reached for the tiny ceramic bell to summon the night nurse.

Dinner was over.

Chapter Eight

The next day was Saturday. The day of Save the Bay.

I woke up late and had to dress in a hurry. This was a problem because Save the Bay is always a costume party. This year CiCi DiCarlo chose the theme of a Western hoedown. Denim was the obvious choice, but it was hotter than blue blazes outside. I ended up in a chambray sundress, slip-on sandals of tooled leather, and a straw cowboy hat. It would do. I grabbed my keys and some notes I had made for Kymbyrlee, and flew out the door.

Keeping the Western theme in mind, I had ordered my '54 Chevy truck for the day. Fred stood next to it, rubbing away invisible smudges.

"It looks great, Fred. Thanks." I tossed him the keys to the Jag.

He caught them in one hand and tossed me the keys to the truck.

"Who's gonna park this out at the DiCarlo place?" he asked gruffly.

Fred views valet parking like an Orthodox Jew views Santa Claus.

"I promise to park it myself," I swore, fingers crossed behind my back.

"Where?"

"I don't know where! Probably in one of the fields where they keep the horses."

He grunted and gave one last swipe with a chamois cloth cleaner than your toothbrush. "Be careful of ruts. This one doesn't have the clearance you would think."

I promised to steer clear of ruts, climbed up onto the bench seat, and drove away before he gave the truck a curfew.

Along with the cashier's check and the cash, Kymbyrlee had given me the address to her new digs. She'd taken a condo in the neighborhood at the north end of Malibu Beach. I cruised up the hill at Pepperdine and maneuvered a hairpin turn toward the ocean. Kymbyrlee had moved into a condo complex clinging to a cliff.

The complex was one of those generic beige structures featuring an endless stretch of beige doors on the ocean side and another stretch of beige carports on the other. Not a house number in sight. I drove slowly, hoping to catch sight of Kymbyrlee. No such luck. I reached a dead end. Turning the truck around required a ten-point turn and cursing.

Back at the entrance stood Kymbyrlee Chapman, waving for my attention.

As if she needed to.

Kymbyrlee's interpretation of Western wear was a denim miniskirt slit up to just short of indecent. Her feet were shod in turquoise and black cowboy boots, her bouncy breasts restrained in a black leather corset. Silver jewelry so big, she must have lifted it off a saddle somewhere. Her hair was pulled back into a high ponytail and she carried a flashy patent leather bag large enough to stash the saddle. The only thing missing from the ensemble was a matching pimp.

"Hi, Alana!" Kymbyrlee said as she opened the door. "Nice truck."

She frowned at the height of the ascent, turned her butt to the seat edge and vaulted in.

She wore red satin panties.

"You must be joking," I said.

"About what?" Obviously, she had not looked in a mirror.

I put on my sternest Mother Superior face and laid down my rules.

"The boots, the bag, and the ponytail can stay. The rest has to go."

Kymbyrlee did not look happy about it. Not a bit. "What is wrong with what I have on?"

"You look cheap," I said. "If you want these people to do business with you, they have to think you are one of them. None of them would dress like that."

"This isn't how people in LA dress?" She sounded honestly surprised.

"Maybe in LA," I said. "But this is Malibu. You need to hit just the right note today. Your business plan should leave the impression, not your cleavage."

She got it. Swinging around, she slid off the bench seat, tugged her skirt down to crotch level, and led the way to a wardrobe change. I locked the truck and followed her to her new digs.

"I'm still settling in," she said, as she opened a beige front door. "The place did come furnished. I haven't decided if that is a good or a bad thing."

I followed her into a nice enough living area with a good enough ocean view. The furnishings were beige, the carpet was beige, and the walls were painted in off-beige. The only color in the place was a glass vase filled with red tulips on the breakfast bar. The whole setup had an OK-for-now sort of feel.

"What do you think?" Kymbyrlee asked me.

"Did someone get a discount on beige paint?"

"No kidding," Kymbyrlee grinned.

I followed her to the bedroom, a beige-on-beige symphony of mediocre taste. She tossed her clothes and boots on the floor and stood in front of the closet dressed in only the red satin panties. Her skin was the same smooth tan all over and those damn breasts had the nerve to stand up all by themselves.

"Most of my clothes are still back in Stockton," she said. "I don't have much to choose from."

That was the understatement of the day. I flipped through her stuff. Kymbyrlee's clothes ran the gamut from sexy to slutty. Heavy on the cleavage-baring items. Not a sleeve in the entire collection. After some searching, I got her into a pair of black leggings tucked into the cowboy boots with a black halter dress worn over. I secured her waist with a red bandana. I took the oversized silver and turquoise earrings off her ears, gave a silent thanks that they were the clasp style, and attached them in her hair. She produced a stunning amber, turquoise, and green jade necklace out of nowhere to wrap around her neck.

"Much better." I stood back to admire my handiwork.

Kymbyrlee turned around and around in front of a full-length mirror. First looking over her left shoulder, then over her right, then bending down to touch her toes. Stretched her arms over her head and ended in a full spin.

"It's pretty comfortable, Alana. I have to say, I never would have put this together on my own."

"I love the necklace. Where did you get it?"

Kymbyrlee kept turning. "It's from one of the artists I know in Jakarta," she said.

"Perfect. You can use that as an opener for a conversation about the business. Let's get going. CiCi hates it when her guests are late."

"CiCi has a lot of rules, doesn't she?" Kymbyrlee gave a final turn, grabbed a cell phone from the bedside table, and tossed it in her bag.

"Oh, you just wait. Did I tell you about her cell phone rule?"

"No. What's that?"

"I'll explain on the way."

Back in the truck, I drove north on PCH and took a right on Kanan Dume road. The DiCarlo Ranch is in Hidden Valley, a picturesque basin of gentlemen farms about twenty miles northeast of Malibu. I used the travel time to bring Kymbyrlee up to speed.

"CiCi doesn't allow cell phones at her parties," I began. "She doesn't want any unauthorized photos leaking out to the media."

Kymbyrlee glanced at her handbag. "Do we leave our phones in the car?"

"No. I'm afraid CiCi's security will confiscate them at the door."

"Great. Is there anything else I should know?"

"Don't flirt with the help, don't ask CiCi about her film career, and whatever you do, don't apply lipstick in public."

"Why?"

"She firmly believes it is bad luck to reapply makeup in public."

"She sounds like a barrel of laughs. Is she someone I should consider for a client?"

"Only if she could get to Indonesia by train. CiCi doesn't fly, and after the last Save the Bay, I've heard she doesn't sail, either."

"What happened?"

"The theme was 'Sailing the Seven Seas' and she held the party on one of those big old-fashioned sailing ships—you know, the kind you see in pirate movies? Anyway, the idea was to cruise around Santa Monica Bay during the party. Worked great until the wind kicked up. People started getting seasick, and by the time the ship pulled back into harbor, the waves were so rough that food was flying off the serving platters. It was a mess. Come to think of it, I wouldn't mention last year's benefit to CiCi, either."

Kymbyrlee laughed. "Don't worry, I won't. But, seriously, Alana, who should I consider for my clients?"

"I made a list." I pulled my notes out of my tote bag and handed them to her. "I'll introduce you to the first three as soon as we get there. Then I need to touch base with some of my other clients. I'll get back to you before the auction and introduce you to the rest."

We reached the 101 Highway and I turned north toward Westlake Village. Before I knew it, we were off the 101 and heading into to Hidden Valley.

Hidden Valley is a world away from Malibu. Crisp white fences neatly portion off the valley floor, horses graze quietly under hundred-year-old oak trees. Just enough cattle roam around to allow the gentlemen ranchers to pay taxes at the agricultural rate.

Ranch parcels start at twenty acres and twenty million. The DiCarlo Ranch is average in size for the neighborhood and is supposedly a historically accurate replica of an early American farm. That is, if the farmer had need of a tennis court, a six-car garage, and nine indoor bathrooms.

We zipped down the hill, passed a few meadows of cows, and joined a queue of luxury cars forming at the DiCarlo gates.

"Any questions?" I asked, as Kymbyrlee folded the paper I had given her.

"No. This list is great, Alana. It would take me months to meet all of these people."

"Glad to help," I said. I had to admit, I was proud of my thorough work. I had found it hard to sleep the previous night, what with the annoyance of Tori and the threat of having to date again. Around midnight I had decided that, regardless of the state of Alan's business, I would proceed on legitimizing my own venture. If for no other reason than to rid myself of the threat of the IRS. So I sat down and produced my first bit of official work—a list to help Kymbyrlee familiarize herself with potential clients. The list included names, addresses, approximate incomes, and decorating tastes. If Kymbyrlee followed my directions, she would book her first trip to Indonesia on Monday.

The gates to the ranch were manned by two security guards. Their biceps bulged out of semi-official uniforms. One took a slow lap around the truck and used a mirror-on-a-stick to check underneath. No doubt looking for party crashers. The other one stepped up to the driver's side window.

I rolled down the window and waited for the interrogation.

"Invitations." A hand the size of a doormat thrust into the cab.

I handed over two invites. "Kymbyrlee Chapman was added to the list just this week," I explained.

"IDs," he said.

Kymbyrlee and I handed over our driver's licenses. The guy compared the licenses to the names on the invites and then cross-checked both against a list secured to a clipboard. Made a note. Double-checked it. Looked at our IDs and looked at us. His gaze may have lingered just a tad longer on Kymbyrlee than on me.

"Cell phones. Alana Fox first."

I handed mine over. He dropped it into a Ziploc bag, wrote FOX on a piece of tape stuck to the bag, and then filed it in a bin behind him. He handed back my license. I stuck it under my leg for safekeeping.

"Cell phone, Chapman." Kymbyrlee complied and he repeated his task.

"OK, ladies, you are free to go. You can collect your phones right here on your way home."

He waved us on through. An invisible force swung open a white wooden gate and the two guards prepared to repeat the process with the BMW behind us.

"That was ridiculous!" Kymbyrlee said irritably, as she tossed her license into her bag.

"CiCi just wants to ensure her guests' privacy," I said, although I did agree with her.

"So she plants the Incredible Hulk and his twin brother at the gate?" Kymbyrlee laughed derisively. "Anyone could get past those two!"

"How?"

"Like this."

Kymbyrlee licked her lips slowly, slid her hands under her halter dress, pushed her breasts up and together, and then batted her eyes at me. I had to admit, the act was a traffic stopper.

"So you could get their attention," I admitted. "How would that get you through the gates?"

Kymbyrlee wiggled back into her dress. "It wouldn't get me in, but I could distract them long enough for a dozen others to hop the fence."

That caught me by surprise—what do you say to that?

We joined an orderly procession of Mercedes, Range Rovers, and Hummers. The main house of the DiCarlo property lies carefully tucked away between a small rise and the steep, sagebrush-choked Santa Monica Mountains. To reach the house you first pass a series of pastures defined by the requisite white fences. CiCi's tax-dodging cows graze under the shade of lanky alder trees and ancient oaks. A huge white canvas tent shaded an exercise paddock. Balloons danced and the strains of a fiddle floated happily in the breeze. Smoke rose beyond the paddock and scented the air with the mouthwatering aroma of barbecue. Cars were parked in an empty pasture just below the tent. An excellent use of the property except for one small hitch—the line of cars waiting to park stood as still as the 405 during rush hour.

Kymbyrlee squirmed in her seat. "I have to pee, Alana. Why don't I get out here and meet up with you after you park?"

"Yeah, fine. Where should we meet?"

"It looks like there is a check-in area near that tent. How's that?"

"Sounds great. See you in a few." A few hours at this rate.

Kymbyrlee slid out of the truck and disappeared into the crowd. I entertained myself by drumming my fingers on the steering wheel in time to the fiddle and wondered what the hell was holding things up. As far as I could see, a large vacant area lay open, ready to fill with the backed-up traffic. But the parking attendants ran around pointing and yelling and generally not directing traffic. I was this close to joining Fred in his assessment of valets when the real traffic stopper showed up.

First, a line of alder trees began to sway. I thought it was a gust of wind, but then came the unmistakable sound of whirring rotors. A helicopter no bigger than a grasshopper floated over the vacant space. The chopper hovered for a second as the parking attendants ran around shouting at the cars, to no avail since no one could hear anything over the din. The chopper floated to a landing, the rotors slowed, the passenger door opened, and out hopped Jorjana's favorite gazillionaire, Donald Wesson.

Donald, all six foot five of him, broke from the chopper and raced away as fast as his two left feet could go. He ran like a hobbled, half-blind giraffe and kept his glasses in place with the middle finger of his left hand. As soon as Donald cleared the rotors, the pilot fiddled with the controls, the chopper grew light on its runners and off it went.

Marvelous, I thought. *How did Donald get invited to this?* Then I remembered that the purpose of Save the Bay was to raise a gazillion dollars. Donald Wesson could have just written the check and saved us all the aggravation of trying to park.

Eventually, the non-gazillionairs were allowed to park. I secured the truck in a rut-free space, threw my driver's license into the depths of my tote bag, found my way up the drive, and took my place in line for yet another checkpoint. Young women dressed as Old West barmaids checked IDs against a master list.

"May I see your driver's license, please?"

The barmaid attending to my check-in looked barely old enough to read. Requisite blonde highlights, sprayed on tan, electric blue eyes.

I dug around in my tote, located the license by feel and handed it to her. Her master list was computerized. She scrolled down her screen, clicked on something and handed back the ID.

"Thank you, Ms. Chapman," she said. "Please proceed to the corral, and have a great time!"

Ms. Chapman?

I turned over the license in my hand. Sure enough, it was issued to one Kymbyrlee Chapman. Apparently, the Hulk at the gate had given me Kymbyrlee's ID and in all the hassle I hadn't paid attention.

Good citizen that I am, I was about to straighten out the mix-up when a hand grabbed my elbow in a very decisive grip and pulled me aside. The grip belonged to the CEO of a local biotech firm. Mr. CEO had recently hired a new sales manager from the Midwest. Then he hired me to help the guy's wife find a social circle. To make a long story short, I had run into some problems with that assignment.

"Dorothy Fries is not happy," Mr. CEO told me in a this-is-your-fault tone of voice. "And if Dorothy is not happy, then Steven is not happy. And if Steven is not happy, he is going to move back to that godforsaken hamlet in Minnesota and work for my competition. What the hell am I paying you for?"

"I'm working on it. They will be here today and I am sure that they—"

"You're missing the point, Alana! It's not *them*! It's *her*!"

Mr. CEO ran his fingers through his hair as if a nice comb out would put everything in order.

"Steven could walk buck naked through midnight Mass and convince the congregation they were over-dressed! Which is why I hired him to head up my sales staff!" Mr. CEO closed his eyes and pulled back on his scalp. He massaged the back of his head and took a deep breath.

"Dorothy needs a friend," he said—slowly, carefully, a little too quietly. "A nice, polite friend to keep her busy while Steven makes my company a ton of money. So get off your ass and find that woman a companion!"

He turned and stormed away like a bighorn sheep looking for a tree to ram.

I looked back to the check-in table. I saw the length of the line. The hell with being a good citizen, I was already in.

I tossed Kymbyrlee's ID back in my tote. I needed a drink.

Drinks were served under the canvas canopy stretched over the exercise paddock. Casablanca-style fans stirred the air and mixed the fragrance of the hay floor with the sweet smell of barbecue. Long bars rimmed the perimeter and were staffed by bare-chested male bartenders. Waitresses dressed in cowboy hats and not much else circulated with trays of extra-salty appetizers. Strolling fiddlers serenaded those who cared to listen. Customers bellied up to the bars, plopped down big bills for the drinks, and then turned their attention to game tables gathered in the middle.

I took a quick turn around the paddock, searching for Kymbyrlee.

I paid the ransom for an ice-cold beer and wandered around the games. I spent a few minutes watching a session of Spin the Wheel. For a mere hundred dollars a pop, players could spin a huge roulette wheel marked with prizes. The grand prize was a shiny new one-person sailboat. Lesser prizes included such treasures as gift certificates to local restaurants. One hapless woman spun the wheel, and clapped and squealed and made a genuine spectacle of herself as she spent three hundred dollars to get a hundred and fifty dollars in restaurant certificates. It was all I could do to pull myself away and search for Kymbyrlee.

I took another lap around the paddock. Then I followed the aroma to the barbecue.

Picnic tables were set under the welcome shade of three ancient oak trees. Cooks busily grilled up chicken, ribs, and whole ears of corn on enormous barbecues. A lively country band played an up-tempo tune as guests filled aluminum pie tins from groaning buffet lines. Servers circulated with trays of ice-cold root beer. The overall effect was that of a ritzy country fair—simple, fun—the polar opposite of the disastrous pirate ship. I silently applauded CiCi for her efforts.

I took a lap around the picnic tables.

I walked past the line at the buffet table.

I peeked behind the country band just in case Kymbyrlee was a closet groupie.

I spent some time schmoozing in one spot, just in case Kymbyrlee and I were circling in the same direction and missing each other.

Bingo was available for one hundred dollars a card. I found two of the couples I had corralled into attending already fast friends with fellow rabid bingo players. Another of my couples was in deep discussion over fiberglass versus aluminum hulls with a local boat maker. All my invited guests were happy; feeling a little silly in their costumes, but thrilled to see and be seen.

Where the hell was Kymbyrlee?

Then I spotted Mia Kaplan. Mia, good little client that she was, had followed my advice to a T. First of all, she was there, which put her head and shoulders ahead of Kymbyrlee. Secondly, she wore a tasteful strapless yellow dress with a tight bodice and a full skirt. Her thick auburn hair was up in a loose bun. An exquisite coral and turquoise necklace circled her throat and her face was shaded by a wide straw brim. She looked as cool and delicious as a slice of watermelon.

And she stood just behind Steven Fries and his miserable wife, Dorothy.

I felt a plan forming.

Dorothy and Steven sat at a table where he held the attention of all around him and she picked at her coleslaw. Dorothy Fries is one of those women who ages like your grandmother. Full bosom, pale complexion, and short gray hair frizzing in the growing heat. She looked as if she would be happier churning butter.

I made my way over and sat down across from her. I motioned Mia to join us.

"Mia," I said, "this is Dorothy Fries. She and her husband just moved here from Minnesota. Dorothy, Mia Kaplan."

Mia reached across the table and shook Dorothy's limp hand. "Welcome to Malibu, Dorothy. That is an amazing vest you have on. Did you make it?"

Dorothy perked up and admitted that she did, indeed, make the vest. It was a quilted thing, tiny squares of fabric stitched together and fitting the ample lines of Dorothy's bosom like a glove.

"I'm a quilter, too," Mia said. "Have you been to that vintage fabric store in Santa Monica yet?"

And they were off on one of those strange conversations those artsy women have. Bobbins and yardage and selvages, and sure enough, Dorothy and Mia bonded. Mr. CEO would be thrilled.

Before dying of boredom, I excused myself.

I left the picnic area and walked up to the tent. Workers were busy breaking down the game tables and setting up the chairs for the live auction.

I wandered out to the check-in table to see if "Alana Fox" had signed in. The table was empty. I tried the

Porta-Potties. Opened each door to see if Kymbyrlee had fallen in. I wandered down to the parking area, up and down the aisles of Hummers and Land Rovers. I checked the truck, lest it had fallen into a rut.

I wandered past the landing space for Donald Wesson's helicopter. I waved at the two Hulks chatting by the front gate.

I was irritated and well on my way to truly pissed off. I don't expect much from my clients—really, I don't. Just do exactly what I tell them. How hard is that?

Why did Kymbyrlee bother hiring me in the first place if she wasn't going to follow my instructions? How did she intend to meet these people? How many more opportunities like this one did she think she was going to get? I worked up a nasty little lecture to deliver to Kymbyrlee and looked forward to giving it to her.

I stormed back to the tent, lassoed a bartender, and convinced him to sell me a beer in order to save another dolphin. I took a long draft and distracted myself by observing the paddock transformation.

The canvas walls of the tent were rolled up. A welcome, if warm, flow of air circulated through. The overhead fans set the hay floor astir. At the far end of the paddock stood a raised stage, complete with spotlights and an array of loudspeakers. On stage, a man quietly adjusted a microphone and tested the speakers.

I recognized him immediately. He was Sterling Scott, a professional auctioneer with a chokehold on local fund-raisers. Hostesses such as CiCi DiCarlo don't so much as think about scheduling a shindig unless

Sterling is available. To his credit, the auction would be a lively romp with him at the microphone.

I finished my beer just as CiCi DiCarlo's voice rose from a loudspeaker.

"OK, all you city slickers! Mosey on up to the paddock and be prepared to part with your gold!"

To hurry the moseying, she added, "The liquor up here is on the house!"

Oh, sure, now it's free. A good-natured cheer came from the crowd. I positioned myself at the entrance to the paddock. The better to grab Kymbyrlee when she waltzed through.

The wait staff formed a line on the approach to the paddock gate. The girls handed out wet bandanas to sop up sticky barbecue sauce and the guys bore trays laden with frosty beers and ice-cold vodka shots. The crowd filed through in an orderly fashion, satiated from the feast, happy about the free booze, and resigned to the fact that CiCi intended to wrestle more money out of them.

The guests laughed and chatted and began the Dance of the Seats.

In a land where appearances are everything, where one sits at an event is as important as oxygen. A seat too close to the stage makes one appear too eager. A seat too far away deems one unimportant. The best seat is midway down on the middle aisle. In a paddock set for two hundred, this leaves six seats that everyone wants. And, just like in junior high, people know if they are worthy of jockeying for those seats or not.

I let the silliness ensue and kept looking for Kymbyrlee. I saw a lot of people, including those I intended to introduce Kymbyrlee to, but still no Kymbyrlee. The seats were nearly full when Mia Kaplan caught up to me.

"Have you seen him?" she whispered.

"Seen who?" I whispered back.

"What do you mean, who?" she whispered just a little louder. "Dimitri Greco, of course! You said you had a plan!"

Right, my plan. Silently I cursed. I cursed Kymbyrlee for absorbing all my attention. I cursed myself for forgetting the one client who had done everything I asked of her from the start. And then I looked for Dimitri Greco.

Fortunately, he was right where I expected. Midway down on an aisle seat, one of the six. I whispered instructions to Mia and sent her on her way.

Mia took a deep breath and scurried down the side aisle to the stage. I saw her cross in front of the stage, square her shoulders, lick her lips, and then strut down the center aisle, pretending to look for a seat. Her bright yellow dress swung suggestively with the sway of her hips. Her lightly tanned skin glistened—probably with sweat, but the effect was sultry. Her eyes searched back and forth, as if she expected to join someone. She caught Dimitri's eye, all right, and just as I told her, let her gaze sweep past him as if he were some schmuck. He turned to watch her stroll past him and kept on watching until she found a seat.

Good job! I congratulated her silently. *He'll wonder who she is, and when they do get face-to-face, he'll be delighted to see her.*

The paddock was full to bursting at this point. The servers begged me to find a seat. I obeyed and ended up in the equivalent of Outer Siberia—back row, last seat on the outside.

"Welcome! Welcome one and all!" CiCi beamed at one and all from center stage. "Please be seated!"

CiCi is sixty if she is a day. She doesn't look a week over forty-five. She wore a denim halter dress, the better to display the legendary DiCarlo cleavage. Her hair, abundant black tresses marked with one silver streak, was pulled back into a ponytail and decorated with white roses. From her ears sparkled another CiCi legend—the DiCarlo diamond earrings. The earrings, a major footnote from her second marriage, are two-carat black diamonds encircled with white diamonds. The diamonds are renowned for alternately sparkling and sucking up all the light. CiCi nodded, and the diamonds sparkled and sucked until the crowd quieted down.

"Thank you all for coming! Are you having a good time?"

Appreciative applause came in response.

"Now, in a minute, our good friend, Mr. Sterling Scott, will take all of your money!"

CiCi beamed, the crowd laughed. And the fans above spun like crazy, to no avail. The canvas covering kept the sun out but the heat just spun around. I took off my hat and fanned myself to supplement the breeze. No luck.

"But first, folks, let me tell you what your tax-deductible contributions will provide for."

And she launched into her spiel about how the Santa Monica Bay was dying and what must be done to save it. She skipped her usual parade of earnest but boring scientists. She kept the speech short enough to make her point, but long enough for the wait staff to liquor up the crowd. The booze went down quickly. Almost as quickly as the temperature went up. By the time CiCi finished, I was ready to write a check just for some fresh air.

"I'm going to turn it over to Sterling now," CiCi said. "Be generous."

The crowd applauded as Sterling Scott took the microphone. Expectations ran high. Everyone knew Sterling was capable of raising a bidding war to a fever pitch. People were already ten grand in the hole, but they were all ready to show off what more their checkbooks could handle. And Sterling was the man to push their limits.

The first item for bid was a weekend getaway to Palm Desert, complete with a tennis lesson from the latest teenage sensation. Female, of course. Sterling won the crowd over by refusing to take bids. He insisted that a guy known for his terrible backhand and his penchant for young women "just hand over yer cash!"

Item number two took the stage.

"What we have here, folks, is a real Western getaway!" Two barmaids carried a poster onstage and paraded it back and forth as Sterling laid out the details.

"This here is a week for two at the Bar S Dude Ranch in Arizona!"

In the background came the sound of pounding hooves. Silently, I gave kudos to CiCi for leaving no detail unturned. Sterling gave the pitch, "And this is no ordinary dude ranch! No, siree!"

The hoofbeats grew louder.

"This is a whole seven days at the most luxurious spa you ever saw! Folks, the Bar S will wear your saddle sore for you!"

Louder hoofbeats.

The crowd roared with laughter. Sterling chuckled at his own joke while slyly casing the sea of faces. He knew the crowd. Knew what they were worth. He ambled casually across the stage, winking at the ladies, grinning at the guys. His right hand hung loose at his side as his fingers discreetly sent signals to his assistants planted in the audience. I know this because Sterling pays me for information. Me being a consultant and all.

The pounding hoofbeats stopped just as Sterling made a graceful turn. His usual tactic is to gaze off to stage left, then spin around and shout, "YOU! Start the bidding with…!" And, having caught someone off guard, the bidding begins a hundred dollars over the suggested price. Works like a charm. Usually.

This time, Sterling gazed stage left, his mouth dropped open, and he stood stock-still. The crowd followed his gaze and gasped in unison.

Horses surrounded the paddock. Mounted bareback on each horse sat a masked rider. Cradled under each rider's arm was a rifle. The crowd muttered nervously.

"It's a joke," someone whispered. "Stupid pun about taking our money."

"I think it is in very bad taste," someone sniffed.

Silence fell; a heavy, confused quiet as all struggled to get the joke.

One of the riders slid off a horse, vaulted over the fence and bounded onto the stage. In a split second a handgun was pointed at Sterling Scott's head.

A collective gasp burst from the crowd as each one of the masked riders raised a shotgun.

Onstage, the gunslinger shouted, "Everyone stay in your seats!" The voice was sharp, angry.

And female.

"Put your hands on your heads!"

Like an obedient classroom all hands went up. The mass movement seemed absurd. It had to be a joke.

"Hey, Sterling!" someone shouted. "How does it feel to be held up yourself?"

The crowd laughed nervously, more than ready for the punch line.

"SHUT UP!" The gunslinger kept her gun at Sterling's head while producing another gun to sweep over the crowd. She looked serious enough. Small black eyes glared over a blue bandana that masked her nose and mouth. She wore jeans—not fashionable hip huggers, but serviceable, well-worn dungarees—and a long-sleeved white T-shirt. Petite and built like a gymnast, she was alarmingly at ease with her guns. The crowd tittered nervously.

"Wasn't she in the last kung fu film?" someone whispered.

The horses stood at attention all around the paddock. Two guarded the gate, close enough for me to smell the horses' sweat. I counted ten horses and riders.

All dressed in jeans, white T-shirts, and blue bandanas.

All sporting accessories of rifles and mascara.

Women. All ten of them.

Four of the riders dismounted and entered the paddock. They carried small burlap sacks.

"Whatcha gonna do, Sterling?" someone hollered. "Auction our stuff back to us?"

The crowd doubled over in laughter at that. Good humor restored, certain after all that it was a very bad joke, arms came down.

Oddly, the woman on the stage did not appear amused.

"SHUT UP!" She fired a shot into the air. The abrupt blast startled the crowd right back into confusion. "PUT YOUR ARMS UP!"

The circulating fans spread the acrid stench of gunpowder. Arms flew back into the air. The riders with the sacks hurried down the aisles, snatching watches from the raised wrists.

Someone whispered, "Blanks."

"CiCi's gone too far this time," someone complained.

My raised arms were killing me. My knees began to shake as the roaming riders hopped up on stage to join the petite one.

Sterling Scott stood unnaturally still, hands aloft and eyes watering. One of the riders pulled CiCi from the recesses of the stage and pushed her roughly into the spotlight.

"This should be good," someone whispered. "CiCi's Academy Award performance!"

CiCi stood trembling, hands over her ears, trying to hide the DiCarlo diamonds and doing a lousy job. Her face was as white as the roses in her hair.

"CiCi isn't acting!" someone else whispered.

Everyone around me gasped in horror. It was true; CiCi was a lousy actor. This was no joke.

"You!" The petite one nodded at CiCi. "Put your hands down."

CiCi shook her head.

One of the mounted riders raised a rifle.

"Put your hands down. Now."

Slowly, CiCi lowered her hands. She shook so hard, a rose fell out of her ponytail. It hit the stage with a thud. CiCi jumped back as one of the riders reached over to grab the DiCarlo diamond earrings. Trickles of blood dripped down CiCi's lobes as the rider tossed the earrings in her burlap bag.

The petite one yelled, "Everyone put your faces on your laps!"

For a little girl, she had a commanding voice. The crowd obeyed. I left my head up just enough to see the stage.

Sterling and CiCi lay facedown on the stage. The riders raced back to their horses and leapt up. The petite one shouted, "Now!"

M.A. Simonetti

The riders raised their rifles and fired.

The supports holding up the canopy snapped.

The structure collapsed on the crowd like a canvas soufflé.

Chapter Nine

The wooden supports snapped like toothpicks. A warm *whoosh* of air shot out the sides of the paddock as the canvas tent fell solidly on top of the crowd. Clouds of dust and hay chased out after it. Following the dust came screams.

I found myself standing barefoot just outside the paddock, my toes curled tightly in the dirt. I stared stupidly at my bare feet. Bloodied partygoers crawled out from under the fallen tent in front of me.

I vaguely remembered diving under the fence. I couldn't recall kicking off my shoes.

"Are you OK?" A woman wearing a starched white shirt and navy shorts faced me. A walkie-talkie crackled in her hand. My first thought was to ask her if she knew where my shoes were.

"We've radioed for help," she said briskly. "But the electricity is down. Go to the front gate and make sure it opens."

I obeyed without question, oddly grateful for the responsibility. I started toward the drive, tiptoeing over the loose stones.

"RUN!"

Her shout jolted me out of my stupor. I took off like a shot, leaping and scurrying over the stones like a ballerina with tendonitis. I was halfway to the front gates when a gust of wind nearly knocked me back to the paddock.

The gust of wind was followed by a staccato *pat-pat-pat* and Donald Wesson's helicopter landed lightly in the parking paddock.

Donald stood in the open landing space waving his arms wildly. In each hand he held one half of his glasses. The pilot set the little chopper down lightly. Donald tumbled into the passenger seat. The pilot fiddled with the controls. Donald held the two pieces of his glasses up to his eyes. And then he spotted me.

Donald grabbed the pilot's arm. He pointed at me, jamming his finger into the windshield. The pilot shook his head at Donald. Donald appeared to disagree. To no avail. The helicopter grew light on its runners. It hovered for an instant and then flew quickly away. And left me standing barefoot halfway between the wails of injured partygoers and the cry of approaching sirens.

By the time I made my way to the front gates, the cavalry had arrived. The gates opened just fine. In swept the cops.

Two police cruisers raced up the drive to the house. A third cruiser stopped just outside the gate. One cop jumped out of the car and asked if I was OK. Then he yelled at me to stay out of the way.

I stepped out of the way, found a nice little tree and slid to the ground.

There were more cops. Then came the fire trucks. Then the ambulances.

I was perfectly fine sitting on the sidelines. Not a bit frightened. A little dusty perhaps, and my shoes were still missing, but I was fine. Except for the fact that I broke out in a cold sweat and had to fight the urge to vomit into CiCi's decorative fern border.

I was fine. Until I heard the moans.

Not painful moans. These moans were angry and frustrated, and came from just behind me. I peeked around the trunk of the tree.

Just a few yards away lay the two Hulks, bound together, gagged, and as angry as two bugs stuck to flypaper.

Just about then I remembered Kymbyrlee saying, "I could distract them long enough for a dozen others to hop the fence."

Remarkably, no one was killed, but dozens were injured. A triage center popped up on the manicured lawns in front of CiCi's house. Ambulance after ambulance carted away the most seriously hurt. The aroma of barbecue and the strains of fiddlers were replaced by the crackle of police scanners and the smell of diesel fumes from the fire trucks.

Helicopters swarmed overhead. In Southern California, no crisis occurs without the accompaniment of a flock of helicopters aiding or archiving the event.

Be it earthquake, flood, fire, or fleeing suspect, the choppers always show up.

Some of the helicopters airlifted the wounded. Some searched for the robbers on horseback. Some circled for the story. On the ground, the rescue crews brought order to the chaos. Injuries were inventoried and given priority. Iced drinking water appeared out of nowhere. The slightly injured were bandaged up and sent to the house to talk to the police. The not injured at all were given a drink of water and told to sit in the shade until the cops got around to us.

Which took just about forever. At sunset, I sat on CiCi's front porch nursing a cup of water and desperately willing it to turn into vodka.

Mia Kaplan sat next to me, holding an ice pack to a nasty black eye. Hay clung to her hair, dust covered everything else. We watched with dulled interest as CiCi's party guests limped to their cars like a parade of war refugees. An unsteady Steven Fries hobbled by, leaning heavily on Dorothy of the quilted vest. Mia rose.

"I'm going to give her a hand with him," she said wearily. "Are you coming?"

"I still have to talk to the police. You go ahead."

Mia gave me a gentle hug and groaned as she got up. She caught up with the Frieses, put Steven's arm over her shoulders, and the three of them joined the grim procession to the parking paddock.

Just outside the gates, the road was clogged with TV news vans. The two Hulks, released from bondage, strutted angrily back and forth. Two motorcycle cops stood silently at attention. Blonde and blow-dried TV report-ers, hustling for the story, had sense enough to leave the cops and the Hulks alone. But every Hummer and Land Rover trying to leave the scene had to squeeze through a swarm of microphones thrust at its windows. I could just see the morning headlines.

"You can come in now."

A female detective stood at the threshold of CiCi's front door. Thirty-ish, trim in a Gym Rat sort of way, she wore brown slacks, a white blouse, and a gun that outweighed her. I followed her to CiCi's dining room.

The dining room overlooked CiCi's pond—perfectly accessorized with weeping willows and decorative swans. The swans swam in slow circles, apparently oblivious to the circus around them. Inside, CiCi's dining table was fully extended. A whole posse of police detectives inter-viewed disheveled guests. The room smelled of dust and blood and bewilderment.

Gym Rat took a seat at the head of the table. To her left sat a guy who looked as if he had just been plucked from a casting call for "gruff, middle-aged cop." Forty-something, full head of dark hair, either a former line-backer or a Sumo wrestler, he was just a doughnut shy of becoming a cop caricature.

"I'm Tina Driscoll," said Gym Rat. "This is Detective Sanchez."

Gym Rat turned on a tape recorder. A stack of paper lay next to it. A notebook with scribbled notes lay next to that. A cell phone, a pen, all in neat order.

In front of Sanchez—nothing. I figured he was the ideas guy.

"Your name, please." Gym Rat picked up the stack of papers.

"Alana Fox."

She gave Sanchez a look.

"You have some identification, Ms. Fox?" This from Sanchez. His voice matched his caricature. Gruff, originating from deep down in his shoes somewhere.

"Well, actually…"

I had two problems here. One was I had no idea where my tote bag was. The other was that the ID in the tote bag wasn't mine.

"There's a pile of personal belongings over there."

Sanchez pointed to somewhere outside of the dining room. He leaned over to whisper something to Gym Rat as I left.

I found the pile of belongings in a room decorated with dainty gilded chairs and needlepoint pillows. A cop stood guard. I described my tote bag. He retrieved it. On a whim, I described my shoes. He retrieved them, too.

That part was easy. Now I had to explain why I had Kymbyrlee's ID.

"Is your ID in there, Ms. Fox?" Sanchez asked as I sat back down.

"Well, actually…" I dug around thinking it would be very convenient if Kymbyrlee's ID were not there. Sadly, I found it.

The part of me that is basically honest handed it to him.

"This is for...," he began, and stumbled over the spelling of Kymbyrlee.

"Yeah, it's for Kymbyrlee Chapman." I explained the mix-up at the gate.

Gym Rat consulted some list just a little too intently. When I finished, she gave Sanchez the look again. She handed him the list and left to make a call on her cell. Just out of earshot.

"You got any other ID that says you're Alana Fox?" Sanchez asked as he scanned the list.

I pulled out my wallet. I produced an insurance card, a voter ID, a Neiman Marcus credit card, a Saks Fifth Avenue credit card, a Nordstrom credit card, a Barneys' credit card, and a Ralphs' grocery card.

All engraved with the name Alana Fox.

Sanchez's lips twitched as he picked up each one. Like there was something funny.

Gym Rat returned. Snapped her phone shut. Consulted more notes. She sure was big on lists.

"What's your address, Ms. Fox?" she asked.

I told her. She consulted her notes.

"What's your weight on your driver's license?" she asked.

I told her.

"You're kidding." Sanchez leaned over the table to get a better gander at me.

"I'm not kidding," I said indignantly. "If you guys want an accurate weight on driver's licenses, you need to put in a scale at the DMV."

Sanchez's lips twitched again. Gym Rat stayed on the task at hand.

"OK, Ms. Fox," she said. "We'll just assume you are who you say you are. Can you explain your relationship to Kymbyrlee Chapman?"

I could and I did. I told them everything that wasn't of interest to the IRS. Called myself a consultant. Called Kymbyrlee a new client. Confirmed that I had brought her to Save the Bay but hadn't seen her since she went to pee. Skipped the part about giving her a list with the clients' personal information on it. Skipped the part about how she said she could sneak a dozen others past the Hulks. It took a good ten minutes to spin the story the way I wanted it told. Still, there was no way to avoid making myself look like a fool.

The detectives shared that look again. Some sort of silent agreement passed between them. Gym Rat handed yet another list to Sanchez, then gathered up her stuff and left without a word.

Sanchez held the list in both hands like it was a bird about to take wing.

"Interesting story, Ms. Fox," Sanchez said. "Gotta be honest with you, I'm not sure I believe you." The twitch was gone.

How could he not believe me? I'd been 80 percent honest with the guy.

"I got some problems here." Sanchez laid the list on the table and pointed at it with his finger. "We got the list of all the guests. According to our list, the only guest who didn't show up today was one Alana Fox. Now here you are and you have this Chapman woman's ID. And, yeah, you have a story about how you ended up with it, but ya know what?" He paused and leaned back in his seat. "I don't believe you."

That was just rude.

I fought the urge to tell him just what I thought of his opinion. Something told me to respond only when asked a question. And, rude or not, he had not asked a question, so I kept my mouth shut. The silence grew long. Eventually he spoke first.

"Why did you bring a woman who lied to you to the most exclusive shindig in town, Ms. Fox?"

"I told you. She explained herself."

"But she ditched you when you got here."

"Yes."

"And you haven't seen her since?"

"No."

"Don't you find it just a little strange that she never checked in at the desk and no one has seen her since you brought her on the premises?"

"Yes." Strange didn't begin to explain it. But I didn't like his attitude so I wasn't about to get all warm and fuzzy and share my feelings. I didn't like his insinuation that I had anything to do with Kymbyrlee disappearing. Yeah, I was worried that Kymbyrlee had disappeared. Yeah, I knew it looked suspicious. But he was acting like I was guilty of something and I hadn't even told him the stuff that looked really suspicious.

And, frankly, no one had any proof that Kymbyrlee was involved in all of this. I sure as hell wasn't going to be labeled an accomplice before anyone knew for a fact that she had done something. For all I knew, she really had fallen into a Porta-Potty and been too embarrassed to call out for help.

I tossed my wallet back into my tote. I was stalling for time. I was also wondering if I needed to call an attorney.

And then a woman's scream brought everything in the room to a halt. It was as if an invisible force pushed the pause button. The woman screamed again. Something was seriously amiss upstairs.

Sanchez shouted something. Every detective in the place responded as if he or she had memorized a twelve-page document on Official Responses to Unexpected Screaming. Some ran outside, some scattered through the house. Gym Rat and Sanchez ran toward the screams. I followed them.

We raced up the sweeping staircase in the grand foyer, past the oil paintings of the DiCarlo ancestors, and down a hallway laid with a floral carpet runner. Sanchez skidded at the end of the passage, collided with a Queen Anne console and sent a vase of roses crashing to the floor. Gym Rat leaped gracefully over the rubble, gun at the ready, and raced through a set of double doors. I arrived on her heels to find CiCi DiCarlo standing in the middle of the master bedroom.

Gauze bandages adorned CiCi's ears. She pointed with a manicured finger to the wall behind a brass bed. There, a quarter-sized hole stood out on the flocked wallpaper, bits of wallboard poking through. From the hole protruded two electrical wires. From the wires hung a device that looked like a transistor radio.

"They stole it!" CiCi cried.

"Stole what?" Gym Rat and I asked in unison.

"My painting! My priceless Balinese painting!"

A pit in my stomach grew as I recalled Kymbyrlee saying, "I've traveled extensively in Indonesia."

And then I noticed another damn list on the floor. This one didn't belong to Gym Rat. This one was the list of potential clients I had drawn up and given to Kymbyrlee Chapman.

I still didn't know where Kymbyrlee was, but I sure as hell knew where she had been.

Chapter Ten

The cops were extremely interested in my list.

Gym Rat scribbled her own little inventory of the names.

Sanchez had someone take it away for prints.

I explained, yet again, my relationship to Kymbyrlee Chapman, and why in the world I would provide her with the names, addresses, and phone numbers of people attending Save the Bay.

Try as I might, I couldn't explain it. And I tried damn hard. It might have been easier if I had told the whole truth. But then there was a stupid issue I had with avoiding the IRS. Can't begin to tell you how much I was wishing I had just paid the damn taxes in the first place.

So I stuck to my story that Kymbyrlee had paid me as a consultant and the list was just part of what a consultant does. I got the impression the cops didn't buy it. Frankly, I was a little surprised when they let me go home.

My truck was the only vehicle left in the pasture. I barreled out to the driveway, ruts or no ruts. The Hulks remained on guard.

I pulled up to the gate and leaned my head out the window.

"You guys have my cell phone?" I asked one of the Hulks.

He shook his head. "They've all been picked up."

"But I didn't pick mine up!" I protested.

"Sorry, lady," he said. He wasn't the least bit sorry.

The drive home seemed endless. When I finally got there, I left the truck parked at the curb and went straight to the kitchen. Poured gin and limoncello straight up into a container I normally use as a flower vase. Found my way to the office. Propped my feet up on the desk and dialed Jorjana's most private number. I knew she would be awake and waiting to hear from me.

"It's me," I said.

"Tell me."

I heard her TV in the background and the somber voice of an anchorman reading the latest. I told her my side.

"It sounds as if the police suspect you of having a hand in this tragedy," Jorjana commented.

"You think?" I replied sarcastically.

"Remember that I am on your side, Alana," she reprimanded me gently.

"Sorry," I sighed. "I am guilty of bringing Kymbyrlee there."

"That was not a crime. You must cooperate with the authorities. Justice will prevail and your name will be cleared."

Her support cheered me a bit. "What about CiCi? She'll be furious when she figures out I brought Kymbyrlee."

"Do not be silly," Jorjana snorted. "CiCi DiCarlo will turn this to her advantage in no time. She will be on the cover of *People* next week, you mark my words."

"You're probably right."

"I am always right," Jorjana replied, believing it completely.

We agreed to talk in the morning at Sunday Brunch and rang off. I poured myself another tankard of gin, straight up. Took a long, hot shower and fell into bed.

My phone rang through the night. I let the calls go and tossed and turned until dawn. Then I brewed an extra-strength pot of coffee and stood in the shower again until the hot water ran out. I drank the pot of coffee, set another to brew, and went to see what was going in the world. As if I didn't know.

The online newspapers were full of it.

The Internet gossip sites were positively hopping with updates.

All news sources were big on the "Maidens on Horseback" details and light on the injuries.

Much speculation centered on the "Curse of the DiCarlo Diamonds."

The cops named a person of interest—one Kymbyrlee Chapman.

Oddly, there were no reports of the Balinese painting stolen from the house. Fortunately, there was no mention of my list.

Eventually, I mustered the courage to face my phone messages. Most of the calls came from reporters. No surprise there, since reporters are yet another group I trade info with on a regular basis. I deleted the reporters. They couldn't tell me anything I didn't already know, so there was nothing in it for me to return their calls.

This left only six messages.

The first was from David Currie.

"Darling! Jorjana told me. Call me."

The second message was from Fred, received that very morning.

"Are you OK? I can come by or something."

That was touching. Sunday is Fred's day off. It was a gesture of epic proportions for him to offer to come by. I made a note to thank him for his kindness.

The other four calls came from a frantic Donald Wesson, pleading for my forgiveness. Apparently, Donald did not know how to fly a helicopter or he would have tossed the pilot out and let me in.

"Nice, Donald," I said to the machine. "Never occurred to you to give me your spot?"

I drank the second pot of coffee.

Medicated an oddly persistent headache.

I told myself that I was innocent. I told myself that Jorjana was always right. I told myself that I had nothing to worry about. If it turned out that I did, Jorjana had access to the best legal talent in town.

Somehow, I didn't feel all that much better. Still, I got in the truck and headed to Sunday Brunch at the York estate.

I found Jorjana by the pool. She presides over Sunday Brunch from a round table shaded by a large umbrella.

She wore a bright orange hat, a linen tunic cut from a colorful madras cloth, and sunglasses the size of saucers. She was on the phone.

Brunch preparations sailed along smoothly. Buffet tables groaned under the weight of freshly sliced melons and strawberries, chewy bagels with cream cheese and lox, lightly dressed pasta salads, grilled vegetables with peppers, sweet muffins, scrambled eggs with Portuguese sausage, roasted red potatoes, and the ever-popular carved roast beast. Servers carefully packed ice into the stand designated for desserts. Three fully stocked bars stood at the ready. I snagged a plain ginger ale and joined Jorjana.

"Good morning, Alana!" Jorjana snapped her phone shut. "Franklin is out. He sends his love."

"Sorry to miss him." I took the seat across from her. A gentle breeze blew in from the ocean. The day was pleasant in that offhanded way that Malibu Sundays are. Clear sunny skies, endless views, the Pacific Ocean rolling lazily at my feet. I took a shot at enjoying myself and sipped the ginger ale.

A jazz trio played an up-tempo song. Scattered around the pool deck were tables of eight—open seating to encourage mingling. Bartenders stood at attention. The sushi chef's knives flew as he sliced and chopped up raw everything. The day was sunny and bright and the perfect breeze kept the temperature hovering around just right. The only thing missing were the guests.

"Where is everyone?" I asked Jorjana.

She glanced at her watch. Then lowered her sun-glasses and rechecked the time. She shook the watch.

"Traffic delays?" she suggested.

I looked over my shoulder to the house. The doors to the front foyer were wide open. Through them I saw the army of valets waiting for cars to park. I turned back. Around the pool stood the wait staff, trays in hand. The jazz trio picked up the beat as if to pull guests out of thin air.

I checked my watch. It was well past the fashionably late hour. I was just about to check a calendar when David Currie blew in.

David wore a white linen suit accessorized with a look of vexation. He gave Jorjana a peck on the cheek and fell into the chair next to me.

"You look dreadful, darling! I have terrible news! CiCi has been working the phones since *dawn*! You won't *believe* what that woman is saying about you! She is telling everyone that you not only brought that dreadful person to Save the Bay, but you gave her a list of names and addresses and what-have-you! Can you *believe* it?"

I felt my heart sink. Right down to the cement lining of Jorjana's pool. Jorjana's mouth made a little O. She picked up her phone and started dialing. David took one look at me and groaned.

"Oh no! It's true?"

I had to admit that it was.

"You can't be serious! Darling, what were you thinking?"

"I was thinking that I was being thorough." I explained my decision to turn my consulting for Kymbyrlee into a full-time legitimate business. I mentioned my concern that Tori was right and Alan's business was going under. I explained my motive to end the threat of the IRS showing up. I was getting to the good part about how valuable my Rolodex was when David waved his hands in front of his face to hush me.

"You gave a woman you just met private information on your friends? Have you lost your mind? Don't answer that, I have to think." He leaned back and closed his eyes.

Jorjana ended her phone conversation. Her face was pale. I flagged down a server and requested a round of drinks. He rushed off to fill the order. It wasn't as if the guy had anything else to do.

Jorjana gently set her phone on the table.

"I have learned some disturbing news, Alana. It appears the police spent the night visiting the homes of the guests on your list who attended Save the Bay. The police are very interested in your relationship with Kymbyrlee Chapman. In addition, questions have been raised regarding your knowledge of the private affairs of others."

"Oh no. Now what?"

Jorjana, of course, knew. "You must cooperate with the police. They will come to understand that you are innocent. Do you not agree, David?"

David opened his eyes. He was not happy with me.

"This mess is *exactly* what Jorjana and I were worried about when we told you to give up on your vendetta against Tori! For God's sake, Alana! What were you thinking? Don't answer that!"

The waiter appeared just then with a tray of drinks. Mimosas for Jorjana and David. Gin, ginger ale, and limoncello for me. I downed mine before he served Jorjana and David. I sent him back for a refill.

"Listen to me, Alana. And for once, do as I tell you."

David was as serious as I have ever seen him. I felt it prudent to pay attention.

"Jorjana is right about the police. Cooperate with them. But you need to have an attorney with you." David turned to Jorjana. "Can you get someone for her?"

Jorjana nodded, picked up her phone and started dialing.

"We need to counter CiCi's hysteria to save your reputation," David said. "Here's what I will do for you. I will spread the word about how loopy she gets on painkillers—what with those horrible injuries to her earlobes. The poor dear must be delusional to spread such a ridiculous story about our darling Alana!"

David looked immensely pleased with himself. "Thank God the papers said nothing about that ridiculous list of yours, darling! It will be her word against mine. I believe I will come out ahead on this. And I will pay a little visit to CiCi to get her to back off. I do have something on her that I have been saving for a rainy day!"

He held his hand out, palm up. "Was that a raindrop I just felt?"

I felt better immediately. Gratitude welled up as I rose to give him a hug. He did not hug me back.

"Sit down, darling. I am not through with you."

I sat. Jorjana hung up her phone.

"I will get you out of this mess under one condition," David said. "You do not continue your vendetta against Little Miss. I am *serious*, darling! I am not going to give up what I have on CiCi DiCarlo unless you promise to back off of Tori."

I started to protest. But the looks from Jorjana and David made me pause. And made me think. Maybe I had accomplished all that I needed to regarding Tori. She was safely isolated. She had no influence over the court documents that allowed for my alimony. And my anger toward her sure had led me into one hell of a mess. For the first time, I felt just the tiniest shift in my attitude toward Tori. Frankly, I needed to focus my energy on saving my reputation. And for that, I really needed David. I agreed to back off Tori. I didn't even choke on the words.

David rose and returned my hug. "Then I am off to pay my respects to CiCi. I'll call you later, darling."

And he was off. Just as a pitiful few nobodies arrived for Sunday Brunch.

As Jorjana graciously greeted the new arrivals, I sat silently and considered my situation. I had plenty of time to do this—no one acknowledged me. A week ago, I would have been sought out and courted at this very table. But a week ago, I hadn't yet met Kymbyrlee Chapman. A week ago, I had the respect of the whole town. A week ago, I had no idea how lucky I was.

After what seemed like forever, Perry—Jorjana's social secretary—appeared with news.

"A Detective Sanchez and a Detective Driscoll wish to speak with you, Mrs. Fox." Perry efficiently presented their business cards. "I have shown them to the library." With a shudder, he added, "They arrived in a patrol car, Mrs. York, and they refuse to let the valets put it out of sight."

Jorjana was thrilled.

"Let the car stay, Perry." To me, she exclaimed, "I will tell our guests that the police are here to seek your advice! GO! Talk to them, Alana!"

I rose reluctantly. Jorjana would have none of it. "Chin up, Alana! You must not look guilty!"

Chin up, I dragged my innocent little butt to the library.

The York library is an octagonal-shaped room, two stories high, with the requisite mahogany paneling and endless stacks of musty books. A massive fireplace dwarfs a seating area of bulky leather chairs. The detectives stood by the fireplace. Neither of them had wasted time on a shower since our last meeting. Sanchez looked like he had slept in his suit. Gym Rat ran her tongue over her teeth as if to rub off the fuzz.

"Good morning." I greeted them as warmly as one greets an oral surgeon.

"Good afternoon," they corrected me.

We negotiated seats, staring at each other across a tiled coffee table that could double as an ice rink. The detectives turned down my offer of refreshments.

Had I cared, the silence that followed would have been uncomfortable.

"Where were you last night, Ms. Fox?" Gym Rat skipped the niceties.

"At home."

"Alone?"

"Yes."

"Can you prove it?"

"I spoke with Mrs. York on the phone around nine o'clock."

That and the empty jug of gin could verify this.

"You didn't leave the house, go anywhere, see anyone?" Gym Rat made it sound like a night at home alone was suspicious.

"I was home. I spoke to Jorjana and went to bed. If I had been out, you likely would have run into me on PCH. I understand you two were busy last night."

Sanchez's lips twitched.

Gym Rat smiled. Not a pleasant smile—a small, superior smile, like the one an older sister gives a younger sister before turning her in for swiping Mom's lipstick.

"Kymbyrlee Chapman turned up this morning," Gym Rat said.

I had the sense she was trying to catch me off guard. I wasn't about to give her that satisfaction. I merely asked, "Where?"

"Her sister found her body floating in the pool. Gunshot to the chest. She wasn't wearing anything but the DiCarlo diamond earrings."

Chapter Eleven

"Do you own a gun, Ms. Fox?" This from Sanchez.

"No."

"Any idea how Kymbyrlee Chapman ended up in her sister's pool?"

"No."

"Anyone that can verify your whereabouts last night?"

"I told you, I called Mrs. York around nine o'clock."

I had a bad feeling about where this line of questioning was going.

"So you have nothing else to add to your story?" Sanchez, on the questions like a bulldog on a bone.

"I've told you everything."

Well, mostly everything. That's when it occurred to me that I just might need access to Jorjana's legal team. "If this interview is going to drag on, I would like to call my attorney."

There's nothing like the threat of a lawyer to sweep cops out of a room.

Sanchez and Gym Rat decided they had enough of whatever it was they wanted from me. Sanchez gave me one of his cards. He suggested I stick around Malibu for the time being.

I let them find their own way out.

Kymbyrlee was dead? But she had just been with me. Chatting about her future. Lying to me about it, yeah, but at least looking toward it. And now she was gone. But I had nothing whatsoever to do with any of it. And yet, it was quite obvious the cops didn't believe me. And I had no idea how to change their minds.

Gym Rat was so rigid she probably couldn't bend at the waist. Sanchez was too focused on my whereabouts and my associations to even consider my innocence. So there I was, completely innocent, for once, and looking as guilty as hell. It was definitely time for a lawyer.

Or time for a drink. A pour-to-the-rim tumbler of gin and a let-me-dive-in-alone-and-swim-around-in-it drink.

I scribbled a hasty note to Jorjana, promising to call her later. I left the note with Perry, the social secretary, collected the truck from the valet, and sped home.

I made it home in record time—probably because every cop in town was busy trying to find me guilty of anything but doing eighty on PCH. I parked the truck outside the house, took the time to set the brake and lock the doors, opened the gate at the top of the stairs and came to a sudden stop.

I had company.

It was the Diversion from the Country Mart parking lot.

He stood ramrod straight, cooling his heels on my stoop. He wore a tropical wool suit cut for his build and his alone. His hair was a bit long in that impoverished

European royalty manner. His complexion was clear and tanned in a manner that connected all the angles of his face just beautifully. His brown eyes were fringed with the most remarkable lashes. He was fit, too. Not a muscle out of place. I know this because I spent a full thirty seconds hunting for imperfections.

I would have kept staring but he spotted me at the top of the stairs.

He smiled. Perfect teeth, of course.

"Mrs. Fox?"

I made my way to the bottom of the stairs without tripping and falling on my face. With all the poise of a fourteen-year-old, I confirmed that I was Mrs. Fox. Please call me Alana.

He handed me an embossed business card. No wedding ring on the hand that presented it.

"My name is Jackson Jones. I am here on behalf of CiCi DiCarlo. If I could have a few moments of your time?"

The card read:

Jackson Jones

Hong Kong - New York - La Jolla

"La Jolla?" I asked.

"I winter there."

Of course he did.

"How do I know CiCi sent you?" My bullshit detector, badly bruised though it was, rose.

"I have a letter of introduction from Mrs. DiCarlo."

That he did. Handwritten on CiCi's personal stationery, it read:

Alana,

Cooperate fully with Mr. Jones or I will see to it that Tori and Alan Fox are added to my A-list.

CiCi

Great. Just great. Running off her mouth about me wasn't enough. Now CiCi was threatening to extricate Tori from social solitary confinement. Sadly, CiCi was the one person who could do just that. I was at her mercy, until David came through with his "little tidbit" to keep CiCi at bay.

Under the circumstances, I let Mr. Jones in.

I led the way to the kitchen, threw my bag on the counter and opened the fridge.

"Can I get you a drink?"

As long as he wanted gin straight up, I could accommodate him. If he wanted something else, I could accommodate that, too.

Although it did seem more civilized to start with a drink.

"No, thank you. I won't be long."

That disappointed me on more than one level.

Jackson Jones unbuttoned his suit jacket and sat on the couch. His jacket parted without so much as a wrinkle. He sat forward, forearms on his knees, hands clasped together. I opted not to hop onto his lap and sat on the other side of the couch.

"I am working with Mrs. DiCarlo to retrieve her stolen Balinese painting," he began.

"Are you a cop?"

This I just could not picture. He was as different from Detective Sanchez as a Rolex is from a sundial.

"No, I am not with the police."

"Private detective?"

"In a manner of speaking." He smiled again. Just enough for the corners of his mouth to turn up. I resisted the urge to part his lips with my tongue.

"I am something of an expert in Asian art. There is reason to suspect that Mrs. DiCarlo's piece will be sold on the black market. She retained me to help her recover the painting."

"Aren't the police doing that?"

"As a private citizen, I am able to approach the problem, ah, differently than the police."

I could just imagine.

"What can you tell me about Kymbyrlee Chapman?" he asked.

"I know she is dead."

"Yes, unfortunate, that." Jackson Jones did not appear too terribly cut up about it. "Mrs. DiCarlo is relieved that her earrings will be returned, but her main concern is with the painting."

"I don't know anything about the painting," I said irritably. "I've gone over all of this with the police. I took Kymbyrlee to Save the Bay to meet clients for this new business she said she was starting. She left to use the bathroom before I even parked. I haven't seen her since then and I had no idea what she was up to."

Jackson Jones leaned back on the sofa. His right arm stretched out over the top. His left ankle crossed over his right knee. His left hand, the one without the wedding ring, straightened his pants leg.

"Tell me how you met Kymbyrlee."

I knew that speech well enough. I avoided eye contact with those deep brown eyes and delivered the whole Kymbyrlee story in just under ten minutes.

"You are certain she said her travels were in Indonesia?"

"Yes."

"Interesting." His mouth tightened. He stood and walked to the sliding glass door, but his eyes were not focused on the view. He stuck his hands in his pockets and absentmindedly jingled his loose change. It surprised me that he carried cash at all.

"Can you describe her?"

"About five feet five inches tall, honey-blonde—"

"No, describe her mannerisms, how she walks, the things that cannot be changed cosmetically."

That took some thinking.

"Still five foot five," I began. "About thirty. Flawless complexion, a copper undertone to her tan. Fine hair, dark naturally. The way she poured her tea made me think she spent time abroad. Amazing figure, or she's seen a great plastic surgeon."

I paused, remembering seeing Kymbyrlee in the altogether when making her change her outfit for Save the Bay. Then it dawned on me what was unique about her. And it wasn't those damned perky breasts. I recalled following her into the living room of Mallory's mausoleum and watching her trip lightly away from the truck in search of a Porta-Potty.

"She moves smoothly—like a cat."

His face relaxed, as if I had handed him a map to the location of the missing painting.

"You have very good powers of observation, Alana."

"I like to think that I am a good judge of character."

"Kymbyrlee Chapman aside."

That hurt. I must have winced.

"Please forgive me."

He came back to the couch and sat close enough to me that our knees nearly touched.

It was at that moment, just before I threw myself at Jackson Jones, that Donald Wesson flew through my front door.

"Alana! We have to talk!" Donald Wesson, arms and legs askew, stumbled into the room. Paused. Adjusted a new pair of glasses with his middle finger.

"Who's he?" Donald pointed at Jackson Jones.

Jackson blinked, recovered in a nanosecond, stood and extended his hand to Donald. The equivalent of Cary Grant greeting Jerry Lewis.

"Mr. Wesson," he said graciously. "It is a pleasure to meet you, sir. My name is Jackson Jones. I am discussing the unfortunate event at Save the Bay with Mrs. Fox."

"Oh, right." Ignoring Jackson, Donald turned to me. "Alana, I'm sorry about the helicopter. The pilot wouldn't let me get out. You didn't return my calls. Are you mad at me?"

"I'm not mad at you," I reassured him. "Is that all? Because we were—"

"I need to talk to you alone, Alana." Donald blushed, rocking back and forth on his giant feet.

Jackson barely hid his amusement at Donald's discomfort. With a quiet cough, he buttoned his jacket and said, "I was just leaving. Thank you for your time, Alana. Mr. Wesson? A pleasure, sir."

And he was gone.

An uncomfortable silence came over the room. I glared at Donald, torn between the desire to race after Jackson Jones and the desire to kick Donald's bony butt out the door after him.

"I don't like that guy, Alana." Donald plopped down on the sofa like he was a welcome guest. "I don't like him at all."

"I didn't ask your opinion," I said snottily.

"You are mad, aren't you?" Donald whined.

Something in Donald's voice, whiny or not, tugged at my conscience. Donald didn't deserve my snotty attitude. Although socially retarded, he was a kind soul. "I'm sorry, Donald." I sat next to him, gently patted his knee, gave him my attention in spite of myself. "You said we needed to talk. What is on your mind?"

Donald regarded me warily, like a caveman suspicious of a suddenly tame woolly mammoth. "Are you sure you aren't mad at me? I did try to get the pilot to stop."

"I'm not mad at you. Is that all? Because I really need…"

But Donald wasn't done. He buried his face in his hands and gently rocked back and forth. I knew this routine. I'd seen it a million times. I got comfortable and waited for Donald to calm the tornados in his head. Eventually one of the twisters would work its way out. Eventually it did, but I could have downed four or five drinks in the meantime.

"I want to get married," Donald began. "But not to you."

I kept quiet. Donald mistook my silence.

"I'm sorry, Alana! Did I hurt your feelings?"

He was so off the mark there that I made a special effort to set him straight.

"NO!" I cried.

Donald jerked back, looking for all the world like a startled ostrich. A beeper attached to his belt snapped off, bounced on my tile floor, and emitted a high-pitched screech. Its little lights blinked furiously. Donald leaned over to pick it up, banged his head on the coffee table and fell to the floor.

"Ouch! My head!" He lay on the floor clutching his head while the beeper continued to screech. I bent over to help him as the front door burst open.

"Hold it right there!"

Two thick necks dressed in navy blue suits towered over me. I could not help but notice they had guns. And the guns were pointed at me.

"Oh, for crying out loud!" I said.

"Back away from Mr. Wesson."

That did not sit well with me. I stood up and kicked Donald.

"These jerks with you, Donald?"

Donald scrambled to his feet, squared his shoulders, straightened his glasses and said, with more authority than I thought possible, "I accidentally dropped the pager. Thank you for your timely response. That will be all."

"Is there anyone else here, sir?" One of the Necks swept through the kitchen and great room, gun held up like a leaky syringe.

"Who are these guys, Donald?" I asked in annoyance.

"Bodyguards," Donald explained. "I apologize for their rudeness." To the men, he said, "There was someone here a few minutes ago. If you didn't see him leave, then I need to worry about what kind of job you are doing. Please wait outside."

Remarkably, the guys re-holstered their guns. One of them picked up the mischievous pager, reset its buttons to make it shut up, and handed it back to Donald.

"Sorry, Mr. Wesson. We'll be just outside the door." They left without acknowledging me.

"Bodyguards?" I wasn't sure what was more surprising, the bodyguards or Donald's authoritative stance with them.

He shrugged. "My head of security thinks you might be dangerous after everything that happened yesterday."

"Dangerous?"

"I told him he was being stupid but he wouldn't listen. He might tell my board of directors that I'm acting foolishly. And I don't want to go through that again."

"Again?" I slumped onto the couch, almost afraid to wonder what new travesty would burst though my front door next.

Weakly, I patted the couch and invited him to sit. The sooner I dealt with him, the sooner I could drink.

"You said you want to get married?" I prompted.

"Yes."

"Do you want me to help you find a girl?"

Donald smiled shyly. "I do."

This would not be easy. Gazillionaire or not, Donald was an acquired taste. With hours of coaching, a fashion makeover, and a boatload of luck, Donald might become socially acceptable. Maybe. And then he would need some serious practice in conversation skills before I inflicted him on anyone.

Still, I warmed to the possibilities. I might have luck diluting him in a crowd like Sunday Brunch. He had attended Save the Bay and not caused a spectacle there. Although there had been a lot of competition for that dubious honor.

I could have David and Jorjana spread the word that Malibu's biggest gazillionaire was available. And that I was the one handling his social calendar. If that didn't repair my reputation, nothing would.

Donald would still need some clothes and coaching on conversation, of course. Lucky for him, I happened to have some free time on my hands.

"Let's start by having you come to a Sunday Brunch at Jorjana York's," I suggested.

"What time is Sunday Brunch?"

"It starts at eleven and goes until two thirty or so."

The time posed a problem.

"I go to church at nine on Sunday and then my cook has my cornflakes and strawberries ready at ten thirty. I never miss my Sunday cornflakes and strawberries and I'm not hungry again until three. Do you ever have Brunch on Saturday? I have breakfast at seven on Saturday, so I could eat again at noon."

I didn't bother to point out that Sunday Brunch was less about the meal and more about the seeing and being seen. Those nuances were beyond Donald. I managed to convince him that the staff at the York estate could provide cornflakes and strawberries for him and that his cook would not mind the change in schedule.

I promised to call him with the details, and then I sent him and the Necks on their merry way. I even waved good-bye to them from my front courtyard.

Which left me alone to wonder how Jackson Jones had managed to leave my house through the front door and out the courtyard—the only exit from the house—without the Necks seeing him go.

Chapter Twelve

I didn't waste a lot of time wondering what became of Jackson Jones. I sat right down on my own front doorstep and wasted time wondering what the hell had happened to me. How I had gone from a respected member of Malibu society to a suspect in a robbery and a murder? Not to mention the type of person who has private investigators knocking at her door.

And then there was CiCi DiCarlo's slander campaign.

Things were definitely not rosy. I granted myself a full five minutes of self-pity. And since I didn't get where I as by lying around feeling sorry for myself, I picked myself up and set about straightening out the mess.

I went back into the house and brewed a pot of coffee. Took the coffee into my office, sat at the desk and began dialing.

First, I left a message at the York estate asking Jorjana to send over one of her best attorneys.

Then I turned my attention to what was left of my life.

I listened to my phone messages. All two of them.

One was from Dorothy Fries: "Steven's ankle is broken and they kept him in the hospital. I'm so sorry we won't make the Brunch. Is it possible to go another time?"

The second was from Mia Kaplan: "I have bruises everywhere! I look like hell! How am I going to get Dimitri to cast me in his damn movie when I look like this? I'm going to skip Brunch today, sorry. Do you know Steven Fries is in the hospital?"

I called the Fries home and left a message for Dorothy, expressing my concern for her husband and extending another invitation to Brunch at their convenience. Then I arranged to have flowers delivered to Steven Fries and his broken ankle.

I called Mia Kaplan.

She was home. She was distraught.

"You have no idea how awful I look! What am I going to do?"

"Don't worry. When you do meet Dimitri, the bruises will be a great topic of conversation. He'll be impressed with your pluck."

"Pluck?"

"An underrated virtue."

Mia remained skeptical, but agreed to rest and wait for the next phase of my plan.

I made a note to think of one.

I left a message for Fred. I thanked him for his concern, assured him that the truck was fine, and asked him to surprise me with Monday's car. The freedom to choose the car would thrill him to no end.

Then Jorjana returned my call.

"Tell me," she said.

I told her about my interview with Sanchez and Gym Rat. I told her about the visits from Jackson Jones and Donald Wesson. Then I asked for her opinion.

Her opinion gave me pause.

"You did escort that woman to Save the Bay and it does appear that she had a hand in the robbery. And now she is dead."

"I'm not feeling better, Jorjana."

"You will not. Not for some time."

"Great. Now what?"

"I have given this matter a great deal of thought. Do you wish to hear it?"

"By all means."

"I have consulted my attorney on your behalf. He will represent you. In the meantime, he recommends that you not speak with the authorities unless he is present. Do you understand the importance of this?"

I did. I agreed to mind my own business. I took down the attorney's numbers—office, cell, home, weekend home, plane—and promised to call the next time a cop appeared on my doorstep.

The next time. How had things come to this?

Jorjana wasn't done. She had more bad news. "Alana, you must now maintain a low profile. The police will sort this out. Keep your head high and you will be exonerated."

"How long do you suppose that will take?"

"Before you know it. Meanwhile, use this time to review your actions and learn how that woman ingratiated herself to you. You cannot afford to make this mistake again," Jorjana advised. "Let us hope that David is successful in his visit with CiCi. If not, he may then counter her accusations with questions regarding her state of mind. CiCi is well-known to exaggerate."

"Thank you, Jorjana."

"My pleasure. Now tell me more about this Jackson Jones."

I sidestepped that question by asking for her help with Donald Wesson. As I had hoped, she reeled off a dozen names of possible brides. Unfortunately, one of the names was mine. It took a good ten minutes to talk my way out of that one.

By the time we hung up, I was starved. I grabbed the keys to the truck and went in search of dinner.

It was late afternoon, seductively warm. I rolled down the windows of the truck, set it in low gear, and cruised north along Malibu Beach Road. Parking is tight in my neighborhood, so as usual the road was clogged with my neighbors' Range Rovers, Mercedes, and BMWs.

Which is why I noticed a battered white van parked up the street. In another neighborhood it would have been a teenager's starter car. But my neighbors' teenagers drive hand-me-downs. Meaning BMWs, Mercedes, and Range Rovers.

So, I took a curious, neighborly look at the van as I passed by. The windows were tinted. The van appeared empty. I remembered to mind my own business for once and drove on. At the end of the road I turned left to catch the light for PCH. And that's when I noticed the van in my rearview mirror. It appeared to head toward the gated community of Malibu Colony.

That was strange. A rusty white van was as likely to get through the Colony gates as last year's Oscar loser.

Then the light turned and I headed north on PCH. I was more hungry than curious. My dinner plans were taking me to the Beach Shack.

It was that time on a Sunday afternoon just before the weekend crowds pack up the collapsible beach gear, roll up the towels, lug the kids back to the SUV, and clog PCH on their way back to somewhere else. I sailed past Pepperdine University and the gates guarding the mansions on the bluffs. I zipped right along, soaking up the sunshine and trying to keep my eyes on the road and off the brilliant blue Pacific Ocean. The only thing lacking was a proper CD player to belt out a beach tune. Fred would not allow installing one in the '54 Chevy truck. Assuming, of course, you could cut into the solid metal dashboard. But the mere thought of broaching the idea with him was hilarious. I chuckled out loud as I approached the turn to the Beach Shack.

The Beach Shack lies on private beachfront property. To get there legally requires a series of right-hand turns. Or one illegal turn from the northbound lanes of PCH. I was just taking aim to illegally cross the south-bound traffic when I spotted the white van again. And this time it caught my attention. I couldn't imagine what a van like that was doing cruising around Malibu.

Or maybe I could.

Maybe the van was packed with cops wasting their time following me.

Only one way to find out—I made the illegal turn. Sure enough, the van slowed as if considering the turn but then continued north on PCH. Which just proved to me that it was packed with law-abiding cops.

Didn't those guys have anything better to do?

I drove down the hill to the parking lot and squeezed the truck between a litter of Harleys and a '68 Corvette. Locked the truck and entered the Beach Shack.

The Beach Shack is just that. A low-slung wooden shack squatting right on the sand. It avoids the regulations of the California Coastal Commission by merely having been there forever. It houses a restaurant, a bar, and picnic tables right on the beach. No one I usually associated with would be caught dead there.

OK, bad choice of words, but the Beach Shack had everything I needed. Food, booze, and a clientele that didn't give a damn about my troubles.

The restaurant was jammed. I left my name with the hostess, who said she would do what she could but wasn't promising me anything. Fine by me. I pushed through the swinging doors to the bar.

The Beach Shack bar was decorated in 1942 and no one has seen a reason to replace spent light bulbs, much less update it. Red vinyl booths line the walls. Maple tables crowd the center space. Long bar, well-used stools, mirrored wall stocked with liquor bottles. You've seen the setup in every B movie ever made.

In one booth, two older couples squabbled quietly over a game of cribbage. At the bar, an aging actor sat hunched with his back to the room. Dressed in white leather pants, white leather vest, black polyester shirt, and white patent leather loafers, he clung to a beer mug like a fading beauty queen clings to a compliment. A pair of actress/model/wannabees sat at a table behind him and giggled into their cosmopolitans.

The bar's gloomy lighting hid any stray desperation.

I made my way to the bar. The actor turned stiffly and greeted me.

"Alana Fox! How do! How do!"

"Hi, Wes," I said in return. "That Corvette of yours still looks sharp. You sure you won't sell her?"

"I'm never letting her go! Only female I can count on!"

"Let me know if you change your mind. Fred would take good care of her."

"I'm not letting another man get his hands on her! I'm going to be buried in that car!"

Somehow, I didn't doubt it. I ordered my usual, finished the niceties with Wes, set up a tab and took a corner booth. I settled in, took a long drink from my cold glass, and let my thoughts wander.

There is something comforting about a corner booth in a dark bar. Drinking etiquette decrees that those sitting in the corner wish to be left alone. Be it a couple cozying up or a foursome in deep conversation or a single savoring a drink, when in the corner, you are ignored. And I really wanted to be left alone. I took another long sip and felt myself relax.

There is something to be said about drinking alone. A nicely made drink is a good companion. Always refreshing. Never interrupts or disagrees with you. Allows you time to think. Of course, there is the possibility of a hangover, but whose fault is that, really?

I amused myself by watching the other drinkers in the room. I eavesdropped on the wannabees' scheming about their next audition. Little did they know that Wes had access to every producer they discussed. I watched the cribbage game wind down. And then who should walk in but Jackson Jones.

He stood just inside the door, took the joint in with one glance. He wore a long-sleeved polo shirt and perfectly rumpled jeans. His hair was damp and his presence changed the whole dynamic.

The men at the cribbage table sucked in their guts. Their wives licked their lips. The wannabees upped their giggle volume to "Look at me!" levels. Even Wes made a stiff attempt to turn around and take a gander at Jackson Jones.

Jackson was either used to the attention or chose to ignore it. He made his way to the bar, gave the bartender an order and nodded at Wes. That's when he spotted me in the mirror. I drained my glass and pointed to its depleted state. He nodded, spoke to the bartender. My usual appeared. Jackson crossed the bar with the eyes of every woman following his every step.

He slid into the booth next to me. I distracted myself by reaching for the drink.

"Thirsty, Alana?"

"Yes."

"Cheers." He held up his drink, beer in a frosty mug. Interesting. I would have figured him for a Scotch-and-something man. But he handled the mug like he had held one before.

We clinked our glasses in a toast. I forced myself to take a ladylike sip.

"Did you resolve Mr. Wesson's problem?" Jackson asked.

"Yes, maybe," I replied, ever the articulate conversationalist. Then I remembered that I had forgotten to have Jorjana add Donald to the Sunday brunch list. Hand over Donald's nutrition concerns to her. For all I knew, cornflakes were out of season.

"He did seem anxious to talk to you," Jackson prompted.

"Donald is very single-minded at times," I said, not really wanting to get into it. "I think we straightened his problem out."

"I'm happy to hear that." Jackson Jones sat back and surveyed the place. The wannabees giggled and puffed out their chests. Wes eyed Jackson in the bar mirror and lifted another quarter inch out of his hunched back. The cribbage couples argued a bit louder. If Jackson Jones noticed the commotion, he didn't let on. He simply asked, "Do you come here often?"

"Often enough. It's good for a drink and a bite to eat if you aren't too particular about either. How did you hear of it?"

Jackson smiled a crooked, self-deprecating grin. Charming, of course.

"I'm lost, actually," he said. "I was looking for a place called Neptune's Net. My directions were a little fuzzy."

"It's about five miles up the road," I said. "Other side of PCH, too."

I said this in my most neighborly manner. But my bullshit detector went up when he mentioned Neptune's Net.

Men like Jackson Jones don't arrive in Malibu and eat an early dinner alone in a roadside stand like Neptune's Net. Men like Jackson Jones grab a supermodel and head to Nobu around ten p.m. for sushi and sake. Something was fishy—and it wasn't the daily special at the Beach Shack.

"Don't you agree, Alana?" Jackson finished whatever it was he was saying with a just-between-us smile.

"What?" I said. I pulled my mind out of its gin-induced haze and focused on him.

"I said that I am cooperating with the police regarding the theft of Mrs. DiCarlo's painting. Since I can approach this matter in ways they can't, it proves to be a mutually beneficial arrangement. Don't you agree?"

"What kinds of things can you do that the police can't?"

"Suffice it to say that the police are bound by regulations that I am not."

He was certainly right about the cops and their damn rules. As evidenced by their refusal to make an illegal left turn against oncoming traffic on PCH. Not to mention their stubborn insistence on investigating me.

"I'll help in any way that I can," I said. "Please let CiCi know that I'm cooperating."

"I certainly will. She is not overly fond of you, is she?"

"You could say I'm not one of her favorite people."

"I'll do what I can to change her perception of you."

That intimate smile again. My guard wavered. And then who should show up but Detective Sanchez.

Sanchez pushed through the swinging bar door like it was resisting arrest. He wore jeans and a pressed dress shirt with the sleeves rolled up to his elbows. There were bags under his eyes heavy enough for him to store extra bullets. He took the joint in with one glance. Spotted Jackson and me in the first pass. Picked up the beer the bartender had waiting for him and headed our way.

The attitude in the bar changed again. Probably had something to do with the gun holster strapped to his side.

Sanchez slid into our corner booth without so much as an invite. Or a fresh drink for me. The nerve of the guy.

Sanchez spoke first.

"Jackson," Sanchez said to Jackson.

"Stan," Jackson said to Sanchez.

"Stan?" I didn't mean it to sound as incredulous as it came out.

Sanchez gave that little twitch of a grin I first saw in CiCi's dining room.

"I'm the twelfth of fourteen kids. All the good Mexican names were taken when I came along."

Sanchez was trying to make me feel guilty about making assumptions. It wasn't going to work. The guy had a Mexican last name, a dark complexion, and, I was willing to bet, drove an ugly white van. Of course I had assumed his first name was Jose.

"I didn't picture you two for Beach Shack customers," Sanchez continued. "I sort of figured you for Nobu people."

OK, so I thought the same thing, too. Didn't make me feel all warm and fuzzy toward him.

"I visit Mr. Matsuhisa's restaurant in Tokyo whenever I am there," Jackson said. "But I find the Malibu Nobu a bit too flashy for my taste."

It was a nice comeback. Countering Sanchez's intended insult about living high on the Malibu hog with an allusion to traveling internationally. Sanchez likely only made it to Tokyo in his dreams. When he bothered to sleep at all. What with him so busy harassing innocent citizens, the man probably only had time to dream of attending the Gilroy Garlic Festival.

I decided to give Jackson Jones the benefit of the doubt on our chance meeting. He obviously ate well when traveling internationally. Truth be told, roadside stand or not, the fresh fish at Neptune's Net was fabulous. Jackson was probably one of those sophisticated travelers who preferred local hangouts. And was bored with supermodels. I could only hope.

"Is there anything we can do for you, Detective?" I asked.

Yeah, I was rude. I wanted to get to know Jackson Jones better. Hadn't Sanchez ever heard of being a third wheel?

"Nothing in particular, unless you want to explain where you were last night, Ms. Fox," Sanchez replied.

"Nothing has changed since the last time we talked."

"You sure you didn't have company?"

Sanchez looked at Jackson and me like we were a couple of deviant teenagers. Jackson coughed and shifted in his seat.

"I only met Mrs. Fox this afternoon, Stan."

"Just checking. You two seem pretty cozy over here."

"Detective Sanchez." I drew myself up and spoke just a little louder than was necessary. "Unless you have *official* business with me, I would like to continue my conversation with Mr. Jones. *Alone.*"

The bar got really quiet with that. The wannabees actually shut up.

Sanchez wasn't the least bit put off. The twitchy grin came back. He took the time to take a long draft of his beer. A regular Sir Laurence Olivier with the act.

"No, Ms. Fox, I don't have *official* business with you. But since you were here I thought I would just stop by."

"Thanks. Is there anything else?"

"Yeah, since you brought it up. The more we learn about the robbery at the DiCarlo place, the more it seems likely that there was an insider involved."

I didn't like what he was insinuating. But I knew better than to answer.

Fortunately, Sanchez picked up his beer, nodded at Jackson Jones, and said, "You two have a real nice evening, now." And left.

"You were a little harsh, don't you think?" Jackson asked me.

"The man is an idiot," I said. "He'll never get to the bottom of this if he doesn't stop following me around. I had nothing to do with it!"

"Following you?" Jackson's brow furrowed.

"Yes, following me." I told him about spotting the white van and my theories on who was driving.

Jackson's gaze wandered from my face to the bar. Stan had taken the stool next to Wes. Jackson looked back at me.

"You're right," Jackson said. "I saw Stan leave Mrs. DiCarlo's ranch in a white van today."

My better sense fell right to the floor.

"I knew it! I've had enough. I'm going to tell him to arrest me or leave me alone!" I started to slide out of the booth.

"Alana, wait a minute!" Jackson looked startled. "Making a scene is not a good idea."

"Why not?"

"You are obviously a person of interest. You don't need a roomful of witnesses watching you threaten a police officer, do you?"

"I suppose not."

"Take a moment to think about this. You don't want to give Stan any reasons to concentrate on you. The police have procedures they follow to eliminate suspects. I know it must seem intrusive, but look at it from their perspective. You brought a woman to the DiCarlo ranch that was involved in the robbery and then ended up dead. Of course the police have questions about you. They will work through it in time. Just stay out of their way and don't give them any more reasons to suspect you. Of anything."

I hated to admit that he was right. But I liked the fact that he believed me to be innocent. And I really liked the feeling that he was looking out for me.

I slid back into my place. Jackson pulled a vibrating cell phone out of his pocket.

"Excuse me, Alana, I've been waiting for this call." He had the good manners to walk out of the bar before answering.

I watched him leave. As did every other female in the place. Stan Sanchez was too busy yakking it up with Wes to notice. Explains why ol' Stan was not humiliated by the glare I sent his way. Figured. If he spent less time harassing innocent citizens or schmoozing with over-the-hill movie stars he might have solved the robbery and murder. But no. I had almost convinced myself that it was worth making a scene when Jackson returned.

"I must go, Alana. Something has come up."

And then he was gone.

In his wake, the hostess appeared to tell me a table was ready.

So I dined alone on grilled halibut instead of Stan Sanchez's ass.

Chapter Thirteen

Monday morning my house intercom woke me at the crack of nine a.m.

"Where's the truck?" It was Fred.

I felt like hell. Was it the flu? Or too many usuals? I rolled over in bed and punched the button on the intercom.

"I took a cab home last night. The truck is in the parking lot at the Beach Shack," I said, and braced myself for a lecture.

"You sound awful. You OK?"

More worried about me than the truck? That was really odd.

"Yeah, fine," I said. "Just have a lousy headache. You want me to drive you up there?"

"No, I'll find my way. I brought the Thunderbird. I'll leave the keys in the mailbox."

"OK. Fred?"

"Yeah?"

"Thanks for the phone call on Sunday. I really appreciated your concern."

"No problem."

I sat up, half expecting to find myself in some alternate universe where doughnuts were good for you and Fred cared more about me than the cars.

Sun poured in through the French doors leading to the little deck off my bedroom. The waves carried on as usual. My pillows lay strewn about the room where I apparently had thrown them in my sleep. All as usual. Except for a damn headache. Which, I hated to admit, was becoming more usual than not.

I rolled out of bed, wandered into the bathroom, swallowed a couple of aspirin, and then stood in the shower for about ten thousand gallons. Managed to pull myself together in a reasonable manner and headed downstairs just as the doorbell rang.

On my doorstep stood David Currie.

"I come bearing lattes, darling!" David sang as I opened the door. He waltzed in carrying a cardboard tray filled with two grande coffee cups and a paper bag that smelled of cinnamon.

"I love you," I said.

"Of course you do!" David sauntered into the great room, sank into the couch, pulled the cups from the tray and handed me one. Then he smoothed two paper napkins out and pulled two cinnamon rolls from the bag. He leaned back against the couch and gingerly pulled the lid from his cup. The aroma of roasted beans filled the room.

I took the chair opposite him, grabbed a cinnamon roll and wolfed it down. Gulped down the coffee. Pointed to the other roll and asked, "You want that?"

"No, darling. You go right ahead."

He perched on my couch like a king about to grant a royal interview. He wasted no time in getting to the point.

"A little bird told me that you were busy drinking your dinner last night at the Beach Shack—what were you *thinking*, by the way—and that you had some very handsome gentlemen callers."

"A little bird?" I put the second cinnamon roll down long enough to read his smirk.

Who did David know at the Beach Shack? Actually, the question should have been who *didn't* David know—anywhere? I did a mental tally. Who had seen me and was likely to report it to David? I put my money on the obvious culprit.

"Wes told you this, didn't he?"

"Wes just passed along a little tidbit. That man owes me," David sniffed. "But that's not why I am here. Jorjana and I are very worried, darling."

"Oh no. You didn't tell Jorjana?"

He ignored me.

"Darling, the papers are just full of stories on the murder of that Kymbyrlee person. Everyone seems to think the criminals are still lurking around and Jorjana is frantic that you are in grave danger. What if they come after you, darling?"

"The criminals are not lurking around," I scoffed. "Why would they stick around here and risk getting caught with that damn painting of CiCi's?"

"But what if they aren't? What if they intend to kill you, too?" David, to his credit, seemed honestly worried.

"They won't. There is no reason for them to waste time on me. Unlike the *police*."

I filled David in on Stan Sanchez and his trusty white van.

"Surveillance? How *dramatic*, darling!" David's smirk came back full strength. "Jorjana will be so relieved to hear you have around-the-clock protection." Without taking a breath, David switched subjects. "Who was the handsome stranger who plied you with drinks last night, darling?"

No question who that was, but I downplayed Jackson's allure by saying, "His name is Jackson Jones and he is working for CiCi to try to find her painting. He is some kind of art expert and wanted to ask me some questions about Kymbyrlee. No big deal. He left after one drink, by the way."

I diverted David's attention by asking how his meeting with CiCi had gone.

He put the lid back on his coffee, placed it gingerly on the table, and said, in the kind of voice you use when you tell a kid the hamster died, "Not as well as we hoped, darling."

"What do you mean, 'not as well as we hoped'?"

"CiCi was not as appalled as I expected. Apparently, hiding one's cosmetic surgery is passé." He shrugged. "Who knew?"

"Cosmetic surgery? All you had on her was that she's had work done? Jeez, David, everyone knows that. That woman's arms are as solid as fireplugs."

"It's not the surgery, darling. It's how she paid for it that's shocking."

"How did she pay for it?" I could only imagine.

David smirked his smirk and said, "Let's just say what she spread open wasn't her wallet."

My turn to shrug. "She isn't the first one to sleep with her plastic surgeon."

David's smirk got a little more confident. "I didn't say she slept with her plastic surgeon, darling."

"Really? Who, then?" Again, only imagining.

"My sources tell me that the surgeon's wife and CiCi were *very* good friends." His turn to shrug. "But apparently CiCi feels a little girl-on-girl time is good for her reputation, now that she is of a *certain age* and all."

"Are you saying CiCi is gay?"

David was appalled at the mere suggestion. "Good heavens, *no*! The woman is a *screaming* hetero! I'm saying that she and the wife, shall we say, *experimented*. And that CiCi is finding the rumors of her *open-mindedness* useful to spice up her image."

David took a delicate sip of his coffee. "My plan backfired. We will have to be content with questioning CiCi's judgment. Fortunately, CiCi will soon be too busy with her *People* cover to spend much more time on you. If you lie low, you will rise back to the top. Just like cream does after the churning."

He seemed very pleased with the metaphor. I tried to hide my incredulity.

"The Learning Channel, darling," David explained. "Lovely little documentary on dairy farms. Before you know it," he continued. "This nasty business will be a thing of the past. So *yesterday*. CiCi will turn it into a Movie of the Week starring *her*. Your part in the whole drama will be relegated to a background extra. Everyone will talk about how *brave* CiCi was, how *heroic* CiCi was. I'm sure in the movie CiCi will apprehend the criminals herself."

"But what—"

"I'm not finished, darling." David put up a finger, shushing me. "Everything will work out just fine in the end. Meanwhile, you need to lie low and stay safe."

I opened my mouth to protest, but he ignored me.

"Do not be impatient, darling. You always want to be the captain of the ship. But this trip, darling, your ship is a sailboat and there is no wind."

"Learning Channel?" I hazarded a guess.

"History Channel. Special on Christopher Columbus."

I squeezed in a question before he briefed me on upcoming programs.

"I get it. Lie low. Stay safe. Let things work themselves out. But what am I supposed to *do* while all of this is going on?"

David smiled at me like a preacher greeting a new member of the congregation.

"You must forgive, Alana."

Forgive? Forgive what?"

David sighed. "Forgive Kymbyrlee for all she inflicted on you."

"Let me guess, Oprah?"

David took both of my hands in his.

"Alana, you hang on to anger for too long. It harms you. You made a bad decision about Kymbyrlee because you have so much hatred toward Tori. And look what happened. Jorjana and I are really worried that you have lost all of your good sense. Right now you should let the police do their work. CiCi will tire of talking about you and shift the focus on herself. Her little vendetta will fall by the wayside as soon as she is the center of attention. And then you, darling, will benefit by having a little notoriety."

"Notoriety?"

"Yes, darling. A little notoriety is not bad for a woman your age."

I honestly had no response to that. But it did occur to me that he and Jorjana had burned the midnight oil discussing my life. His little speech was just a bit too well rehearsed. I felt a mixture of irritation and gratitude. There were so few people on my side. With Jorjana, David, and Jackson Jones there were three. A veritable crowd of supporters.

"It is imperative that you lie low until this blows over," David continued. "Look to your future. Maybe you *should* start a business. By the time you come up with a business plan, the police will have made their arrests and everyone will be on to the next thing."

I was too weary to argue with him. Or maybe I was starting to accept that it was time to change my ways. Leave Tori alone. Start a business. Date. Good grief, what had happened to my life?

The phone rang just as David left. It was Todd, my contact at the insurance agency.

"Alana, I have a lunch date with Jennifer today."

"Jennifer who?"

"Jennifer, you know, Dimitri Greco's assistant? I did what you told me and set up a lunch date as soon as possible."

"Oh, Jennifer, right." I cursed under my breath. Was I so distracted that I had forgotten about the one client I still had left?

"Give me the details, Todd. I'll set things up with Mia right away."

Two hours later, Mia and I sat in her car at the far end of the Greco Productions parking lot. Mia was mess. One eye was bruised and swollen. She had scratches on her neck and arms. She looked as bad as I felt.

Her nails, however, were freshly polished. She kept a cell phone from leaping out of her grip by strangling it with both hands.

A beige sedan pulled into a parking space near the Greco front door. Todd emerged from the car and gave a tiny wave in our direction.

"Do you have the phone number ready?" I asked Mia, more to give her something to do than anything else.

She let go of the phone long enough to produce a slip of paper with a number on it.

"Let's review," I said calmly. "Todd is picking up Jennifer for lunch. Hopefully, she will duck into Dimitri's office to inform him that she is leaving. While she is gone, Todd will then do whatever it is to send incoming calls to Dimitri's office. If he is successful, he will give us a thumbs-up on his way out."

"What if he isn't successful?" Mia whispered.

"Then we go to Plan B." I refrained from revealing that I had no idea what that would be.

Before Mia could quiz me on Plan B, Todd and Jennifer exited the building. Ever the gentleman, Todd opened the door for his date, saw to it that she was comfortable, shut the door firmly and gave us a thumbs-up.

"You're on, Mia!" I said, to hide a sigh of relief.

Mia drew a deep breath, shrugged her shoulders and dialed. I heard the muffled sound of Dimitri's phone ringing.

"Dimitri here."

"Mr. Greco? This is Mia Kaplan calling. I just wanted to check that your car was taken care of to your satisfaction. I am sorry for the inconvenience."

Mia adopted a tone that was several octaves lower than her usual voice. A tone that suggested smoky bar-rooms and clandestine strolls on the beach.

Dimitri took the bait. I couldn't hear his reply, but she gave a deep, sensuous chuckle.

"I agree," she said. "What's that? A drink? Oh, I don't..." More chuckles. "I see...I guess I do owe you at least that...fine...no, I'm afraid I can't today. What does your schedule look like tomorrow? Six is fine. Geoffery's will be lovely. How will I know you?"

Moments later she hung up.

"Oh my God! I have a date with Dimitri Greco! Alana, you're a genius!"

Recent events considered, I was only too happy to agree.

Chapter Fourteen

Mia drove me home. I went straight to my office, plopped down in the desk chair, and before I had a chance to get bored the phone rang.

It was David and he was out of his mind with giddiness.

"Darling, have you heard?"

"Most likely not."

"Pay attention, darling, I am only going over this once. I have just returned from Mallory Price's reception. Her 'Welcome Home from Cancun' party turned into a 'Condolences Reception,' what with her sister being dead and all. But Mallory hardly looks bereft, darling."

"You mean she isn't upset that Kymbyrlee is dead?" Join the club, Mallory.

"She is more upset about having to drain the pool! Her water bill will be outrageous!"

"That's too bad. Who was there?"

"Go see for yourself, darling! Mallory wants to see you *tout de suite!*"

"What does she want to see me for?"

"Who cares? Darling, GO! The food is fabulous, and there isn't a single person there that has connections to CiCi, if you know what I mean."

Did I ever.

"Oh, and Alana, wear white."

"White?"

"Yes, it's the new black."

Who knew?

I threw on a generic outfit of white linen slacks and a white tank top. Locked the house. Fired up the Thunderbird that Fred had delivered and headed out.

My '56 T-bird is a cherry red convertible with red and white leather seats and a red metal steering wheel. Has an automatic transmission. Very handy when driving with a hangover. I made it to Mallory's place in no time.

The road in front of Mallory's glass and concrete house was packed. I scooted the Thunderbird up the hill and hoofed my way back to the enormous front door. A waiter dressed in white slacks, white shirt, and white tie welcomed me inside. I followed the sounds of a mournful harp and the quiet chatter of a crowd and ended up in the room that reminded me of an aviary.

The guests were all in white—like a flock of doves. It was a mixed group of Malibu Players and lesser beings that looked to be out-of-town family. Waiters circulated with silver flutes of champagne and the air was perfumed with the scent of white lilies. A crowd milled about Mallory. Next to her was a table cluttered with white floral arrangements and one of those books that is put out to write notes of sympathy to the deceased's family.

I saw no sense in wading through the mob to get to Mallory. Mainly because I was starving. It seemed to me that the last time I had something to eat, Kymbyrlee Chapman was still alive and my life was still in order. Fortunately, the all-white theme did not extend to the buffet. I grabbed a plate and loaded it with tiny rolls filled with roast beef, stuffed mushrooms, and stinky cheeses of every color. I ate standing up and peering out the French doors.

Outside, two guys dressed in green coveralls supervised a giant rubber hose as it drained the pool. Remnants of yellow crime scene tape fluttered from the fence. All in all, it wasn't as macabre as you might have thought. Certainly didn't harm my appetite. I polished off the food in no time, grabbed a flute of champagne, and went to give my sympathy to the surviving sister.

Mallory Price stood very near the spot where I had accepted my fee from Kymbyrlee. One by one, she received her due condolences. At her side stood a guy with such perfect features, I thought at first Mallory must have ordered him straight off the cover of *Romance Monthly.*

Mallory showed little of the strain of having lost a relative. Also, little of the tan you'd expect to bring back from Mexico. Of course, given the guy, I figured she never left the hotel. Her hair, the color of a palomino's hindquarters, was pulled back into a low ponytail. She wore a white wrap dress and flat white sandals. She had the unnaturally white teeth, dermabrasioned skin, and liposuctioned chin of every Malibu woman over twenty-five. When she spotted me, she broke away from the crowd.

"Alana, thank you for coming." She extended both hands as if I were the one needing consoling. Apparently, she didn't suspect me of having a hand in her sister's murder. Or she didn't care. Hard to tell.

"Mallory, I am so sorry," I began.

She waved away my words, took me by the hand. Called out to the guy, "Sven, I need to talk to Alana for a minute. See that everyone has what they need, will you?"

Sven wasn't much of a talker. He nodded and turned to a crowd of women circling him like hyenas at the kill.

Mallory led me away down a cement and steel hallway into a study lined with black leather walls. She sat down in an original Eames chair and got right to the point.

"What was my sister doing in Malibu?" So much for grieving her loss.

I found a seat in an original Wassily contraption. Fed her the story in less than nine minutes. Mallory was the first one to hear the story and be amused.

"A tour business? Oh, that's rich! How did she plan to find all those artists?"

"She said she had traveled extensively in Indonesia and had contacts."

Mallory regarded me with pity.

"The only place my sister has been in the last three years is prison," Mallory said grimly. "She was serving ten years for fraud. She was released early for good behavior, if you can believe that."

I have to say I could have believed anything at that point. What was left to surprise me, anyway?

Mallory stood and began pacing. "The family was devastated by Kym landing in prison. My grandmother was so upset she even changed her will. I didn't think it could get any worse—and now this." Mallory collapsed back into the Eames chair. "Why did you believe her?"

That again. Like I hadn't spent the last two days trying to figure it out myself.

"She seemed to have a lot of ready cash," I said in my defense. "She had some stunning jewelry and a new set of Vuitton luggage. If she had been in prison, where did she get the money?"

Mallory shook her head as if shaking away a bad idea. "She got some attorney to challenge the will. She ended up with about a hundred thousand dollars. Sounds like she blew through it in a hurry."

Mallory resumed her pacing. "Typical of Kym. She could have invested the money, or gone back to school and turned her life around. But no."

Mallory stopped, took a deep, ragged sigh, and then thick tears poured down her cheeks. I got the impression that a lot of emotions were about to boil over the top of her reserve.

"The police asked me a million questions about who her friends were, where she went after she got out of prison, that kind of thing. Do you know how painful it was to tell them I had no idea who my sister's friends were? That I will never know?"

I was just the littlest bit curious about Kymbyrlee's friends myself; on the outside chance they did have some vendetta against me. "You haven't been in touch with her since she left prison, then?"

"I saw her about six months ago. She showed up for my father's birthday dinner. Suffice it to say, the family's reception wasn't exactly warm. The last I heard, her parole officer was looking for her."

Mallory sat back down, folded her arms tight across her chest, and gave big, deep sighs. The kind of sighs that just make room for more pain. "After everything she put us through, I did still care about her. But you reach a point where you have to distance yourself or risk falling in the muck, too. And Kym consistently made the stupidest choices. She hung out with the biggest losers. She dressed like a tramp. I mean, really, she was never willing to put in the work to make her life any better. I finally decided that I couldn't help her and I wasn't going to let her drag me down with her."

Mallory looked at me for something—understanding, maybe. "But you know, her story about her and I going into business together? That could have been fun. We could have taken groups to Mexico, anyway. We both spent a lot of time there when we were younger. I sort of figured she went to Mexico when her parole officer couldn't find her. I wonder where she came up with the idea of Indonesia?"

"She probably thought it sounded exotic enough to attract a Malibu crowd," I suggested.

"Maybe," Mallory mused. "But Kym wasn't the brightest girl around. Someone else must have given her the idea. Do you know if the police have any leads yet?"

"No, I haven't heard anything." I wasn't about to get into the discussion of where the cops thought I landed in all of it.

Mallory seemed inclined to reminisce on the life and times of her sister. That was the last thing I felt like doing, so I made noises about "so sorry about Kymbyrlee" and left Mallory and her thick tears in the study.

The walk back to the crowd in the aviary felt ten miles long. Something Mallory had said about Kymbyrlee didn't add up.

Kymbyrlee was a liar? Check.

She dressed like a tramp? Double-check.

She wasn't the brightest girl around? Who was that?

I remembered her articulate conversation. Remembered the reference to her sister being on "holiday." Remembered how she steeped her tea. The girl Mallory described sounded cheap and vacant. The woman I met in Coogie's was neither cheap nor vacant. I wondered if Kymbyrlee had taken a crash course in culture while hiding out from her parole officer. I wondered if I could sign up Donald Wesson for the same course.

Back in the aviary, the crowd was even bigger. Cocktail chatter had replaced murmured condolences, likely fueled by all the champagne. The harpist strummed a plucky little tune. The buffet table was packed. There were so many flower arrangements that they spilled onto the floor amid the brass planters of saguaro cactus.

I headed for the table with the condolences book. Had every intention of scribbling something and heading out.

I did wonder what to write.

"*Sorry the bitch is dead*" seemed a bit harsh.

I opened it up, scanned the other entries. I opted for a generic "*Sorry for your loss*" scribbled badly so no one could read it. I put the pen down and then noticed a photo of Kymbyrlee tucked behind a bouquet of daisies.

And then everything made sense.

The woman I had met in Coogie's had almond-shaped eyes and a smooth copper complexion. The girl in the photo in front of me was a cheaper-looking version of Mallory with acne scars the size of quarters.

The woman I had met at Coogie's wasn't Kymbyrlee Chapman at all!

Chapter Fifteen

This changed everything.

And nothing.

I would never have taken the girl in the photo to Save the Bay. Acne scars aside, her whole appearance screamed cheap, vacuous. She could have come to me with a referral from CiCi herself and I would have ended the interview on the spot.

On the one hand, it was nice to know I hadn't lost my ability to judge who was suitable for Malibu society and who wasn't. And the woman at Coogie's had certainly met my standards. Small comfort, I know, but at the moment, what else did I have?

Nothing.

Precisely. Because on the other hand, I had no idea who the woman I had met at Coogie's was. Or how she had found out about me.

Suddenly, I felt terribly alone in a crowd of people dressed in white. The proverbial chill ran down my spine. Followed by a wave of nausea. I tossed the photo back on the table and made a quick escape.

I made it back to the Thunderbird without throwing up. Sat in the car and drew a few deep breaths and really concentrated on keeping everything down. I hate nausea. I might actually prefer to be locked in a room full of small children. Not the best scenario to focus on when battling the urge to puke, however. I forced myself to think of lavender fields, cold snow. I thought briefly of trekking back to the house and begging for ginger ale. But that would force me to walk past the photo of Mallory's dead sister, and that just made me want to throw up more.

It passed eventually. But it took longer than you would think. By the time I was able to draw a calm breath, people were leaving Mallory's place. I fired the Thunderbird up and joined the parade to PCH.

I hate not being in control. Nausea, CiCi's slander campaign, divorce court, not to mention suspicion of murder. If I'm not in charge, I'm not happy about it. The whole Save the Bay fiasco irritated the hell out of me because I had not known what was next. And now I had no idea who had dragged me into the nightmare in the first place. It was like being a fish on the line—just swimming along, minding your own business, and all of a sudden a nice little worm turns into something you never expected and you're being pulled out of the water against your will. It was enough to make a vegetarian out of you. But then you could get into the whole discussion of a tomato growing quietly on a vine and suddenly it gets plucked at the height of its beauty. You could go on and on.

I took the left onto PCH and drove south. Another glorious day. All that sunshine, the ocean the particular shade of blue that it turns in the mid-afternoon. Zuma Beach was packed: volleyball players lined up at the nets, colorful umbrellas dotted about, parking lot full up and the overflow crammed tightly along the highway shoulder. I really didn't feel like going home. I needed a second opinion.

I glanced at my watch. Three forty-five on a Monday afternoon. I knew where I would find Jorjana. I left Zuma behind and headed to the Malibu Country Mart.

Jorjana doesn't leave the York estate all that often. She doesn't have to, since everyone gladly comes to her, but Jorjana always has enjoyed the energy of a crowd. Once upon a time, she tooled herself out and about in a flaming red Jaguar convertible, the stereo blaring and her foot heavy on the gas. Now she ventures out in the world with a driver in a specially equipped van, a nurse by her side and a sizable lump of humility in her soul. But every Monday, she goes to the Country Mart.

I found a parking spot right in front. Ducked into the Coffee Bean and Tea Leaf for an iced ginger tea for my stomach, a mocha latte for Jorjana, and a triple espresso for one of my paparazzi buddies camped outside. I put the espresso down next to the pap just as he zoomed in on the latest celebutante parking her car. I wished him luck and went to find Jorjana.

I found her with her nurse, settled too close to the swings for my liking. Jorjana wore a canvas hat, a khaki blouse with oversized pockets, and dark glasses. An olive-colored blanket covered her legs. Binoculars lay in her lap and she paged through a book titled *Birds of the Pacific Coast.*

"You look like you're about to join Franklin on a safari," I greeted her.

"Alana! What a lovely surprise!" Jorjana turned a cheek to accept a kiss from me. "I just purchased this manual at Diesel Books. It is very informative."

"Sounds interesting." I handed the mocha to her and signaled to the nurse that I wanted to talk to Jorjana alone. The nurse nodded and headed over to the Coffee Bean.

Meanwhile, all hell broke loose in the sandpit under the swings. A little red-haired girl kneeled proudly by a pile of sand she had constructed. Before her mother could snap her photo, a little boy stomped ruthlessly on the creation. Screams, pouting, and the behavior that I abhor in children ensued.

"That is Tucker Tanner's son," Jorjana said, referring to a particularly ruthless local developer.

"The nut doesn't fall far from the tree," I observed.

"In Tucker Tanner's case, the tree often falls first," Jorjana returned.

"Let's find somewhere else to sit," I said. I took the handles of her wheelchair and found a quiet shady spot near a picnic table. I set the brake and took a seat facing her.

Jorjana looked back wistfully at the playground. Why she insisted on hanging out at a playground after she had lost her own daughter was beyond me. But she claimed she enjoys watching children play. I gave her a few moments before pulling her attention back to me, where it belonged.

"I'd like to run something by you," I said.

Jorjana turned to me. Her eyes held that faraway gaze someone gets when she remembers when. She snapped out of it, though. "Tell me."

I told. I watched her expression change from a hazy contemplation to shock and then outright fear. Telling the story gave me time to sort things out. By the time I was done, I felt better about everything but her face was gray with concern.

"That woman was in prison?" Jorjana was shocked.

"No, Kymbyrlee Chapman was in prison. The woman I met wasn't."

"How do you know this for certain? Perhaps they met in solitary confinement."

"They couldn't have met if they were held separately," I pointed out patiently. "And I doubt the woman I met ever went to prison. She didn't have that edge."

"She deceived you in so many ways! You would not know!" Jorjana was on a roll now. "You are in danger, Alana! I am certain of it! You will move into my home this afternoon! I will send for your things!"

I was touched by her concern. Curling up at the York estate surrounded by servants was tempting. Waited on hand and foot, no doubt safe, but hiding out nonetheless. And therefore, not in control.

I was about to explain this to Jorjana when she lowered her glasses and stared at something behind me. I turned to see what had caught her attention.

"What" was none other than Jackson Jones.

Jackson made his way through the Country Mart wearing a silk T-shirt and silk slacks that fit well but not too tight. Sunglasses perched on his head, he squinted in the sunlight just enough to emphasize his laugh lines. He carried a folded newspaper in the hand without the wedding ring. He headed in our direction. As he passed the playground, the air stirred as all the mommies whipped their heads around to stare.

"Good afternoon, Alana," he said pleasantly. "Isn't it a lovely day?"

I agreed it was and managed to introduce Jorjana without tripping on my tongue.

"Mrs. York, your reputation does not nearly do justice to your beauty." Jackson took Jorjana's hand and kissed it lightly.

"Why, thank you, Mr. Jones," Jorjana blushed. "Why have we not met until now?"

"I rarely leave La Jolla when I am in America," he explained. "Did Alana inform you of the nature of my association with Mrs. DiCarlo?"

"She mentioned you only in passing," Jorjana replied. "Perhaps you will enlighten me?"

"Certainly."

I watched this exchange in awed silence. Few people can decipher Jorjana's formal speech, much less respond in kind. Jackson conversed with her as easily as if they had been childhood buddies at the weekly etiquette lessons in Queen Victoria's parlor. Jackson not only explained his "association" with CiCi, but also allowed Jorjana to establish his place of birth, education, and marital status. St. Thomas, Oxford, and single. Satisfied, Jorjana then let me back into the conversation.

"Alana, please tell Mr. Jones what you learned from Mallory Price."

Jackson sat next to me on the picnic bench just close enough to be distracting. I managed to get the story out, anyway.

Jackson's jaw twitched ever so slightly when I told him of the discovery of whom Kymbyrlee Chapman turned out to be. When I finished, he put the newspaper on the picnic table. Tucked inside was a manila envelope. He pulled out an eight-by-ten photo.

"Do you recognize this woman, Alana?" He handed the photo to me.

It was a shot of a woman in evening dress walking down a grand staircase. The place had to be a museum, what with the stone lions, gargoyles, and ornate gilded everything in the background. The woman held up her satin skirt with a hand that sported a gold cuff bracelet. Her hair was honey gold and held back in a low ponytail. Her eyes were almond-shaped. I could just hazard a guess on how she steeped her tea. I handed the photo to Jorjana for a look-see.

"That's the woman I thought was Kymbyrlee Chapman," I said. Then, to Jackson, "Who is she?"

"Her name is Carly Cortez," he replied. "She is an art thief. I've worked for clients who have been victims of

Carly's in the past. So I had reason to suspect her planning the robbery at Mrs. DiCarlo's. The lead that came while we were having drinks confirmed it."

"Drinks?" Jorjana's ears perked up at that.

"Confirmed what?" I asked.

"Confirmed that Kymbyrlee Chapman was in prison with a known 'associate' of Carly Cortez. I suspect that Kymbyrlee was recruited while in prison. Carly used Kymbyrlee's identity to get herself introduced quickly around Malibu. As Mallory's sister, Carly had the 'in' she needed to attend Save the Bay."

"Why did she require an invitation?" Jorjana asked. "Why did she not ride in with the rest of the robbers?"

"The robbery was merely a diversion while Carly stole the painting," Jackson replied. "That little miniature is worth millions and was heavily secured. Carly had to be on the property ahead of time to disarm the alarms and get out of the house undetected."

"Why do you think they killed Kymbyrlee?" I asked.

"Carly Cortez has assembled and trained a gang of women," Jackson said. "A brilliant idea, really. She has a knack for finding troubled young women and giving them something they don't have—a second chance. She takes very good care of them and only requires their loyalty. I believe that Kymbyrlee was the newest member and the robbery was a test of her loyalties."

"And she failed?"

Jackson shook his head. "More likely lost her nerve. A call was made to 911 after the robbery. The caller said she had information about it, but was cut short. The call was traced back to a motel in Camarillo. All of the horses were found within a couple of miles of there."

"Why has there been no report of this in the local press?" Jorjana asked.

"The police tend to keep some details of a crime like this out of the media," Jackson explained. "And since the public is more interested in the lurid details of a nude young woman found floating dead in a swimming pool, the media feeds them that story."

"But the stolen painting hasn't been mentioned, either," I said.

"That was at my request," Jackson said. Then, noting Jorjana's interest, he went on, "Mrs. DiCarlo hired me to recover her painting before it hits the black market. I feel there is a better chance of recovering the painting if there is no publicity."

"Why is that, Mr. Jones?"

"Carly Cortez's potential buyers are people who are not concerned with obtaining items legally. Often, in these cases, the buyers are more interested in the thrill of owning an item that is under pursuit. By eliminating the publicity, I have some advantage. As long as Carly has the painting in her possession, I know where it is. It is only a matter of finding her to recover the painting."

"How do you know she hasn't sold it already?" I asked.

"I have ways of knowing these things, Alana."

Of course he did.

"Do the authorities know of this Carly Cortez?" Jorjana asked.

"They do. But they are working their way through their investigation as they see fit."

"Are you dissatisfied with the investigation by the authorities?"

"Let's just say that they have rules and procedures they must follow." Then, turning to me, he said, "You know that the police consider you a person of interest."

"Detective Sanchez made that pretty clear," I said.

"I'm sure he did. But I must warn you that the police are reluctant to share information with you even if it means you may be in harm's way."

"I knew it!" Jorjana gasped. "I knew you were in danger!"

I shushed her. "He said 'may.' May be in harm's way. I'm fine."

Jackson took my hands in his. "Carly Cortez is a very dangerous woman. As was proven by Kymbyrlee Chapman, she is not afraid to kill anyone that gets in her way."

"I'm not in her way," I said, pulling my hands away. "Why would she be worried about me?"

"You can place her at the DiCarlo ranch where the robbery occurred. There is no other evidence to place her there. No fingerprints, no security photos as she dismantled the entire security system. Very cleverly, I might add."

"What about the two bozos at the gate? They checked us in."

"I've shown them Carly's photo and neither of them could identify her. You did say that she was dressed, um, differently that day."

No kidding. I looked at Carly Cortez's photo again. No boobs bursting out from the evening dress. No wonder the two Hulks couldn't identify her.

"So I can say she was there. Why is that important?"

"She is known for leaving no witnesses alive."

Jorjana gasped again. "Alana, please. Please agree to stay with me. We can protect you!"

Jackson smiled warmly at her. "You are a very good friend, Mrs. York." Then he turned to me. "Alana, it might be a good idea to stay with her until Carly Cortez is in custody."

"And when exactly will she be in custody?" I asked indignantly. "Stan Sanchez is spending all his time following me. Why isn't he looking for this Carly Cortez person?"

"*Stan* Sanchez?" Even Jorjana, that paragon of diplomacy, couldn't believe it was the guy's name.

"Yes, our friend Detective Sanchez has been following me around like a lost puppy."

"You are still spotting Stan's van?" Jackson asked.

"All the time. Maybe if Carly Cortez shows up on my doorstep he might actually be able to find her."

I paused. I didn't like the look on Jackson's face. Then I connected all the dots. And it did not sit well with me.

"He isn't looking for her, is he?"

Jackson hesitated. "The police are not as convinced that Carly Cortez is behind this. They are still hunting down clues that point in the direction of an insider planning the robbery. They are investigating Kymbyrlee

Chapman's associates and trying to link them to the staff at Mrs. DiCarlo's ranch or the catering staff."

"Well, that's a colossal waste of time. I didn't take Kymbyrlee Chapman to Save the Bay. I took this Cortez woman. Haven't you shown the cops this photo?"

"Yes, but you are the only one claiming that Carly was there. There are no surveillance photos of her. No one else claims to have seen her. And Kymbyrlee Chapman did end up wearing the DiCarlo diamond earrings."

I didn't like the sound of that. And I really didn't like the logical conclusion that followed.

"Don't tell me, let me guess. Stan and his buddies are so convinced that I am an insider that they won't even consider looking for Carly Cortez?"

Again, that look on Jackson's face.

"So what you are telling me is that the cops are following me because they still think I am the one who planned the robbery and killed Kymbyrlee?"

"Yes, I am afraid the evidence, however circumstantial, does point to you, Alana. The police have not been, shall we say, open to my suggestions to look for Carly."

"Alana, I beg you! Stay with me!" Jorjana was nearly in tears.

I felt the fishhook dig in even deeper. So I did what comes naturally—to hooked fish and to me—I fought back.

"No, Jorjana. I am not going to hide out and wait for Detective Sanchez to figure out that he is wasting his time on me! The next time I see him and his stupid van, I'm going to give him a piece of my mind!"

"Mr. Jones! Please convince her to change her mind!"

Jackson seemed unsure of what to do. Jorjana's eyes welled with tears. I sat, arms folded, fairly steaming in frustration. Jackson looked at me, and then at Jorjana, and then back to me. And to his credit, he took pity on Jorjana. He knelt in front of her, took her hands in his, and said, "Mrs. York, do not be frightened. Carly Cortez is dangerous, but as Alana pointed out, she is under police surveillance. I didn't take that into consideration when I warned Alana of the danger. It is reassuring that the police are following Alana, but they may suspect her further if she retreats into your home. Perhaps it is best if she carries on her life as an innocent woman."

"Thank you, Jackson. I'm glad someone believes me." It was the first time I had said his name out loud. I liked it.

Jackson stood and faced me. "Nonetheless, Alana, be careful. There is no telling where Carly is now. Do not try to elude the police surveillance."

I assured him that I would be careful. Between the two of us we managed to calm Jorjana down. I promised to lock my doors, turn on the security system, and keep my cell phone at my side at all times. Jackson promised to do his level best to convince ol' Stan to look for Carly. By the time her nurse returned, Jorjana was nearly calm.

Jackson gave her one of his cards, bid us good day and left.

Left me alone to explain to Jorjana about having drinks with him at the Beach Shack. The nerve of the guy.

Chapter Sixteen

I mulled over the conversation with Jackson and Jorjana as I headed back to the T-bird.

I had come to the Country Mart to chat with Jorjana and try to make sense, yet again, of the mess I was in. Jorjana, as always, was fully on my side, and desperate to keep me safe. But Jorjana's support couldn't change the fact that I had innocently taken Carly Cortez, an art thief, to Save the Bay. Or the fact that Kymbyrlee Chapman was dead. Or the fact that the cops were still keeping an eye on me. Which, while it was a waste of time, did grant me some protection. Just in case this Carly Cortez was not done with me.

All things considered, I was almost relieved to spot Stan's stupid white van in the parking lot. It tried its damnedest to hide between a black Lincoln Navigator and a red Chevy Suburban, but it stood out like a gap-toothed smile on an orthodontist. But my almost relief was swept away by a tide of anger. I had a few things to discuss with Detective Sanchez. The first of which was his inability to see that I was as much a victim as the other guests at Save the Bay. I was innocent. It was high time he got his nose out of my business and into tracking down the real criminals. I couldn't wait to see the look on ol' Stan's face when I told him exactly what I thought of his investigation. I marched right up to the van and knocked on the window.

Imagine my disappointment in finding the van empty.

I walked around to the front windshield and peered in. The rear windows were tinted and the sides paneled, so the interior was dark. I could barely see that the inside of the van held shelving instead of seats. I looked around, half expecting to spot cops crouching in the bushes, guns drawn. No such luck. Not only was Stan a lousy investigator, it looked as if he was a lousy surveillance man. Here I was, ready to flee the premises and he was nowhere to be found. Where was he?

I trotted back to the pile of paparazzi hanging out at the CB&TL. My buddy with the triple espresso lowered his camera as I approached.

"Did you see who drove that white van over there?" I asked.

He raised his camera and focused in on the van across the lot.

"Yeah, a couple of big dudes got out just after you drove up," he said. "Nobodies."

"Where did they go?"

He shrugged. "I don't get paid to shoot nobodies."

I thanked him anyway. I got my answer. Stan and another big cop had followed me to the Country Mart. I supposed I was relatively safe. Mad as hell, but relatively safe.

I drove the T-bird to Ralphs and purchased a balanced dinner of take-out Chinese and diet ginger ale.

Drove straight home, put the Chinese in the microwave, mixed up the usual, and chatted with Fred about Tuesday's car. Ate alone, drank alone, and didn't bother to check for messages.

But before heading to bed, I set the security system. Just in case.

Tuesday morning, I traded keys with Fred and then entered my office with a cup of coffee. I started with phone messages.

There were precious few.

Donald Wesson, beside himself with joy, left the first message.

"Alana! I have an invitation to the new Disney movie! You know, the one with all the talking animals? They filmed it on my ranch in Montana so they sent me two tickets to the premiere! And to the party afterward! So I need to get a date."

I wondered where to dig up a girl. One willing to endure an evening of Donald's juvenile enthusiasm and sloppy manners. I did know the premiere he talked about. It was a family movie about buffalos or some other smelly creature. The after party was going to be held in Malibu in the space vacated by the old Granita restaurant. It was one of those themed affairs with servers dressed in animal costumes and boring speeches given by studio execs. I had my invite in the trash somewhere.

Message two came from Jorjana. "Alana, call me the moment you arise. I am worried about your safety."

I called the York estate; got the social secretary on the line, told him I was still alive and would be by later in the day. I asked him to talk to Jorjana about Donald Wesson's need for a date. He promised to send the message along to Mrs. York.

Message three was from none other than Little Miss Tight Buns. "Alana, this is Tori, and don't you dare erase this message. Meet me today to settle this alimony thing or I am calling my attorney. Meet me at Leo Carrillo Beach at ten thirty this morning!"

According to my caller ID she had yet another new cell phone. I was betting on a pink one with rhinestones. No wonder she needed more money.

I looked at my watch. It was 10:03 a.m.

"You forget who you are dealing with, Tori," I muttered. Unfortunately for Tori, this was one aspect of my life I still had control over.

I opened the office safe and pulled out a copy of the divorce settlement. Dug through my files and found a copy of my investment in Alan's company. Tucked the papers safely in a tote bag, checked the locks on all the doors and windows, and set off to remind Tori just where her place was.

The car of the day was a 1966 Ford Mustang, my least favorite. I hate the color—Aspen Gold—although it reportedly makes the car a real gem. I only drive it when Fred insists it needs a run. And I was too tired the night before to argue with him.

As I pulled onto PCH, I planned my counterattack on Tori. I thought about giving the nanny a call to see what she knew. Might be nice to know what I was walking into. But then again. I patted the tote bag beside me. If all Tori did was threaten lawyers, I was fine. My alimony arrangement was ironclad, whether she liked it or not. However, in the unlikely event that Tori persisted, I could pull out the legal documents and put an end to that discussion.

And start a legit business anyway. The first step in reclaiming my life would be to eliminate the worry of the IRS and the possibility that Alan's business was tanking.

I wondered how long it would take to launder a hundred grand or so. I wondered how much I would have to up my fees to cover the income tax. I wondered how my life had gotten so complicated so quickly. I was still wondering as I turned into Leo Carrillo State Park.

Leo Carrillo Beach boasts a scattering of tide pools, unusual for a Malibu beach. This makes it an attractive spot for zealous mommies who hanker after educational outings for their kids. And a lot of them appeared to be there. The parking lot was packed with the type of vehicles one needs to haul around kids and their accessories. I left the Mustang parked in the shade of an SUV and headed for the beach.

The parking lot lies east of PCH and the beach is accessed through an enormous storm drain running under the highway. I emerged just behind a lifeguard station. Dozens of children swarmed the beach. Sandcastles were busily under construction, kids scrambled over the slippery tide pools, and mothers chatted under the shade of beach umbrellas. Just off the beach, surfers straddled their boards, waiting for the next set of perfect waves. Tori was nowhere to be seen.

I ventured south for no reason other than I had to look somewhere. The beach curved east just out of sight of the lifeguard station. I know this because dozens of signs warned beachgoers of the legal ramifications of swimming in a rough current without lifeguard supervision. Suffice it to say, the State of California frowns on it.

I pulled off my shoes and slogged my way through the sand. Sure enough, Little Miss Tight Buns lurked just around the bend.

A blanket lay on the sand with a protective umbrella shading it. A wicker basket was open next to that. A few feet away, Tori played with Chaucer. She swung him by his arms in a wide circle and he giggled gleefully.

Tori wasn't far enough along in her pregnancy to show, but she did wear a longish T-shirt over her usual too-short shorts. She had the kind of long legs that are meant to be shown off. Her long blonde hair was pulled back into a ponytail—that all-American look popular among cheerleaders and other sluts. She wasn't young enough to pass as my daughter, but no one would mistake us for peers.

Spotting me, Tori let Chaucer down gently and directed him to the shade of the umbrella. She produced a juice box from the basket and a book. He greedily grabbed both, blond curls tumbling down over his forehead. He smiled at his mother, brown eyes full of adoration. It was a cute scene if you are into that kind of thing. She walked over to me and got right down to business.

"I'm glad you finally came to your senses, Alana," she said. "I brought the checkbook. How much do you want?"

I said, "Thirty-three million dollars."

She let out an exasperated sigh. "I thought this was going to be a civil conversation."

"I'm being civil."

"I meant serious."

"Oh, you mean serious. If you wait a sec, I can calculate the exact amount for you."

Tori looked at me like I was the one being unreasonable. "I only came here because you said you wanted to settle this once and for all."

"I said that? What are you talking about?"

"I'm not kidding, Alana! You said you wanted to settle, which is the only reason I dragged Chaucer out here when he is so upset about the nanny quitting and—"

"I never said anything—"

"You did, too! You said you wanted to meet here and we would settle the alimony thing! I can't believe you lied to me again!"

Something was wrong here. Tori thought I called her? Just how confusing were pregnancy hormones, anyway? I was about to suggest a psychiatrist when Tori's shorts rang. She held her hand up to silence me, like she was in charge or something, and pulled a cell phone out of a pocket.

"Hello? Dr. Patterson? Is that you?" Tori squeezed her eyes shut and put a hand to her ear. "I can't hear you, hold on a second."

She put her hand over the phone. "I have to take this, it's my OB. We aren't finished, Alana. Keep an eye on Chaucer. I'll be right back." She stormed around the bend, phone to her ear.

And left me babysitting. Of all people.

Chaucer looked up from his book and stared forlornly after his mother. He turned to me with eyes full of tears. "Mama?"

"She'll be right back." I wondered if he was old enough to understand.

Satisfied, as if he were used to his mother leaving him in the care of total strangers, he pulled something out of the wicker basket. Holding it aloft, he asked, "Ball?"

He held up a deflated beach ball. The last thing I wanted to do was to play ball with Tori's kid. But ignoring his request might make him cry. And then Tori would likely add child abuse to her complaints about me.

So, I took the thing and blew it up. Then I sat on the blanket and handed it to him.

He surprised me by asking, "Play?"

"No, you go ahead." I turned to see if Tori was coming back. She wasn't.

Chaucer's eyes puddled again. His lower lip stuck out. The kid was really a wimp.

"All right, all right."

I took the ball and tossed it back to him. He wasn't much of a ballplayer. He stood stock-still and let the thing bounce off his head. Good thing I didn't lob a softball his way. The ball bounced to the sand and a puff of breeze carried it down the beach. Chaucer waddled after it, giggling all the way.

The breeze carried the ball safely away from the water. So I stayed put on the blanket. Chaucer picked up his pace, closing in on the ball as it approached a hedge of chaparral. I expected the ball to get wedged on the hedge where Chaucer could reach it, and then Tori would be back and I could recommend a good shrink to her.

But no. The ball inexplicably reached the hedge and dropped out of sight.

In a heartbeat, Chaucer dropped out of sight, too.

Great. That's all I needed. To misplace Tori's kid.

I scrambled to my feet and raced down the beach. Just before the hedge, the beach sloped down quickly. Plenty of room for a toddler and a ball to roll out of sight. Dropping to the sand, I peeked under the hedge. Just beyond the hedge was a steep incline. I slid down the incline and came to a stop just in time to see Chaucer's blond head bobbing out of sight into a grove of oak trees. The kid could really move.

I raced after him.

I scurried through a low growth of sage scrub and into the grove of trees. There, I found Chaucer safe.

Safely ensconced in the arms of Carly Cortez.

Chapter Seventeen

She was exactly as I remembered her. That mixture of mystery and sex and a dash of danger all in one package. But the package now sported short brown hair. And was dressed in Country Club Chic—red polo shirt, striped sweater, and white capris. Not an ounce of maternal instinct, though. She held Chaucer like a sack of rotting potatoes. He, in turn, looked at her like she was Cruella De Vil and he was a Dalmatian puppy.

"You are a difficult woman to find alone," Carly said to me. "With all the cops following you around, I thought we would have to leave the country without you."

She wasn't using the royal "we."

Behind her stood three women, all carrying guns. One was the petite gal who had held the gun to Sterling Scott's head during the robbery. She might have passed for cute, what with her tiny nose and Kewpie doll lips. But up close she looked capable of bench-pressing twice her weight.

The other two women were the large, economy size of Ugly Broad. Like two matching bookends, the Broads stood a head taller and a brick house heavier than the rest of us.

"Planning a trip, are you?" I asked this as nonchalantly as possible.

"We should have been long gone by now," Carly said. "You are a bit of a problem for me."

"I'm a problem for *you*?" Who was she kidding?

Chaucer tried to wiggle out of Carly's grasp. He put both of his fat little arms against her chest and pushed back. Carly responded by hiking him up higher on her hip and pulling him closer. He started to squawk. She put a hand over his mouth.

"Don't interrupt me when I'm talking to you." Carly's words lashed out like a slap. I didn't know if she was talking to the kid or to me.

Before I could clarify this, a voice carried over from the beach.

"CHAUCER! Baby, where ARE you?"

It was Tori.

The Broads—One and Two—and the Petite One looked at Carly, their fingers twitching at their guns.

"Follow me," Carly said. She turned quickly and strode away from the beach, through the sage scrub, a wiggling Chaucer in her arms.

Broad One twisted my right arm behind me and pushed me forward. I tried to complain that it hurt, but then I felt the barrel of a gun push against my back. It seemed best to cooperate.

We zigzagged through the brush. We moved quickly, but not so fast as to attract attention. Anyone watching would have figured our group to be taking a shortcut back to PCH. A prickly shortcut. Sage scrub is scratchy stuff and I felt it catch on and tear my pants. To top it off, I was barefoot. I kept tripping as my feet landed hard on rocks. I did cry out in pain but Broad One was without pity. She kept the gun at my back and told me to shut up.

Tori's voice faded as we got closer to PCH. The traffic ran noisily above us when we came upon a drainage ditch. This ditch was considerably smaller than the one by the parking lot, but it was big enough to crawl through on all fours. The Petite One went first. Carly followed, somehow squeezing through with Chaucer in her arms. Broad One pushed me ahead of her as my knees straddled a stream of green gooey runoff. Broad Two brought up the rear.

On the other side waited a shiny red Suburban. Engine running.

The Suburban was brand-spanking-new. Windows tinted as dark as legally allowed. The door slid open and I was shoved into the very back seat. Chaucer was tossed right next to me. Carly and the Broad One took the middle seat. The Petite One landed in front next to the driver, yet another woman. Broad Two stayed behind. Before you could say "ollie, ollie, outs in free" we were heading north on PCH. Perfectly camouflaged among all the other red Suburbans and black Land Rovers on the road.

I sat slumped in the corner, massaging my numb feet. Chaucer sat at the other end of the bench seat, legs straight out, eyes blinking tearfully. One of us needed a diaper change.

Carly peered out the windows, scanning the scenery from left to right. "Anyone following us?" She directed this to the driver.

"No, we're clear," the driver said in a strongly Hispanic accent. "Those police not follow her to the beach."

"Probably didn't want to get sand in their wingtips," the Petite One said.

Laughter all around. Chaucer and I were the only ones who didn't get the joke.

Satisfied, Carly leaned down and pulled a knapsack from the floor. She rummaged through it as Broad One kept a gun pointed at me.

I got it. Sit still and keep quiet. What the hell did she think I was going to do?

Carly pulled several phones out of the knapsack. Examined each one before settling on the one she wanted. She tossed the rest back in the sack and then dialed a number.

"It's me," she said, when the call connected. "We're on our way back. What do you have for me?"

The answers pleased her. She repeated that we were on our way just as Chaucer slipped off the seat and onto the floor. The fumes from his diaper could have peeled paint off a wall. Broad One held her nose. Carly made a face and turned back to glare at Chaucer.

"Wait a minute," Carly said into the phone. "We've got the kid, too. We need diapers. Yes, diapers. What? Hell, I don't know."

She turned to me. "How old is he?"

I shrugged. "Not my kid."

"You don't even know how old he is?"

I considered it. Tori claimed he would be in pre-school when the new brat was born. How old was that?"

I decided to ask him. "How old are you?"

He tugged at the offensive diaper. Then held up all five fingers.

"He's five," I said.

"He's not five," Broad One said derisively. "He's still in diapers!"

"He says he's five. He should know."

Carly glared at me. Putting the phone back to her ear, she said, "I'd say he's between two and three. Don't go to the marina grocery store. There will be an alert out for him soon."

As if on cue, two CHP cars flew south on PCH, sirens blaring and lights flashing.

Carly tossed the phone back into the sack and grinned at Chaucer. "Looks like your mother has sounded the alarm. The cops are really going to want to talk to your Aunt Alana now!"

They all thought that was hilarious. Again, Chaucer and I didn't get the joke.

"I'm not his aunt!" I said, as calmly as possible. "It seems to me that the cops will want to talk to you! You're the one who kidnapped him."

Silence fell in the Suburban. Broad One's forearms tightened and her gun twitched just a bit. The Petite One turned around, agog. The driver glanced nervously in the rearview mirror. Apparently one did not

M.A. Simonetti

contradict Carly. At least to her face. Or the back of her head, in my case.

Carly turned in her seat and looked hard at me, the way one considers puzzle pieces before deciding which to pick up first. I could see her mentally turning over her responses. I figured she had to save face in front of the troops. It did occur to me that the easiest way to do that might be to shoot me. That's about the time I realized I might be in some real danger.

But Carly gently pushed the Broad's gun away. Broad One turned around. I didn't notice her put the gun away, however. Carly folded her arms on the back of her seat, rested her chin on her arm and smiled a self-satisfied smirk at me. I hate receiving that look. I much prefer handing it out.

"I believe the circumstances point to you as the likely kidnapper, Alana," Carly said. "After all, you did call Tori and tell her to meet you at the beach and you did specify a particularly remote area. And you lied to her about wanting to settle the alimony issue. Why would you do that if you didn't intend harm?"

"What are you talking about? I didn't call—"

Carly pulled something out of her knapsack. Held it up for me to see. It was my cell phone—the one that went missing from the Hulks at Save the Bay. Of course.

Carly then held her fingers up to her ear to simulate a phone call.

"Alana! Meet me at the beach!" Carly's imitation of Tori was so convincing that Chaucer stood up and toddled forward.

"Mama?" His tiny voice was full of relief. He reached up and pulled at the Petite One's arm. Didn't take it well when he realized the Petite One wasn't Tori. Plopped right down on his dirty diaper and wailed.

I knew exactly how he felt. Carly had fooled me, too. And Tori. Not that Tori was that hard to fool, but it did explain why she thought I had set up our meeting. Instead, Carly set up the meeting at the beach by calling me and pretending to be Tori. And then calling Tori and pretending to be me. Damn clever of her.

Chaucer's wails rose to full-out screams.

"Shut him up!" Carly demanded.

The gang was about as knowledgeable in child rearing as I was. And as well prepared. The Petite One put her gun on the dashboard and rummaged through the glove box looking for who knows what. Broad One tucked her gun under her thigh and leaned over to pick Chaucer up. He screamed and kicked, his face turned red. Something brown and smelly oozed down his fat little leg. A box of Kleenex appeared. The Broad held Chaucer aloft while the Petite One tried to wipe the poop off his leg. He kicked and screamed some more. The driver yelled something in Mexican. The Petite One got Chaucer partially cleaned up, tossed the dirty tissues on the floor, and then came up with a water bottle. She twisted the lid off and held it up to him. He batted it away. Water sprayed everywhere.

"I said, SHUT HIM UP!"

"We're trying. We don't have anything in here for a baby." The Petite One came to the back to retrieve the water bottle. Carly shot her a look that sent shivers through me.

"Pull off the freeway. Find a store. Do it quickly."

The driver took the next exit. A convenience store conveniently appeared just as Chaucer's screams turned into rib-cracking sobs. The air was thick with tension and ripe diaper.

The driver pulled up to the side of the store. Broad One clamped a hand over Chaucer's mouth. His eyes grew wide in surprise. The Petite One opened the door to hop out. Carly stopped her.

"Don't buy diapers or anything that really looks like a kid will use it. There probably is an AMBER Alert out already."

The Petite One nodded and was gone. Carly turned back to me. She did not look pleased.

"You better be worth all of this trouble," she said. Like it was my fault.

I didn't respond. I sat in my corner and worried about what she intended to do with me. I felt my skin grow clammy. A knot twisted in my stomach. Chaucer squirmed beside me and the fumes from his diaper filled the van. Talk about a lot of trouble. At least I was potty trained.

While we waited for the Petite One to return, Carly made more calls, using a different cell phone for each one. One call concerned the availability of ripe pineapples. "Tea" was told to clear out her room and move in with "Dee." It all sounded oddly domestic to me.

All the while, Broad One kept her hand clamped over Chaucer's mouth.

The Petite One returned with a plastic bag full of stuff. The driver backed the Suburban out of the parking lot and headed back to the highway. The Petite One climbed into the back and kneeled on the floor as she opened her bag. The Broad took her hand off Chaucer's mouth. He glared at her with indignant brown eyes. He opened his mouth.

"Just stay quiet, kid," she advised. Oddly, he obeyed.

"Here, have this." The Petite One opened a small bottle of Diet Pepsi. He reached for it with both hands and guzzled. Then burped. Adding yet another delightful aroma to the air.

The Petite One pulled out a small package of wet wipes, a pair of scissors, a roll of paper towels, a bag of rubber bands, and a corn dog wrapped in foil. She and the Broad then worked to clean up the kid. His T-shirt, shorts, and diaper came off. His legs and privates were cleaned with the wet wipes, a new diaper was fashioned out of the paper towels, and the offending diaper and dirty tissues were stuffed in the plastic bag. His shorts slipped back on. Then the Petite One took the scissors to his T-shirt. She cut off the arms and part of the back so it looked like a little halter top. Then she pulled his blond curls up into pigtails and fastened them with the rubber bands.

"They're looking for a boy," she said to Carly. "If we get him through the marina quick enough maybe no one will notice."

Carly snapped her phone shut and nodded her approval. The Petite One smiled and blushed, and then looked at the Broad with that triumphant expression one sibling gives another when parental approval is bestowed. I couldn't see the Broad's face but her neck muscles tensed.

The Petite One handed the hot dog to Chaucer. I did wonder if that was such a good idea, but he scarfed it down and followed it with a Diet Pepsi chaser. Gave a big yawn. The Broad picked him up and brought him back to my row. Lay him down and gently stroked his pigtails. Very touching. Probably would make the cover of *Kidnappers Weekly*.

I kept myself busy staring out the back window. We headed north on the 101. Given the references to a marina, I figured our destination was somewhere in Santa Barbara, with its myriad of harbors and yacht clubs. We passed Rincon Point, Carpinteria, and the banana plantation. I stared out the window. There wasn't much to see, but it beat watching Chaucer nap beside me. Then I spotted the van.

At first I thought I was kidding myself. I sat up a little straighter. Broad One turned to look at me. I pretended to stretch. She looked away. I turned as if trying to stretch my back and stared hard out the window.

Sure enough, a rusty white van trailed behind the Suburban. It followed stealthily, keeping three or more cars between us. At times it disappeared behind a bend in the road, but it was always close enough to spot us if we had exited. I was so happy to see that finally Sanchez had found the sense to listen to Jackson Jones.

We took the left exit leading to the zoo and East Beach. Drove past the lagoon and bird sanctuary and headed north on Cabrillo Boulevard. Passed the sand volleyball games, the State Street intersection, and Stearns Wharf. No surprise to me, we turned onto Harbor Way and ended up in the parking lot of Santa Barbara Yacht Club. Parked with plenty of room for Stan and his men to surround the vehicle without harming the innocent public.

The driver and the Petite One hopped out. The Broad opened the door, stepped out and turned around. There was a big bulge in the right-hand pocket of her shorts. Carly got out, turned to me, and said, "We're going to walk to the boat now." Keep your eyes straight ahead and do not look at anyone. Pick up the kid and let's go."

I slid across the seat and climbed out alone.

"You pick him up. You kidnapped him."

I stepped away from the Suburban, intending to be out of harm's way when Stan showed up. Bravado aside, it did occur to me that it was better to leave Chaucer inside out of the gunfire.

Carly laughed at me.

"You know, Alana, I really do like you. You are one cold-hearted bitch. You remind me of me."

She told Broad One to get Chaucer. Then she stepped past the rest of us and led the way toward the harbor. The Petite One grabbed my arm. I stood my ground.

"Hey! Let's go!" The Petite One tugged my arm. I stayed put. At the entrance to the parking lot, the white van had just pulled in. I was about to be rescued.

She tugged hard. I didn't move. The van drove toward us, a little too slow for my liking, but what do I know about police shootouts?

"Let's GO!" The Petite One put all her weight into shoving me toward Carly. I held fast, eyes glued to the van. Carly turned around and her gaze followed mine. Her eyes widened just a bit. I was betting she knew her gig was up. No more pushing me around, it was Carly's turn to be the fish on the line.

The van pulled into the space on the far side of the Suburban. I figured my best option was to drop to the ground and roll under the car.

The driver's door to the van opened.

I held my breath.

And let it out in a *whoosh* when Broad Two emerged, arms laden with grocery bags. All alone. No cops.

Did Broad Two steal Stan's van? Oh, crap, would the cops blame me for that, too?

And then I remembered my paparazzi pal's description of the "big dudes" in the van. And I realized it wasn't Stan and another cop that had pulled in behind me at the Country Mart. It was the Broads. With their short hair, bulky figures, and mean demeanor, they could easily pass for "dudes." Especially if they were "nobodies."

I suddenly felt very, very alone. And very, very afraid. And drenched in sweat.

The Petite One shoved me again. This time I moved.

Carly led us down a ramp to a gate guarding the entrance to the marina. She slid a card key to unlock the gate. The door clicked open and we walked down a set of stairs to the docks. Carly marched ahead. The Petite One and I followed, arm in arm. To look at us you would have thought we were just great buddies, since you wouldn't have seen the nose of a gun pushed up against my ribs. Broad One followed us with Chaucer asleep on her shoulder and looking more like a little girl than I would have thought possible. The Hispanic driver and Broad Two brought up the rear, laden with grocery bags.

We walked past motorboats and sailboats bobbing gently up and down. We passed the twenty-foot boats, then the thirty-five-footers and the forty-footers. The dock got wider as the boats got bigger. At the end of the seventy-five-footers, another gate loomed. Carly swiped another card and we passed into the land of the "Oh My Gods."

"Oh My God" is a nautical term for luxury mega-yachts. Gleaming white, the size of barns, the yachts sat moored in silent splendor. Any hope I had of rescue sank as the gate locked behind us. Yachtsmen at the mega-yacht level are notoriously private. The Petite One could shoot me point-blank and not a highbrow would be raised.

Carly stopped at the last boat. I gauged it at 180 feet. I knew this because I associate with people who own these things. A gangplank hovered about six feet above the dock. A rope chain at the end of the gangplank stated Private. Big surprise there. A woman appeared on the boat and lowered the gangplank to the dock. Carly unlocked the chain and stepped on board. We all followed.

The woman at the head of the gangplank offered her hand to help me step down to the deck. She was barefoot and dressed in navy shorts and a white polo shirt with the boat's name embroidered on it. Brilliantly, I deduced that we were on board the *Delirious*. We boarded the deck closest to the water. Because I know this stuff, I knew the deck would be called the sport deck and the door just off it would open to a storage area stocked water toys like inner tubes, Jet Skis, and snorkel gear.

"Welcome aboard," the uniformed woman said.

I marched past her and followed Carly up two flights of stairs.

The stairs brought us to an outside lounging area with cushioned benches along the perimeter and a covered dining area. A teak dining table large enough to seat twelve held a lovely tropical centerpiece. A bar with six stools stood to the other side, reminding me that I could really use a drink. Between the bar and the table, an automatic glass door swung open. I followed Carly into what I assumed was the main salon.

The salon featured the low padded ceilings and nautical decorating theme you just naturally expect. Not that there is anything wrong with that. Every time I set foot on a yacht someone has decided to decorate in an "offbeat" style, I am slightly disappointed. Where else can you enjoy navy blue upholstery and rope accessories without feeling silly? The salon of the *Delirious* did not disappoint. It was spacious, with two seating areas, a card table surrounded with bookshelves, and a promising-looking bar. The furnishings were plush with no sharp edges. It was air-conditioned and as quiet as a library.

Behind the bar stood yet another woman dressed in navy shorts and a white polo shirt. She was left-handed. I knew this because of how she wore her gun holster. She poured iced beverages into frosty mugs as Carly lowered herself onto an ivory chenille couch.

Carly indicated that I was to sit. I sat opposite her in a club chair. Carly looked none the worse for our dash through the scrub sage. Her sweater draped easily over her shoulders, her hair was in place. Me? I had scrapes and scratches in places that haven't seen the light of day since I was eighteen.

The holstered bartender delivered our drinks. Turned out to be root beer. Turned out I was parched. I emptied the glass in one guzzle. A fresh glass appeared instantly.

"Where is Chaucer?" I asked. Not that I cared all that much, but it seemed like the polite question.

Carly raised an eyebrow at the bartender. The bartender said, "Penelope took him below to get cleaned up."

"Very good." Carly took a ladylike sip of her root beer. And then got right down to business.

"What did Jackson Jones want from you?"

"What?" I was startled. Which was surprising, given how the day had gone up to that point.

"What...did...Jackson Jones...want...from...you?"

She sat calmly waiting. At least she appeared calm. One leg was curled up, one arm was extended over the top of the couch. She held the mug of root beer firmly in one hand. But her knuckles were white. And her eyes flashed in that manner I knew meant trouble. She was tense. And that just pissed me off. How dare she talk down to me after she kidnapped me? And had the nerve to frame me for kidnapping Chaucer, to boot.

"You know, since the day I met you, my life has been turned inside and out," I said. "I've been held at gunpoint more times than I can count. I've been questioned by the police, put under suspicion, lied to, and now kidnapped. I'm not answering any questions until you tell me what the hell is going on."

The air seemed to be sucked out of the room. The bartender stood stock-still, her hand hovering over her gun. Carly's eyes narrowed as she measured her response. She never stopped staring at me as she said, "Sylvia, please leave us alone."

Sylvia hesitated ever so slightly before walking out of the salon and positioning herself and her gun just outside the automatic glass door. I spotted two more women pacing the outside passages. All dressed in *Delirious* uniforms. All armed. I figured it would take a crew of at least twelve to woman the boat. How convenient that Carly had trained bandits at her disposal. And such a flexible bunch—bandits, sailors, candlestick makers.

Making a dash for freedom was out of the question. At least for the moment.

"I suppose I do owe you an explanation, Alana," Carly said. "It's a long story. To save time, why don't you tell me what you know and what you want answered."

Fair enough.

"I know of you, first of all. Which puts me in the minority, since there has been no mention of you in the newspapers. I know you are an art thief. I know you have a gang of women that works for you. I know you planned the robbery at Save the Bay as a diversion while you stole CiCi DiCarlo's Balinese painting. I don't know how you met Kymbyrlee Chapman or why you killed her. And I don't know why you had to drag me into all of this."

Carly listened carefully, I'll give her that. No smirks, no flashing eyes. When I was done, she set her root beer down. Put both feet on the floor and leaned her arms on her knees. No bulging breasts this time.

"Sylvia met Kymbyrlee in prison. Kym seemed like the right fit for my organization. Unfortunately, her loyalty was not up to my standards and we had to dispose of her."

"Dispose of her? That's a tidy phrase for cold-blooded murder."

"There was nothing cold-blooded about it. Kym made her choice and she died from the consequences."

"What do I have to do with all of this?" I held my breath, not sure I really wanted to know.

Carly shook her head. "First tell me what Jackson Jones wanted."

"I'm surprised you don't know. Haven't you been following me?"

"Yes, we have. But Jackson is crafty and I need to know what he is up to."

"Why is he so important to you?"

"Jackson can get in my way. He is as good a thief as I am, and if he figures out what I am up to, he could screw up everything."

"What is it? Some sort of competition among thieves?" I was surprised to hear Jackson referred to as a thief. Maybe she just meant he had as much knowledge about the art world as she did.

"Not among thieves," Carly corrected me. "This is a family matter. Jackson Jones is my brother."

Chapter Eighteen

"Your brother?"

She had to be kidding. Her almond-shaped eyes. Her smooth copper skin. Her whole exotic aura. Jackson, in comparison, was all-American. And he had to be in his late forties. How could they be related?

"Half brother," Carly corrected herself. "Same father."

"Your mother is married to Jackson's father?"

Carly looked at me like I was a half-wit.

"Jackson and I share the same father. There was no marriage involved."

"Very interesting, but what does this have to do with me?"

"Tell me what Jackson wanted and I will explain that," Carly countered.

Retelling my side of the story seemed to help me make some sense out of this mess. So I told her what I knew, starting with Jackson's job with CiCi and ending with the meeting at the Country Mart.

"La Jolla? Jackson said he lives in La Jolla? That's hysterical."

I didn't get the joke again.

She sensed my confusion this time.

"Jackson is about as likely to live in La Jolla as I am."

Well, that certainly cleared everything up.

"You said you would tell me what the hell is going on."

"I did." She gave every indication that she was about to set the record straight when Sylvia reentered the salon.

"Excuse me, Carly. We are ready to set sail."

Carly gave Sylvia a curt nod. To me, she said, "This will have to wait until dinner." Then, to Sylvia, "Have Penelope take Alana below."

Penelope turned out to be the Petite One.

She stuck a gun at my back and steered me to the middle of the boat. We descended one flight down a stately staircase of polished walnut with brass railings. Oil paintings of sailing ships lined the paneled walls. The stairs led to the entrance to a formal dining room which was slightly smaller than a hotel lobby. A table with sixteen chairs anchored the space. The nautical theme prevailed, from the navy blue upholstery on the chairs to the rope details on the stools in a cozy bar aft. A set of glass doors near the bar led to an outside deck. Penelope did not steer me out the glass doors and make me walk the plank. Instead, she directed me to a discreetly hidden door and into the galley. A woman wearing a chef's hat and a linked metal apron stood at a center island and expertly gutted a salmon. I knew the metal apron was a safety feature to prevent the chef from impaling herself when cooking at stormy seas. But under the circumstances, it appeared a bit medieval to me. The chef did not bother to look up as we passed by. At the end of the kitchen, an austere staircase led down. We clankety-clanked down one more flight. At the bottom of this set of stairs was a sparse room featuring a cramped U-shaped booth wrapped around a Formica table. A tiny TV sat precariously above a microwave and faced the booth. With my great powers of deduction, I figured we were in the crew's quarters. Two short steps led forward to a narrow, harshly lit hallway.

There were six doors down the hall, three on each side. At the end lay the laundry area where two industrial-sized washers and two dryers tumbled away. The Ugly Broads flanked one of the doors like two giant redwood timbers. Penelope opened the door between the Broads and indicated that I was to follow her into the room.

"There will be two guards outside," Penelope said. "If you need to use the head, just knock and someone will escort you."

And she stepped out. She shut the door in a manner that indicated there would be no further discussion.

With nothing better to do, I inspected the quarters. The room, nearly the size of a shoe box, contained a set of hard-looking bunk beds, a miniature writing desk, and a closet straight out of a dollhouse. No window. A small TV above the desk.

And Chaucer Fox grinning at me from the bottom bunk.

Someone had cleaned him up. He smelled sweetly of baby powder. His pigtails had bows and he wore a pink sundress. He clutched a teddy bear with one chubby hand. In his other hand was a lollipop the size of his head. He appeared enormously pleased with himself.

"Bite?" He graciously extended the sticky lollipop to me.

"No, thanks." I turned back to the door and pounded on it.

The door opened a hair. "You need to use the head already?"

"No. I want another room."

"What?"

"You kidnapped this kid. You take care of him."

The door slammed shut.

I pounded again. "Let me out of here!"

No response.

I kicked the door. No small task in bare feet.

Nothing.

I leaned against the door and slid to the floor. Exhausted, barefoot, filthy dirty, and held against my will. Locked up with a sugar-laden toddler. My own private hell.

Chaucer held the lollipop out to me again. It slipped from his grasp, fell to the linoleum floor, and shattered into hundreds of pieces. His eyes filled with tears and his lower lip protruded. His cheeks grew blotchy and his face wrinkled up. I sensed something bad was about to happen.

It did.

He let out a little sob, then another. And another. He plopped over to one side and began howling. Really shrieking. Incensed shrieks intended to bring uncooperative adults to their knees.

It worked.

A scuffle sounded outside the door.

"What did you do to him?" The two Broads stuffed themselves into the room.

"Nothing."

They didn't believe me.

"Get him to stop crying!"

"Not my kid. Not my problem."

I was getting tired of explaining this.

Three more women appeared in the corridor. All dressed in the *Delirious* uniform.

"Someone has to shut him up!"

"We're almost under way!"

"They need us on deck!"

Someone said, "Find Ginger!" Broad One tried to get Chaucer to suck on a broken piece of lollipop. He responded with a quick left hook. She jerked her head out of the way and butted it against the upper bunk. She cursed, he screamed.

The room was so packed, I honestly worried that we might all suffocate. Just then, Ginger arrived.

Ginger was of Asian descent with a gentle smile. Her navy shorts swam on her tiny frame. She unbuckled her gun holster and handed it to Broad Two. She produced a cotton blanket out of thin air and expertly swaddled Chaucer. The blanket had the fresh, clean smell of laundry soap. She made soft, cooing noises in his ear.

To his credit, Chaucer did not immediately fall for it. He stiffened, arching his back to get away from Ginger. She hung on tight and then sweetened the deal by gently rubbing his back. Then she swayed from side to side, cooing away. Eventually his sobs faded and the tears subsided. He took a couple of gasping breaths. Then he stopped and lay his head on Ginger's shoulder. Ginger bustled him out of the room. But not before giving me a big smile.

I couldn't help but notice that Ginger's tongue was missing.

The rest of the crew skedaddled for their deck duties.

The Broads stayed with me.

"I think I will use the head now," I said.

No such luck. The Broads stepped in the hall and slammed the door behind them.

The boat shivered. I heard the anchor clunk its way up, one chink at a time. A scent of diesel fuel wafted in from the engine room. A gentle lurch forward, an achingly slow turn to the port side and then forward movement. I heard feet pounding, the thump of ropes and side bumpers landing on the deck. The engines chugged rhythmically and the boat swayed ever so gently as we headed out to sea.

With nothing better to do, I took stock of my situation.

Personally, I was having a hard time keeping track of just what my situation was. The cops, of course, thought I was a robber/murderer and now a kidnapper. Of course they were wrong, as well as incompetent.

What Carly was up to was anyone's guess. Not to mention what her plans had to do with me.

Only one thing was clear. I had to get off the damn boat.

To keep from dying of boredom, I distracted myself by snooping through the cabin. I rifled through the tiny closet. Found four sets of crew uniforms, six white T-shirts, and four pairs of jeans. Gee, wonder where I had seen those before? Four pairs of shoes, two of them size ten. When laced up tightly, they did not fall off my feet. I filed that little piece of data away for future use. I found passports, apparently one for every occasion. The two roommates of the cabin hailed from San Antonio, Mexico City, or Buenos Aires. I guessed where depended on Carly's frame of mind.

I made myself comfortable by lying on the lower bunk. I raised my legs, planted my bare feet on the bottom of the bunk above and stretched. It felt good. I raised my hands over my head and pushed against the headboard. Also good. I turned my head back and forth. The stretching brought some relaxation to my muscles. I could really use a hot shower. And a cold drink.

The boat swayed gently in the waves. I wondered what plans Carly had in mind. And then I wondered about Carly's state of mind. More than anything, I worried. I worried that if pressed, that flash in her eyes would explode. And I felt pretty certain I did not want to be in her way at that time.

The engines geared down to a low purr and then the Broads opened the cabin door.

"Carly said you could use a guest suite to clean up. Let's go."

No argument from me. Broad One led the way. Broad Two flanked me and we retraced the steps up the austere metal stairs and through the galley. Past the cook deftly chopping fresh dill on a wooden block. A pot filled with simmering water sloshed away at the electric stove. I glanced out a porthole above the sink as we passed. We were sailing to the south.

We passed through the swinging doors into the formal dining room. The table had been dismantled and set for dinner for two. Formal china perched regally on thin rubber placemats to keep the dishes from flying off the table. I remembered Carly had mentioned continuing our conversation at dinner. I noted with relief that wineglasses were on the table.

The Broads led me down the center mahogany staircase to a small foyer. The walls were paneled in mahogany, a thick carpet at our feet. There were three wide doors here; one door forward, and one each on the port and starboard sides. Broad One opened the door on the port side.

"You can use this suite. There are toiletries, towels, and a hair dryer in the bathroom. Clean clothes on the bed. Just toss your dirty clothes out here and they will be laundered. Carly said to give you privacy. But don't get any bright ideas. The portholes are double-thick marine glass. Even if you could break them, there are sharks in the water out there."

Chuckling, she shut the door.

The suite was just slightly smaller than a roller rink. Oversized twin beds flanked the walls. My change of clothes lay on one bed—a white polo shirt a size too large and a pair of navy pants also too big. New underwear in a plastic bag and a tank top in lieu of a bra. All in all, a huge improvement over the sand-and-sweat-encrusted ensemble I was wearing.

A large mahogany desk lay at one end of the room and double doors to the bathroom at the other. A comfy leather chair and matching ottoman decorated in soothing shades of tan and navy. Portholes ran the length of the outside wall. I peered out and saw land in the distance. We were definitely heading south and going there at a good clip.

I gave up my lookout post in favor of a shower.

Twenty minutes later, I emerged from the marble-appointed bathroom in a fluffy white robe, my hair wrapped in a towel and smelling of lilacs. I felt oodles better and inclined to snoop. And I knew just where to begin.

I sat at the spacious desk and rifled through the drawers. Boats the size of the *Delirious* are often rented for charter. Much like a pricey hotel, I suspected the *Delirious* had a manual outlining her features. Sure enough, she did. Leather bound, of course, the manual for the *Delirious* listed everything a passenger needed to know about the boat. Everything except who actually owned it.

I skipped past the sections on the water toys, how to use the phone system, and even the wine list. I stopped at the detailed drawings of the boat's layout.

She was quite well laid out. Five decks. Eight guest cabins. A full gym. A theater. TVs with DVD players in each stateroom. Private baths in every room, two baths in the master suite. The dining room could seat sixteen. Outdoor dining on the main deck. And a stash of toys for every sport—water skis, Jet Skis, scuba gear, kayaks, windsurf boards, bicycles, and two custom-built tenders to shuttle back and forth to shore. A sundeck on top and quarters for a dozen crew members. Fully MCA compliant with no restrictions. And a fuel capacity of fifty thousand gallons. All of which meant the *Delirious* could sail anywhere, anchor anywhere, and not run out of things to do until Chaucer was twenty-one.

I studied the deck layouts and determined where the boat's captain slept, where the outside crew stairs were, and which decks were close to water level. I was committing the emergency exits to memory when someone pounded on the door.

"Dinner in fifteen minutes!"

I quietly stashed the manual away and went to dry my lilac-scented hair.

The Broads escorted me to the main salon. I knew from my study of the deck plans that the main salon lay one deck above the dining room. As we ascended the spiral mahogany staircase that lay amidships, I knew that if I bolted and dashed outside through the glass doors in the dining room, I could race down yet another set of stairs to the sport deck and dive off a platform into the chilly shark-infested waters of the Pacific.

Or just hang around and wait for a better opportunity.

The Broads dropped me off at the main salon and disappeared.

Carly sat in a club chair near the bar, a flute of champagne in her hand. She was dressed in a red silk halter dress, a string of pearls, and a haughty smile. Across the salon, a TV was tuned to the LA news.

"Alana! You are a headliner!" Carly laughed.

On the TV screen was a female reporter, dressed in the khaki garb TV journalists reserve for true disasters. The reporter strove to balance humane concern with hard journalism.

Chaucer's kidnapping was the story.

"And there you have it. A tragedy today in Malibu. Two-year-old Chaucer Fox snatched right our from under his mother's watchful eyes. Back to you in the studio.

"You are famous Alana! How does it feel?" Carly drained her glass.

The story closed with a parting photo of Chaucer. Tori had obviously supplied the photo, a formal shot of little Chaucer sitting on his mother's lap, with Tori's cleavage forming the backdrop behind his head.

Sylvia appeared with a refill. She was dressed in an evening uniform of a white linen shirt with epaulets, navy skirt, and navy stockings. Brass buttons all over the place. She picked up Carly's empty and put another in its place. Handed one to me like she was doing me a favor.

I settled into a club chair next to Carly. She pointed the remote and switched channels. There, too, Chaucer's tragic kidnapping played out. This channel boasted the added attraction of the grieving parents. Live.

Alan and Tori Fox stood at the microphone. Their spokesman, one Richard Lafferty, addressed the "shock and dismay" of the parents. The hard journalism neglected to mention that Richard Lafferty was also an attorney.

"...are devastated, as one might imagine." Richard's voice carried all the appalled tones one would expect for the five thousand dollars an hour he charges.

"Does Mrs. Fox have any idea why...," the reporter pressed for details.

I didn't hear the answer. I was too distracted by the scene playing out next to Richard. There stood Tori, dressed for the part of the traumatized mother in a lacy white maternity dress, with a big blue ribbon holding back her hair. All she needed was a shepherd's staff and a flock of sheep.

But that wasn't what caught my attention. It was the look on Alan's face. His complexion was gray, his eyes puffy. His jaw was set in that manner he gets when all odds are against him.

And it hit me like an invisible brick to my thick head. Alan was actually fond of the kid.

Funny, it had never occurred to me before. I had focused on what Chaucer's arrival had done to my house on the hill. The tricycle tracks on my beloved floors. Baby gates screwed into my Italian plaster walls. God-knows-what-spit-up on my pure wool carpets. Tori prancing around my perfect pool and ruining the view in her tiny bikinis.

No, I had never thought about how Alan felt about the kid.

And then another revelation hit me like another invisible brick to the other side of my head. I'd always blamed my divorce on Alan cheating. And hated Tori for being available to cheat. For the first time, I realized that Alan had been drawn to Tori not because of her tight ass, but because she would give him kids. And I would not.

The camera pulled back to show Alan and Tori looking lost and scared. Alan had his arm around Tori's shoulders. Richard stood nearby looking a little lost himself, probably because he wasn't sure who to sue yet.

The reporter closed with, "The police are also looking for Alana Fox, the ex-wife of Alan Fox. She was last seen with the boy…"

A police sketch of a woman that was supposed to be me flashed on the screen. Along with the identifying data of height, weight, and age.

Off by two inches, twenty pounds, and ten years.

Tori's description, no doubt. Great. Just when I was teetering on the verge of feeling sorry for her.

I sipped the champagne. Cristal, not bad. Although under the circumstances I would have drunk warm gin out the bottle with a straw.

Carly switched channels again. Lo and behold, more about Chaucer missing. Where's a good earthquake when you need to divert your thoughts to something else. Like how to get off the damn boat.

"Put something else on," I said, none too politely.

Behind the bar, Sylvia stopped polishing glasses and moved for her gun. Carly muted the TV. Spoke over her shoulder.

"Sylvia, leave us alone, please."

Sylvia folded a bar towel with slow purpose and then walked across the salon and positioned herself outside the sliding glass doors. Carly waited for the doors to close completely. She looked me straight in the eye and said, "Do not speak to me in that tone of voice in front of my crew again, Alana."

"It's OK if we are alone, then?"

I saw a flash in her eyes and braced myself. Her whole demeanor tensed up, just like a cat about to pounce. I felt a nasty energy swirl through the room, like a Santa Ana wind—hot and eerie.

And passed in a nanosecond. Carly brightened and raised her glass in a toast.

"We are going to work very well together, Alana!" Carly announced, as if it were a done deal. "Let's toast to our future!"

I ignored the toast and said, "What the hell do you want from me?"

My tone of voice did not faze her. She drained her glass. She poured another and said, "Let's take a walk outside and discuss your future."

I followed her out the glass doors to the deck. It was now dark but still warm. We were far enough from shore to just make out the lights on land. I figured we were south of Santa Barbara, as the oil derricks were behind us. Nowhere near Malibu, or I would have jumped ship and swum home, sharks be damned.

"Do you like the *Delirious*, Alana?" Carly stared out to sea.

"It's fine. Whose is it?"

"It belongs to a client of mine. In my line of work, I meet the wealthiest people in the world. They pay me well. In cash and in perks. The *Delirious* is one of my perks."

"What did you have to steal to earn this perk?"

She waved the question away. I followed her down the side passage to the front of the boat. We rounded a corner, walked down a short set of steps, and sat on a bench that lent a view up and into the wheelhouse. The moon was full and the air warm. The boat sailed slowly, gently rising and falling on the quiet sea, barely stirring up a wind. Under any other circumstances, it would have been romantic.

"I have a plan for you, Alana. An offer you will find irresistible."

I could hardly wait to hear this.

"I live an exceptional life. The *Delirious* is typical of the kind of luxury I enjoy. I work for people who truly appreciate the things I obtain for them. And I am willing to offer this life to you."

"Thanks anyway. I live pretty well myself."

"In a cramped two-bedroom hovel on a public beach?"

She was right about the public beach. But even I wouldn't call the house a hovel.

"I live in only the most luxurious settings," Carly continued. "Chalets in Switzerland, homes on private beaches in Mexico, penthouses in New York. My clients make all this possible. I go wherever I want, whenever I want. I am obligated to no one. Completely free."

"Except when the cops are looking for you."

"I have the protection of the most powerful people in the world. People who are above the law!"

People who are above the law? Nice company if you like tyrants, dictators, and paparazzi. I still wasn't seeing what all this had to do with me. But Carly wasn't finished.

"My clients have everything money can buy. But they often desire things that cannot be bought. They hire me to obtain those things for them."

"Yeah, good for you, Carly. I get it. You live well. But I live well, too. Why am I here?"

"You are here, Alana, because my organization needs something that you have."

"And that would be...?"

"Class, breeding, sophistication." Carly glanced around to see if anyone was listening. "I have a wonderful crew. Very loyal, hardworking. They would do anything for me. But they are from disadvantaged backgrounds. I need a partner who is able to blend in seamlessly with the crème de la crème of society. That's where you come in."

"I don't know anything about being a criminal."

"That I can teach you."

"Thanks. Not interested. Can I go home now?"

"You will soon see, Alana, that you can never go home again."

Chapter Nineteen

"Sure I can," I said. "Just drop me off at the nearest dock, I'll call a cab."

Carly didn't hear me.

Something shifted in her attitude and I did not like the looks of it. She stared out at the ocean, her lips curled in a half smile that was anything but pleasant. Her shoulders at once tightened and straightened. She brought her champagne flute to her lips and savored it like a vampire would relish blood. I felt a shiver run through me, and it wasn't from the ocean breezes.

"Let me tell you a little more about my crew," she said. "I found each one of them myself. Some in the Philippines, some in Mexico, others in the U.S. They all have one thing in common—something prohibited them from returning to their families and their communities. Sylvia, for instance, did time in jail. Regina was a prostitute. An abusive husband cut out Ginger's tongue and her family took his side. I found each of my girls at a point in her life when she had nothing left to lose. And I offered them refuge, a place to stay, excellent pay—all in return for their loyalty. It has worked exceedingly well."

For once in my life I kept my mouth shut. Carly's demeanor had changed completely. Her posture, her voice, even the way she held her glass was as if a different spirit inhabited her body.

"And I learned a valuable lesson about human nature, Alana. I learned that once a person loses everything, she has a new moral compass. And that is beneficial to someone who knows how to use it."

I hated to admit it, but I got her point. I had seen it, time and again—the lousy decisions people will make when they are convinced they have no other choice. A bad relationship, an illegal business deal, a horrendous—but cheaper—chintz cover for the ottoman. And this among people of means; people that should have other ways out.

Carly's gang members had that look about them that said they came from rough beginnings—the wariness in their eyes, the hard set to their jaws. The kind of women who once believed in fairy tales and handsome princes to the rescue. Forced into a corner and lacking a prince, no wonder the gang was loyal to Carly. Clever of Carly to take advantage of women in such desperate need. How this related to me, I had no idea.

Carly, of course, did.

"What you don't see, Alana, is how is how I've manipulated your life so that you are in exactly the same position as my girls. Your friends can't trust you. You are at best a laughingstock. At worst an outsider."

"Why me?"

"I told you. I need someone with breeding and sophisti—"

"No. Why ME? Why not someone else?"

"Because you were the easiest one to destroy."

Carly's little half smile hardened into an evil grin. She took a sip from her champagne and kept her eyes on me as she drank. Another shiver ran down my spine and settled like a block of ice in my stomach.

"You have no family, Alana. Your life revolves around your image. People flock to you because of who you know. A wonderful life, I am sure, but sadly, a reputation is the easiest thing to lose. Or, in your case, for me to destroy."

"I rebuilt my reputation after my divorce. I can do it again." I said it with way more confidence than I felt.

"Perhaps. But after your divorce, you were the victim of a man who cheated on you. You were a sympathetic figure then because of the harm that had come to you. Now your friends believe that you have deceived them. People are not as forgiving of the one who hurts them. I am offering you an opportunity to start fresh and to make a lot of money while you are at it."

"Again, no thanks. I'll take my chances."

"Are you as willing to take your chances with the police? I'm sure that they have obtained a search warrant for your home by now. How will you explain ninety thousand dollars in cash in the shoe boxes in your closet?"

"Ninety thousand dollars! There was close to a hundred and eighty thousand there! What happened—"

Carly shrugged. "I needed some cash. Thank you, by the way."

"My pleasure." My tone of voice did not sit well with her.

"I told you not to speak to me like that."

"You said it was fine if we were alone."

She didn't like it, but she let it slide.

"How will you explain all that cash lying around your house?"

"I'll say I have a morbid fear of the banking system."

"You really think you can return home, reestablish your reputation, and explain your horde of cash to the police?"

"I do."

"Interesting. Although from what I have seen of you, perhaps you could do just that." She held her glass aloft as if to toast me. I didn't join her; I had a bad feeling coming on, and it wasn't seasickness.

"Could you explain away murder, Alana?"

"Murder? You have some plan to implicate me in Kymbyrlee's murder now?"

"You leave me no choice." Carly's eyes danced. "But not in Kymbyrlee's death. If you refuse to join me, I will arrange to have it look as if you kidnapped and killed your ex-husband's little boy. No one will ever forgive you for killing Chaucer Fox."

Chapter Twenty

Well, that was true enough. A dead toddler would make it damn hard for me to regain my reputation. Which was no longer the least bit important to me.

I felt fear race through me, numbing my fingers and toes, weakening my legs. I couldn't breathe, I could barely think. But on the heels of the fear came anger. How dare she threaten that innocent baby?

I mentally battened down my fear and took a long, slow breath. A courage I never knew I had calmed my thoughts and braced my wits for battle. Instinctively, I knew that I had to outwit Carly to get Chaucer and myself to safety.

Carly mistook my silence for submission.

"What do you say, Alana? Are you ready to join forces with me now, or do I have to dispose of Chaucer?"

"You can't be serious." I put on the scared-stiff act. OK, maybe it wasn't such an act.

"Of course, I'm serious. I have to get rid of him at some point. To dispose of him and point suspicion at you serves my needs very well."

I stared at her wide-eyed, as if the reality of her power was just sinking in.

She loved it. Like every other megalomaniac I've ever met, she just loved feeling like she controlled the world completely.

"Come, Alana. Let's have dinner. We can discuss our future."

Carly stood and walked up the stairs leading past the wheelhouse. I calculated an appropriate lag to my response as if I were still in shock. Then I stood and walked with a heavy step to the dining room.

I deserved an Academy Award.

Dinner promised to be superb. There was a colorful little appetizer of chilled gazpacho at the table as we entered the dining room.

As soon as we were seated, Carly was handed a manila envelope by the Hispanic driver. Carly slid a couple of papers out of the envelope, glanced over them and threw them back at the driver.

"That man is an idiot!" she sputtered.

The driver fled, papers clutched to her chest.

"Something wrong?" I asked.

Carly stared hard at me.

"The first thing I will teach you, Alana, is how to collect payment." Carly picked up her wineglass and swirled it around, watching the liquid spin in the glass. "And how to deal with clients who change plans at the last minute."

She said nothing more, but it was clear that she was fuming over something.

I knew better than to ask questions. I took a long sip of the better-than-average chardonnay I found in my glass and pieced a few things together just from my own observations.

I suspected the yacht had been harbored in Santa Barbara because Carly still had the Balinese painting in her possession. And had not yet received payment. Given her reaction to the message in the manila envelope, her client had changed the plans to deliver the painting and the payment yet again. This did not bode well for me. I doubted Carly wanted to put my services into use in California, what with me in the custody of a missing toddler and all. Once she got rid of the painting we were likely taking to the high seas. I needed to get off the damn boat while we were still close to Malibu.

Carly fumed and I mused while the rest of the meal was served by two young women, both blonde, both American. Both cleaned up well enough, but something about them suggested they were new to the art of fine dining. They moved about the dining room as awkwardly as two strippers in a church vestibule.

They wore nametags stating their names as Lacey and Katie. Over a nice little salad of butter lettuce with a proper French dressing, I tallied up the number of crew that I'd had the dubious pleasure of meeting. The two Ugly Broads, Penelope (the Petite One), the Hispanic driver, Sylvia, Ginger, the cook in the galley, Lacey, and Katie. I'd heard Carly speak on the phone to a Tea and a Dee. That made eleven. Someone was captaining the boat and someone else had to back up the captain. That would be thirteen. Every boat the size of the *Delirious* needed an engineer to monitor the engines. Fourteen. Counting Carly, there were fifteen.

So, there were fifteen people I had to outsmart to get Chaucer and myself to safety. Once I had a plan.

Over a main course of poached salmon with fingerling potatoes, I wondered which of the crew had participated in the Save the Bay robbery. My money was on Penelope, Sylvia, Ginger, the driver, Patrice, Tea, Dee, the engineer, and the backup captain. The Broads were too big to ride a horse, and the captain and the cook were too valuable to risk losing.

And that was it for my musing. I signaled Lacey to bring more wine, in hopes that an escape plan would pour out of the bottle.

Carly stopped fuming just as dessert arrived. She barked an order at Katie to have Chaucer join us.

Seeing as how she was talking again, I took the opportunity to clear up one of the ten million questions bothering me. And lead Carly to think that I was truly curious as to how she ran her business.

"Tell me about the meeting you arranged between Tori and me," I began. "Did you impersonate my voice, too?"

"I didn't have to," Carly said. "I called her from your cell phone and she just assumed it was you. She almost didn't come. Apparently, her nanny quit that morning and packing up the kid was too much trouble for her. I had to convince her that the meeting was then or never. She certainly is keen to have your alimony stopped."

"How do you know all this?"

Carly shrugged. "The animosity between you and Tori is common knowledge. Kym knew a lot of it. I bugged your phones for the rest."

Of course she did. It wouldn't have surprised me if she knew the name of my childhood dentist.

"Why me?" I kept coming back to this. I still couldn't understand why I deserved all this aggravation.

"You have skills that are useful to me. You understand the nuances of life in a sophisticated world. It was just a matter of making sure you lost everything. All you had was your reputation. As I said before, a reputation is easy to destroy."

That again. I'd been so shocked by her threat to kill Chaucer, that I had let her explanation of "why me" slide. She really thought all I had was a reputation?

Carly apparently read my mind.

"Most successful people have something tangible in their lives. A career, a family, a business. Complicated alliances that can be difficult to upset. Your life, Alana, is simple. You have no family, no business. You are a glorified socialite. To your credit, you have used that to your advantage. But your reputation was built on little more than positive gossip. It was simple to change that. People do latch on to malicious gossip so easily."

True enough. God knows, I had used the power of gossip myself often enough.

"So you see, Alana, you have two choices. You agree to join my organization and I let the child go. Or you return to your life and face murder charges. Your decision."

It seemed best to play along. "What would my role be in your...organization?"

Carly gave a sly smile and her eyes flashed. She held up the manila envelope.

"I have been approached by a client in Europe. Unfortunately, the task he has in mind would bring me into contact with people that know me too well. You, they do not know. You will be the one who attends the events and makes the connections I need to complete the task. Think of it, Alana; you will mix with the crème de la crème of society in Venice! How can you say no?"

There was more. She was good at the sales pitch, I'll give her that. She made it sound like a glamorous getaway to the Venice Film Festival. Complete with corporate barons and movie stars. I would have loved to pursue the topic further but we had guests.

Ginger led Chaucer by the hand into the dining room. He wore a pair of pink pajamas and clutched his pink teddy bear tightly to his chest. Fuzzy panda slippers on his feet. Yawns all over his face. Someone had just woken up.

Ginger dragged a chair over to the table and sat down with Chaucer on her lap. A bowl of ice cream appeared. Ginger held a spoonful to Chaucer's mouth.

He shook his head. It seemed to take all of his energy to keep his eyes open.

"How is he?" Carly asked Ginger.

Ginger gave a thumbs-up.

Chaucer yawned and pulled the teddy bear closer.

"Who the hell names a kid Chaucer?" Carly asked no one in particular. She looked hard at him, as if she were seeing him for the first time. A malicious smile spread across her face.

"Do you know how to swim, Chaucer? If your Aunt Alana makes a bad decision, we may have to toss you overboard. Would you like that?"

Chaucer didn't have an opinion. He was fast asleep. I did notice Ginger's eyes widen slightly.

"Bad idea, Carly," I said, as I finished off my lemon tart. "If you want to frame me for murder, you will need to produce a body. He'll be eaten by sharks if you toss him overboard."

Ginger's eyes widened even more.

"That's true. I didn't think of that." Carly looked at me in admiration. "You see, Alana, you and I will make a great team. We will strengthen each other's weaknesses. So tell me, how does a jealous woman dispose of her ex-husband's baby?"

"I wouldn't know. I'm not jealous of anyone."

Carly waved her hand in the air as if she were swatting away a bad smell.

"Fine. We won't go into the lengths you have gone to in order to harass your ex-husband's wife. For the sake of this discussion, though, how would you get rid of a body? Assuming you had to?"

I played along only to buy myself some time. And to convince Carly that I was considering her offer to join up. Also, I found Ginger's reaction to the conversation very interesting. For a member of Carly's "loyal" gang, she seemed mighty uncomfortable with the discussion.

"If I didn't want to have the body found, I would weigh it down and toss it overboard. If I wanted to have the body found, I would place it somewhere more accessible. I have to say, I never gave this any thought until now."

"Very amateurish, Alana. I have a lot to teach you."

I could only imagine.

Chaucer let out a loud snore.

Carly gave Ginger a dismissive wave.

Ginger stood up slowly so as not to wake Chaucer and tiptoed out of the room.

"Alana, I have business to finish this evening so I will say good night." Carly stood to take her leave. "I will give you until tomorrow morning to make your decision. Think about what you have lost. And what I am able to do to you. And to the child."

"I still have questions, Carly."

"Such as?"

"Such as, how does Jackson Jones figure in all of this?"

"There are things I will explain to you once I am certain of your loyalty. Jackson Jones, among others."

"What happens to Chaucer if I agree to join you?"

"I will see to it that he is returned unharmed."

She was lying. I knew that for certain. But I pretended to go along with her.

"Those would be my terms. Chaucer is returned to Tori."

"Of course, Alana. You have my word."

Yeah. Like she had never lied to me before.

Penelope came to escort me to my sleeping quarters. To my relief, I was taken to the luxurious guest suite. The two Broads stood guard outside my door. I heard Ginger cooing a lullaby in the guest cabin across the foyer. Good to know. Just in case I had a chance to run for it, I could pop in and grab Chaucer.

I was bid good night and the door shut was shut firmly.

An oversized T-shirt lay folded on one bed—perfect to sleep in. My own clothes, freshly laundered, lay next to that. I pulled off the too-big clothes I was wearing and put on my own undies and the sleep T-shirt. In the bathroom, I found a new toothbrush and toothpaste. I was so tired; I could barely brush my teeth and wash my face. I climbed wearily into bed, shut off the lights, and lay as wide awake as if I had consumed four double espressos instead of one single bottle of wine.

The boat sailed slowly forward, rising and falling with the ocean swells. The hum of the engines was soothing, the suite as dark as pitch. All the ingredients for a perfect night's sleep, if you aren't being held against your will with the life of a two-year-old in your hands.

I turned over the day's events in my mind, trying not to assume anything. Hard to do when everything and everyone had been a lie from the start. After sorting what I had been told from what I had experienced, I came up with this: Carly planned the robbery, stole the Balinese painting, "disposed" of a traitor in her gang, kidnapped me, and hit the high seas in a borrowed yacht. She was seriously concerned about Jackson Jones. I wondered why/how/if Jackson Jones really was her brother. I wondered about the details of the Venice "task." Once I turned over all the facts and lies, I was just about back to where I started.

I took a deep stretch and tried to sleep.

I gave sleep a good hour to show up. Then I switched on the lights and looked for something to do. I thought about reviewing the boat's deck plans, but oddly, the manual was missing. The magazines provided by the leather chair were sadly outdated. With nothing better to do, I switched on the TV.

Nothing was on.

Seriously, there was no reception. I switched channels, getting one electronic snowstorm after another. Carly's client didn't love her enough to provide satellite service, apparently.

I surfed all the way from channel 2 to channel 99. Then I found something.

The screen switched from snow to a shot of a narrow teak deck and a railing. The deck and railing appeared to rise and fall with the movement of the boat. In the lower corner of the screen was the label "MAIN DECK STARBOARD."

I flipped to the next channel. A different image appeared; this one was labeled "MAIN DECK STERN," and showed a wide deck with a dining table in the lower half of the screen and a bar in the upper half. To the left was a sliding glass door.

I recognized the view. It was the outdoor dining area on the *Delirious*. I flipped to the next channel. It was labeled "MAIN DECK PORT." Then came "LOWER DECK STERN." I kept flipping channels. Apparently, the *Delirious* broadcast the security camera images through the media system. There were images all around the outside of the boat, from the top of its sundeck (labeled "SUNDECK") to the little platform off the sport deck (labeled "SPORT DECK"). I flipped back to "MAIN DECK PORT" and spotted Sylvia and Lacey. There was no audio so I couldn't hear their conversation, but I gathered they were changing guard. The exchange of binoculars and the size of their weapons clued me in.

Interesting.

Since I had nothing better to do, I flipped through the channels and followed the path Lacey took around the boat. She walked the perimeter—sundeck, main deck, landing off the dining room, and down to the sport deck—and then up and around again. And again and again.

Very interesting. I felt a plan forming.

I climbed back into bed and fell fast asleep.

Chapter Twenty-One

I slept hard but quick. I awoke in the morning just after dawn. A brief glance out the porthole revealed the boat had turned around in the night. We were sailing north, and were in no hurry to get there.

I washed my face, brushed my teeth, and put my clothes on. Then I grabbed the TV remote and took stock of what was going on.

Sylvia was the guard on duty. She took the same circuitous route around the boat that Lacey had the night before. She still wore her gun holster for a left-handed draw. She ducked into a door and returned with a cardboard cup that I assumed was coffee.

On MAIN DECK STERN I spotted Carly seated at the outdoor dining table. She wore a tank top with a sweatshirt thrown over her shoulders and a matching headband holding back her hair. She looked for all the world as if she was headed out for a tennis match.

The table was set with placemats and china. Carly sipped something from a cup with a matching saucer and she read from a stack of papers. Lacey was on hand to refill the cup. Lacey looked like she needed a caffeine IV drip.

Penelope came on camera. She looked rested and wore the daytime uniform of white polo shirt and navy shorts. She and Carly chatted for a few moments. Carly appeared to give an order and Penelope left. I heard a phone ring in the hall outside my cabin. I flipped off the TV and waited. I suspected I had been summoned.

Sure enough, a knock came at the door and in walked Broad One. She still wore the evening uniform of a white blouse, navy skirt, and dark stockings. She looked like a gorilla dressed in drag just returning from an all-nighter.

"Carly wants you to join her for breakfast."

In the hall, Penelope stood, gun at the ready. Next to her stood Broad Two, still in evening uniform.

"Good morning, Penelope," I said brightly. "You look like you slept well."

Penelope didn't answer but I noticed the muscles tighten in the Broad's necks.

Interesting. Carly was certain of her gang's loyalty to her, but what of the gang's loyalty to each other? Did Carly even consider how to keep fourteen women from sniping at one another?

Penelope put the gun between my shoulder blades and steered me up the stairs. We passed through the main salon and out to the deck without incident. Carly still sat at the head of the table. But now she had company.

Chaucer sat next to her, boosted by pillows and chomping happily on a bowl of dry Cheerios. A cut-up banana, a glass of milk, and the teddy bear lay on the table next to the cereal. He smiled at me and stuffed a fistful of Cheerios in his mouth. Someone was as happy as a pig in mud.

Ginger stood silently on guard behind him.

"Good morning, Alana. I trust you slept well," Carly said to me.

"Well enough."

I took a seat. Lacey poured a cup of coffee for me and asked what I wanted for breakfast. Just to be difficult, I ordered eggs Benedict.

"You are in the news again, Alana."

Carly handed me the stack of papers I had seen her reading on the boat's TV. The papers were Internet reports from the *Los Angeles Times*. The headline read: Toddler Missing, Ex-Wife Sought. The picture of Chaucer and Tori's cleavage ran next to a new photo of me with a champagne flute in hand standing by Jorjana's pool.

I read the accompanying story. Chaucer and I went missing, it said. No witnesses to the disappearance. Tori accused me of lying to her about meeting at the beach. One could conclude from the story that I had set up the meeting and taken off with the kid.

Or one could read between the lines.

The cops didn't actually name me as a suspect. One was clever enough to note that my tote bag, shoes, and car were left behind. But the one thing I knew, and Carly didn't, was that the photo of me came from Jorjana's private album. This told me that Jorjana was in the background doing what she could.

Maybe my reputation was shot. Maybe the malicious gossip was firing fast and furious. But I had something far more valuable than reputation, houses, cars, and money. I had one thing even Carly could not take from me.

I had a true friend in Jorjana. Jorjana—generous, loyal, well-connected Jorjana—was working behind the scenes to help me. I knew it in my heart as surely as I knew that Carly was dangerous. But with Jorjana at my back, I had the courage to stand up to Carly. I just had to keep my wits about me until an opportunity to escape came up.

I handed the papers back to Carly, pretending the reality of my situation weighed heavily on me.

"There you have it, Alana," Carly said with satisfaction. "You are suspected of kidnapping Chaucer Fox. How will it look if he winds up dead?"

I didn't answer right away. I played up pretending that all was lost. I slumped. I stared forlornly at Chaucer. I thought about conjuring up a tear, but I've yet to meet a circumstance worth crying over. I sighed deeply instead.

"How does this work?" I asked Carly. "Do I sign something, or do you take me at my word that I'm going with you?"

"Your word is enough." Carly dabbed lightly at her mouth with a linen napkin. She had the look of someone who just snatched the bishop from the chess game.

"I will deliver the painting today," Carly said. "We will leave tonight for Venice. I will fill you in on the details of that en route. I am pleased to have you with me, Alana. You will not be disappointed."

"Not so fast, Carly. I want assurance that Chaucer will be unharmed. How do you intend to get him back to his mother?"

"I will make arrangements to return him tomorrow." She paused and her eyes flashed briefly. "It might be easier to leave him in a public place than to actually place him in his mother's arms."

I wasn't going to press the issue. I knew she had no intention of returning the kid. I hoped her unfinished business would take all day. I had a plan forming fast, but I needed some time for it to work. Time and circumstances. Hopefully the business required docking the boat.

"Just get him off the boat and leave him somewhere safe," I said.

"You have my word."

Yeah, right. Her word was as good as mine was.

The eggs Benedict arrived. The eggs were poached to perfection, the Hollandaise sauce appeared to be freshly made, and the whole thing was accompanied by a juicy fruit salad.

Once again, the meal tasted like cardboard.

"I have questions I want answered," I said to Carly.

"Such as?"

"How does Jackson Jones figure into all of this?"

Carly paused. I knew she was smart enough not to trust me yet. So I was surprised when she answered the question.

"This job has been unusual from the start," she said. "I am almost sorry I took it on."

She pulled out the manila envelope I had seen at dinner.

"The client changed the plans yet again. Fortunately, I have the resources to respond quickly to his latest demands. But my brother could be a problem. The client does not care who obtained the painting. He is only interested in who delivers it. My brother is a very good thief, Alana. He knows I have the painting. Now that I have done the hard work, he will try to steal the painting away from me and present it to the client for payment. Is there anything else you want to know?"

"Yes. How much money is in this for me?" Like I was really considering joining this lunatic.

Carly bristled at my tone. She shooed Lacey and Ginger away with her hand. Lacey skedaddled like a well-trained puppy. Ginger swooped Chaucer up in one arm and raced after Lacey. Carly glared at me with enough anger to make the hair on the back of my neck stand up.

"I will not have you speak to me in that tone of voice, Alana. I can dispose of you as easily as I disposed of Kymbyrlee."

Before you could say Jekyll and Hyde, Penelope and her gun appeared to steer me back inside. Within a minute, I was shoved into a cabin in the crew's quarters and the door was slammed shut.

I should have negotiated better accommodations.

Chapter Twenty-Two

So there I was. Locked away in tight quarters. I settled on the lower bunk, turned on the TV, and flipped through the security channels. Ginger came back and collected Chaucer's teddy bear. Carly finished her coffee and Sylvia kept up a lazy rotation around the boat. On SUNDECK, two women I surmised to be Tea and Dee joined Regina for a lounge on the sundeck. This shot gave me the best view of where we were headed. As far as I could tell, the boat continued north.

Time passed slowly. The boat rocked gently and consistently. With nothing better to do, I switched off the TV, lay down and fell asleep. I'd probably still be there if Broad One hadn't burst in with my lunch.

I woke with a start and suffered a second of not knowing where I was. I stared stupidly at Broad One. She had changed into the daytime uniform. She looked haggard. She gave what would have been a giggle from someone weighing less than 250 pounds.

"I brought you some lunch."

She put a tray on the little desk and turned to leave.

"Just a second," I said. "What time is it?"

"It's about eleven. I know it's early for lunch, but we are going to anchor soon and everyone will be busy." She looked at the tray as if to apologize. "It's a cold meal, so it can keep until you are hungry."

"Thanks," I said. Then, trying to stall for time, "Can I use the bathroom?"

"Sure. Follow me."

To my surprise, no one else was on guard outside my door. The Broad led the way into the hall and forward to a common bathroom. I shut the door and took stock.

The bathroom was designed for maximum efficiency. To my left was a dark, damp space with a changing area and a shower. If you were a gnome, it would have been delightful. To the right was a counter with one tiny sink, a rough mirror, and several mini storage cabinets. Just because I am nosy, I opened each one. They contained the usual paraphernalia that women use—shampoo, tampons, hairbrushes, blow dryers, curling irons and flat irons, vitamins, and stuff. One long cabinet to the side contained clean towels. Straight ahead lay the toilet. I did actually use it. I washed my hands after, took another quick look around, and filed what I had found in my newly forming escape plan. Then I joined the Broad waiting in the hall.

She stood against the wall with her head leaning back, eyes closed. She looked exhausted.

"Didn't get much sleep?" I asked her.

"I'm OK," she insisted.

"You look like you were up all night."

"Yeah."

"When do you get time off?" We were back at my door. I waited to go in.

"It just depends on where Carly needs us. I'll catch up on sleep tomorrow."

"While we are en route?" I asked, as if I knew what I was talking about.

"Yeah, I'll sleep for days. Can't wait."

She closed the door behind me.

I took a look at the tray. It looked yummy: ham and cheese in a croissant, pear and walnut salad, a nice big chocolate chip cookie, and a glass of iced tea. Too bad I wasn't hungry. I sat on the lower bed and flipped on the TV.

Things were happening. Regina, Dee, and Tea scurried about on the main deck, pulling out ropes and doing the stuff that needs to be done when a boat gets ready to dock. I flipped back to SUNDECK to see where the boat was headed, but we were still too far out to tell.

On MAIN DECK STERN, I saw that the outdoor dining table was empty of dishes because Penelope was busy setting out an array of guns. She checked each one for ammunition and tried putting each gun in her pants pocket. The smaller guns were left on the table, the larger ones went back into a big metal box. Then she closed the box, secured it with a lock, and carried the box away.

As she passed closer to the security camera, I took note of what she wore. The pants with the pockets for guns were black and had a shiny stripe down the leg. Her shirt was a white tuxedo-style and she wore a black bow tie. She looked like a twelve-year-old boy dressed for a formal dinner. She left the camera's sight for a few moments and returned with a couple of black plastic bags full of something. She put the bags on the table next to the guns and said something to someone off camera.

The someone was Carly.

Carly came on camera dressed exactly like Penelope. She filled out the pants and tuxedo shirt better, but her hair was slicked back and she wore no makeup. For Carly, it was an unobtrusive look. She stuck her hand into one of the bags, pulled out something, and placed it over her head. It was a black penguin mask that covered her head like a hood. The face of the mask was white, with cartoon-like features and a large yellow beak. Carly adjusted the mask and then stuck her arms stiffly at her sides. She walked around, knees locked and swaying from side to side.

"Very funny," I said to myself. "A tuxedo, a penguin, I get it."

Carly took off the penguin mask and tossed it to Penelope. Penelope pulled it on and mimicked Carly's penguin act. Carly pulled another mask out of the other bag. This one was fashioned after a monkey's head. Carly put it on and hopped around the deck like a crazed chimpanzee. The mask was a little too big for Carly's head and the monkey ears flopped like fish out of water.

"Hysterical," I said to myself. "A monkey suit."

Carly and Penelope pulled the masks off their heads and collapsed in laughter. Yet another joke I didn't appreciate.

Sylvia showed up with a package for Carly. Carly pulled herself together long enough to open it. She placed the package carefully on the table, untied the strings around it, and smoothed down the paper wrapping. A small painting was inside, no bigger than the tray my lunch came on. I didn't need subtitles to know it was CiCi DiCarlo's miniature Balinese painting.

Carly held it up for Sylvia and Penelope to admire. The painting itself was very small, I guessed no more than eight inches by eight inches. The subject matter was abstract but done in a manner to suggest sunset on a tropical island. Even broadcast over a grainy black-and-white security camera, I could see the genius of the artist.

The frame was thick, fashioned out of bamboo. Carly gently turned the painting facedown onto the table. Penelope handed her a knife slightly smaller than a machete and Carly pried the painting out of the frame. Sylvia produced a length of fabric that looked like cheesecloth. Carly wrapped the painting in the cloth with care. Then, she put the painting on top of her head and pulled the monkey mask over it. The mask held the painting in place and the painting kept the monkey ears perked up. It was a perfect cover-up.

And suddenly I knew how and where Carly intended to deliver the painting to her mysterious, dramatic client.

The good news for me was that the boat would have to dock and I would have the time I needed.

Carly took the monkey mask off her head. Penelope put the mask and the painting worth millions into the plastic bag. Carly fiddled with the guns on the table before choosing one. She handed it to Sylvia, who checked it for ammunition. Someone off camera caught Carly's attention. I saw the flash in her eyes. She said something and Penelope and Sylvia fled, guns and masks and painting in hand. Carly walked out of the camera's view. I flipped through the channels and found her on MAIN DECK PORT. She walked along the side deck and went through the door leading to the wheelhouse. The boat shifted gears, groaning and moaning as it turned toward land. I flipped the channel to SUNDECK in time to catch a glimpse of Stearns Wharf in Santa Barbara on the horizon. It looked as if we were headed back to dock at the Yacht Club. I couldn't have been happier. I flipped off the TV, opened the tiny closet, and pulled out the size ten sneakers. I sat on the floor to pull off the laces and think more about my plan.

The *Delirious* groaned and creaked and eventually came to a stop. I sat on the bunk and waited patiently. I heard the crew scurry about. The anchor was let out in a series of screeches and scrapes like giant fingernails on a chalkboard. I watched what I could from the TV cameras. We anchored just off the Yacht Club, not at the dock. This required an adjustment to my plans and kept my mind busy for a while. In the meantime, on SPORT

DECK I watched Carly, Penelope, the two Broads, the Hispanic driver, and the two plastic bags leave by tender.

An older woman sporting a captain's hat drove the tender. She wore a short-sleeved white blouse with enough gold braid to tie up the whole *Delirious*. I figured she was the captain. Just by process of elimination.

No matter, eight people left. Lousy odds. I flipped through the channels and watched the remaining crew perform the general duties of tending to a boat the size of the *Delirious*. After about an hour, I heard footsteps outside my door. Laughter and relaxed conversations, doors opening and closing. Things quieted down on the crew deck and on SUNDECK I watched Dee and Tea emerge. They wore bikinis and carried bottles of beer. Lacey and Katie, however, remained on duty, guns at the ready.

After a while, the tender returned with just the captain. From the SPORT DECK cam I watched a woman help tie the tender to the boat. I hadn't seen this woman before. She wore a white short-sleeved shirt with considerably less gold braid than the captain. I figured her for the engineer.

With the return of the captain, I guessed there were nine crew members on board. Two on the sundeck, two patrolling, the captain, the engineer, the chef in the kitchen, and Ginger with Chaucer. That left Sylvia to stand guard at my door. The odds were definitely against me.

My odds got considerably better an hour later. The captain and the engineer emerged from the wheelhouse. The duo turned up on the sport deck. I heard more clanking and creaking, and then caught a glimpse of the engineer on a Jet Ski zipping around the boat. She made a quick trip around the boat and then tied it to the swim platform just off the deck. More clanking and groaning and a second Jet Ski went out for a spin. Then the captain climbed in the tender. The engineer helped push the tender off and went inside. Eight to one.

I made a quick survey of where everyone was. Still two on the sundeck and two patrolling. Sylvia outside my door. The chef in the kitchen. Ginger minding Chaucer. The engineer somewhere.

It was now or never.

I turned off the TV, stuffed the shoelaces from the size ten sneakers into my pocket, took a deep breath and knocked on my door.

"I need to use the bathroom."

No surprise, Sylvia opened the door.

"Let's go."

She stood aside and let me lead the way to the common bathroom. I closed the door, locked it, and silently rummaged through the mini cabinets. I found what I wanted. I put a flat iron on the counter and stuffed a bottle of sleeping pills in my pocket. I actually used the toilet. I didn't flush this time.

I made noises like I was rustling around. Made them louder than was necessary.

Sylvia took the bait.

"What are you doing in there?" She jiggled the door handle.

"I can't figure out how to flush," I lied.

"Just step on the pedal."

"What pedal?"

"The one on the floor."

"Where?"

"Let me in! I'll do it!"

I waited a moment longer than necessary before opening the door. I needed her to be sufficiently distracted. When I finally unlocked the door, she blew past me like I was yesterday's news.

"I can't believe you never—"

Her back was to me. Just as she lifted her foot to flush the toilet, I swung the flat hair iron and brought it down as hard as I could on Sylvia's head.

She went down like dead tree.

I used the shoelaces from the size ten sneakers to tie her hands behind her back. I tied her feet to the base of the toilet with the cords attached to a couple of hair dryers. I made sure her airway was clear. I pulled the sleeping pills out of my pocket and put two under her tongue. Then I took a sanitary napkin and stuffed it in her mouth, And secured it in place with three more stuck together and wrapped around her head. I took the gun from her shoulder harness, thought about it for a minute, and tucked it into my waistband. She was still out cold when I closed the door to the toilet and headed to the galley.

Seven left.

I moved silently down the hall of the crew's quarters. Stopped at the end of the hall and peeked around the corner to the U-shaped booth of the crew's mess. Empty. I tiptoed to the winding metal staircase leading up to the galley and stopped. I heard the chef shuffling around and the sound of water rinsing out pots. Good sign. The sound of a knife chopping would change everything. The chef knew how to handle a knife. I knew nothing about the gun in my waistband other than it was black and surprisingly heavy.

I crept up the stairs. At the top, I peered around the corner.

The chef stood at the pot sink, her back to me, with a stack of pots nearly as tall as she was on the counter next to the sink. She was dressed casually in a T-shirt and jeans. No gun. No linked metal apron that would resist a gun. Completely unarmed. I could use that in my favor.

I took the gun out of my waistband and looked at it. I wondered if it was loaded. I wondered if the safety was on. I wondered what a safety looked like. Was there a little red light somewhere that warned you if it was on or off?

It appeared that I was going to have to fake it. I crept up behind the chef. She hummed happily while rinsing a pot with a metal hose that was attached at the wall and swung up and over the sink. I stuck the gun in her back in the same spot that Penelope usually planted her gun in my back and said, "Don't say anything or I'll shoot."

It worked. The chef stopped rinsing and stood still and quiet.

Now what?

That second of hesitation ruined everything.

The chef spun around, the hose in her hand and sprayed me right in the face. I stumbled back. Blinded, I dropped the gun. I heard it fall to the floor and slide away. In the second it took to wipe my eyes, the chef dove to the floor, hands reaching for the gun. I landed on top of her and swatted the gun away. The chef kicked and waved her arms around as if trying to swim away from me. I hung on like she was Flipper and I was that annoying kid with the blond hair. The little one. His older brother was a stud. And I felt anything but studly at that moment.

We squirmed and wiggled on the floor like two female wrestlers without the cushion of a pool of Jell-O. She planted both hands on the floor and shoved hard. It was enough to roll me to one side, but I held on to her tightly. We rolled against a metal counter in the middle of the kitchen. The counter had a shelf underneath for storing pots and pans. I got my right arm up under her chin, and wrapped my legs around her waist. I reached out with my left arm and grabbed a frying pan. Brought it down hard against the side of her head.

It slowed her down some.

She went limp for just a moment. It gave me time to jump to my feet. The gun was nowhere in sight. But one of those little browning torches used for crème brûlée was within reach. I pulled her to her feet by her braided hair and held the torch against her head.

"Do what I say or I will set your hair on fire."

The chef had a magnificent head of hair styled in one long, thick braid right down her back. I would have bet that she had never cut it. She cooperated in a heartbeat. I grabbed a kitchen towel from the counter and stuffed it in her mouth. I pushed her into the walk-in refrigerator and grabbed a couple of kitchen aprons on the way in. The cloth kind, not the linked metal. Told her to stand facing the metal shelving inside, then got her to tie her own feet to the supports using one of the aprons. Told her to raise her arms up. I put my knee against her back and secured her hands to the shelving with the other apron. I double-checked her feet to make sure they were secure. Took the towel out of her mouth and made her swallow two sleeping pills. Checked her mouth to make sure she swallowed. Reinserted the towel. Found a coat in the kitchen and tucked it in around her shoulders. Then, I pushed and shoved the other set of refrigerator shelving up against her back to keep her in place. Closed the walk-in door and manuevered the heavy kitchen island up against it.

Six left.

I found the gun under one of the counters and stuffed it back in my waistband. Carefully opened the swinging door into the dining room. I crept around to the central mahogany staircase and made my way down to the guest suites. I stood outside the suite where I thought Chaucer was and listened at the door. All was quiet. I drew the gun, took a deep breath and stepped inside.

Chaucer's suite boasted a large sitting area and a king-sized bed. Chaucer was asleep in the middle of the bed, bolstered on either side with rolled-up blankets. Ginger lay on a couch in the sitting area reading a book. She jumped to her feet as soon as she saw me. She made a move for the phone, but stopped when she saw my gun.

"Ginger, wait! I'm not going to hurt Chaucer!"

She froze, eyes wide and mouth agape. It was not a pretty sight.

"I'm not going to hurt Chaucer," I repeated. "I need your help to take him home."

Ginger stood still. She looked me up and down. Her eyes narrowed. I could only imagine what I looked like. I brushed a wet lock of hair out of my eyes and pleaded my case.

"I need your help to get him off the boat. Carly is going to kill Chaucer."

That startled her. She shook her head no. She had obviously heard another story.

"Ginger, think about it. Carly needs to kill Chaucer and make it look like I did it. I know she said she would let him go, but she won't."

Ginger shook her head; she didn't believe me.

Stupid me. Of course, Carly had told her something else.

"Did Carly tell you that Chaucer could stay?"

Ginger nodded slowly.

"She told you that Chaucer could stay on the boat and you could take care of him?"

More nods.

I cursed under my breath. That sounded just like something Carly would dream up. Ginger wasn't going to listen to me unless I appealed to her fondness for the kid.

"Ginger, listen. I know Chaucer's family. Did you know he is going to have a little brother or sister soon?"

That she didn't know. She looked over at the sleeping baby, her eyes softened.

"Do you want him to grow up not knowing his baby brother or sister? Chaucer needs to be at home with his own mom and dad. They are worried about him."

I hit a note there. She looked at Chaucer again. Her eyes welled up. We were halfway home. Ginger looked back at me and pointed to herself. Questions all over her face. She asked something in sign language. I got the gist of her eloquent gestures. She was worried what would happen to her.

"If you help me get him home, I will help you stay out of trouble."

She nodded OK.

Five left.

"How much longer will he sleep?" I pointed to Chaucer.

She indicated about a half hour. Plenty of time.

I switched on the TV facing the couch. On SUNDECK, I showed her where Dee and Tea were drinking beer.

"Go to the bar in the main salon. Pour three beers into frosted mugs and add two of these to each one."

I handed her a bottle of sleeping pills.

"Pretend you are just being nice to them. I am going to go up to the wheelhouse and take care of the woman in there."

Ginger grabbed a pad of paper from next to the bed. She scribbled something and then showed it to me.

Enginer. Sleping.

I got the drift. The woman in the wheelhouse was the engineer and she was taking a nap.

"OK. Wait until the pills start to work and meet me back here. Then we can figure out what to do about Lacey and Katie."

Ginger nodded. She pulled a key out of her pocket and unlocked the cabinet under the TV. Pulled out a holster and a gun. Put both on with such efficiency, I just had to ask, "Is this thing loaded?"

I handed my gun to her. Her eyes widened in more terror that I had ever seen. She took the gun from me, checked it over, and then went to the desk and wrote:

BE CARFL!

I had every intention.

.

Chapter Twenty-Three

Ginger left with the sleeping pills. I flipped on the TV to check everyone's location. Two lounging up on the sundeck. On SPORT DECK, I could see Lacey and Katie dangling their feet in the water, looking bored. The "Enginer" was nowhere in sight. I waited until, on SUNDECK, I saw Ginger appear with frothy mugs of beer. Suffice it to say, she was welcomed.

I turned the TV off and slipped quietly out of the room. Chaucer slept, well, like a baby.

Up the central stairs, through the main salon and out to the side deck. I knew from my study of the layout of the *Delirious* that the captain had a cabin tucked between the wheelhouse and the radio room. The "Enginer" was likely napping there. I tiptoed past the radio room, peered inside. It was full of controls and video screens—some of which I actually recognized. But no "Enginer." Around the corner was the wheelhouse.

The wheelhouse is where you steer the boat. Its windows displayed a panoramic view of the Santa Barbara Yacht Club and the harbor and beach. The *Delirious* appeared to be anchored about two hundred yards off the entrance to the marina. It was a quiet midweek morning. No sign of life anywhere.

The captain's chair, a leather contraption resembling a La-Z-Boy recliner, stood at the helm. A giant steering wheel was mounted amid an assortment of dials, computer screens, and buttons. All at the ready. The room, however, was empty.

Behind the captain's chair was a center island big enough to unfold a map on. Along the back wall was a long leather bench raised up for passengers to sit on and see how the captain went about driving the boat. At the far end was a door. It was the entrance to the captain's quarters.

I pulled the gun from my waistband and held it facing the ceiling, just in case it went off on its own. I walked slowly to the door, took a deep breath and turned the handle. I knew from my study of the boat's layout that the captain's bed was to my right. I pushed the door open, stepped inside and pointed the gun at the bed.

It was empty.

Where was the "Enginer"?

The door to the captain's bathroom was closed.

Oh, great, I was going to catch her on the potty. I covered the room in two steps—not so surprising, it was tiny—and pushed open the bathroom door.

Empty.

Where was the fifth crew member?

A cell phone lay on a tiny table next to the bed. I picked it up. It was fully charged. I tucked it into my pocket and continued my search for the "Enginer."

Back into the wheelhouse.

Empty.

Past the radio room.

Empty.

Down the side passage and back to the main salon.

Around the corner.

Not empty.

I stood face-to-face with the "Enginer."

She was bigger in person than she had appeared on the security screen. Tallish and lean, I figured her to be on the long side of thirty. She had an intelligent intensity to her, like she knew what to do with a quadratic equation. She was coming in from the outside dining area and was damned surprised to see me. She was quick on the draw, too.

"How did you…?" Her gun was out and pointed at me before she could figure out the rest of her question. My gun was up and pointed at her just as quick. I had the advantage of knowing that I had no idea how to shoot the thing. As much good as that did me.

Her eyes narrowed. My hand did not shake much.

She hesitated for an instant.

It was enough. I pulled the trigger.

Nothing happened.

The "Enginer" took a swift step toward me. Her right leg came up and kicked the gun out of my hand. She spun around just like they do in the kickboxing movies and her left arm aimed right for my head. I jerked my head back and missed the blow. She landed to my right and crouched down as if to pounce. I kicked my left leg out like I was aiming at a ball in a dodge ball game and knocked her gun out of her hand. Then I jumped away,

259

just as she dove to tackle me. I headed for the door with every intention of diving off the side of the boat and swimming to shore.

Then I remembered Chaucer. I came to a dead stop. The "Enginer" slammed into me and we fell to the floor. She landed on top. She got her hands under my chin and pulled up, like she was trying to pry a lid off a can. My yoga classes came in handy just about then. I pushed away from the floor with both hands, turning the lid-prying move into a neat Cobra pose. Then I pushed hard with my left leg and rolled over on top of her. I rolled out of her grasp and jumped to my feet. This required me to plant my butt into her stomach and that slowed her down some. She turned to her side, clutching her stomach. I planted a hard kick between her shoulder blades, knocking the air out of her in a *whoosh*.

"OP!" It was Ginger, gun in hand, pointed at the "Enginer." Talk about perfect timing.

The "Enginer" moaned. She looked ready to puke.

I pulled her arms behind her and got her to her feet. Ginger kept the gun pointed at her. I pushed her toward the central stairs while I thought about what to do with her. I knew from my study of the boat's layout that a small guest suite lay off the main salon. I pushed her in that direction. Ginger followed with the gun.

The suite was compact. It was outfitted with a tall, narrow closet. I squeezed the "Enginer" inside and she slumped to the floor. Puking was a definite possibility. No matter. I shut the doors and sent Ginger to the kitchen for something to secure it. She came back with an aluminum baking paddle that resembled an oar. The paddle fit like a charm between the U-shaped closet handles. I wedged it in place with a bath towel.

Two left.

"Go get Chaucer," I told Ginger. "We're getting out of here."

She ran down the stairs. I slipped around the corner and down the deck to the radio room. I had to locate Lacey and Katie.

The radio room was equipped to communicate with anyone in the known universe. Had I known how the stuff operated, I would have radioed for help. And then helped myself to Carly's wine cellar. On my earlier trek to the wheelhouse I had noticed the radio room contained the master controls for the security cameras. The master controls included a screen indicating which rooms/staterooms/service areas were in use. The screen showed a floor plan of each deck of the boat. A little light indicated if a room was occupied (red) or vacant (green). Every five-star hotel has a similar setup. That's how the staff knows when to change the sheets and make the neat little fold in the toilet paper.

First, I scrolled through the deck cameras to SPORT DECK, just in case Lacey and Katie were still lounging. They weren't. I raced through the other cameras, only pausing on SUNDECK to see Tea and Dee passed out cold and on their way to one hell of a sunburn.

"Good job, Ginger," I muttered. "Now, where are the other two?"

The computer screen showed that the crew's quarters were empty but someone was in the crew bathroom. No one wandered around the kitchen but someone was in the walk-in fridge. The guest suites downstairs were empty except for Chaucer's room and the tiny one next to the main salon. The owner's cabin was empty. Someone was in the radio room. And lo and behold, Lacey and Katie were in the theater! And, according to the master controls, they were watching *Thelma and Louise*. Big surprise there.

The theater was on the same deck as the main dining room and the owner's cabin. The movie was twenty-four minutes into its 129-minute run. I took a moment to double-check the exits. And then I thought about the old saying declaring that when the cat is away, the mice will play. So much for Carly's "loyal" crew.

This was going to be a piece of cake.

I left the radio room and met Ginger at the top of the stairs. She had Chaucer in her arms and a bulky backpack on her back. He held his teddy bear in one hand and held tightly to Ginger with his other. His hair was again in pigtails and he wore the cutest little pink sundress and white sandals you ever saw. There was serious therapy ahead for this kid, I just knew it.

"Take him down to the sport deck and wait for me," I told her. I led the way down the stairs, stopping at the main dining room. I put my fingers to my lips and waved at Chaucer as Ginger carried him down another flight.

I made my way along the starboard side hallway leading to the owner's suite. A set of double doors led to the theater. The doors were closed. I could hear the movie playing. Very clearly, actually. Lacey and Katie were of the generation that is used to having music plugged directly into their ears. They had the volume turned up to "major decibel level." That certainly worked in my favor. Now I just had to keep them in there.

The doors did not sport the U-shaped handles of the guest suite upstairs. So much for that easy solution. However, a pair of hefty-looking lounge chairs flanked the doors. It took some effort, but I managed to slide the chairs one in front of the other and block the door. There was still a space between the end of the second chair and the wall. I darted into the owner's suite to find a filler.

The suite was something to see. Sadly, I didn't have time to hang around and check it out, but believe me when I say the space was luxurious. Luxurious and a complete mess. Carly was a slob. Clothes lay tossed about. Shoes littered the floor. A fussy little dressing table swayed under the weight of every cosmetic known to womankind. Tops were off jars of cream and a thin layer of powder covered everything. The bed was unmade. My general impression was that Carly did not pick up after herself and didn't allow anyone else to do it for her.

I pushed another club chair from a sitting area out the door. I managed to turn it upside down and wedge it between the other chairs and the wall. It would be impossible to open the doors from the inside. Lacey and Katie were securely tucked away.

None left.

Time to go.

I scurried down the stairs to join Ginger and Chaucer on the sport deck.

Ginger had Chaucer stuffed into a kid-sized life vest. He sat on the floor picking at the straps of the vest. She jumped as I walked toward her.

"It's OK. Let's go," I said, and pointed to the Jet Ski bobbing in the water.

I grabbed a vest from the overhead rack and slipped it on. Didn't bother to fasten it. Ginger picked Chaucer up. I unfastened the Jet Ski. Ginger handed Chaucer and the backpack to me and stepped back. She was crying.

"Ginger, come on! We have to get out of here!" I put my hand out to help her on.

She shook her head no. Put her hand to her lips and blew Chaucer a kiss. Pulled the sleeping pills out of her pocket. Poured two into her hand and popped them in her mouth. Tossed her head back and swallowed. And turned and walked back into the boat.

She was staying.

I did not have the time or inclination to follow her. I settled Chaucer in front of me, slung the backpack over one shoulder, and pulled the Jet Ski away from the *Delirious*. Chaucer giggled as we chugged slowly away from the boat. I kept a firm grip on the kid as I steered away from the other boats and people in the Yacht Club marina who could call the cops and mess things up for me. We passed out of the shadow of the *Delirious* and down toward Stearns Wharf. I found a spot to mingle among the boats moored off Palm Park before shutting the engine down.

"Hang on, Chaucer," I said. "We're going to get some help here."

I took the cell phone I had stolen from the "Enginer" out of my pocket. Dialed a number I knew by heart. Prayed for an answer.

"Errands, Etc. David speaking. How may we help you?"

Prayers answered. David Currie was on the line.

"Don't say anything," I warned him. "And what the hell are you doing working like nothing happened when I've been kidnapped?"

Silence. Which just goes to show you how shocked he was.

"I'm on a Jet Ski just off Palm Park in Santa Barbara," I said. "I have Chaucer with me. I need you to meet us somewhere without the cops."

"Why, darling?" David sounded like someone had just bopped him in the family jewels.

"Because it will take too long to explain all of this to the cops," I said. "Where can you meet us that won't attract attention?"

More silence. Either David was stumped for a solution or he couldn't talk.

"I believe I can help you with that, Mrs. Fernald," David said finally. "I can be there within the hour. Just turkey and cranberries, then? What's the *point* without the trimmings?"

"I got it," I said, understanding exactly what he was talking about. "It will take me an hour to get there. Can you leave now?"

"Yes, darling, I'm on my way."

"Remember, no cops!"

"I'll do my best."

And we hung up.

To translate, David's message to "Mrs. Fernald" was in reference to a Thanksgiving dinner he and I shared at a beach house located on Fernald Point just south of Santa Barbara. Errands, Etc. is the business David manages and the company was charged with keeping an eye on the place while the owners were out of the country. David and I had spent Thanksgiving weekend there not so long ago. It was the perfect meeting place. Unoccupied, tucked away behind a gate, and accessible by Jet Ski. David was a genius to think of it. The only problem was the fact that he told me this in code, which meant the cops were at his office. Hopefully he could get away.

If not, I could go to Plan B. As soon as I thought up a Plan B.

I tucked the cell phone back in my pocket. "Hang on, Chaucer, we've got a ways to go."

I turned the Jet Ski back on and aimed it south to Fernald Point.

Stearns Wharf, Palm Park, and East Beach are what come to mind when you think of Santa Barbara. Long stretch of sandy beach accented with tall, tall palm trees, dozens of volleyball nets, and the weekly artists' fair all share the picturesque shore at the edge of town. Postcards neglect to point out, however, that just off East Beach are anchored hundreds of small boats, medium-sized tugs, and huge barges. Just short of the horizon are the oil derricks and their necessary watercraft. My point is that driving a Jet Ski just offshore of Santa Barbara is like riding a tricycle on the 405 at rush hour. If you live in Southern California, there is no hell greater than the 405 between six a.m. and nine p.m. (the established rush-hour times). Much less negotiating the 405 on a trike.

We were far enough offshore to avoid the tangled mess of the small sailboats. Steering clear of large surf further out, I wound my way around a group of catamarans and thirty-foot motor yachts, being careful to keep down our wake—the nautical equivalent of tiptoeing. We passed the catamarans, the thirty-footers, and a couple of barges without incident. The Jet Ski cut through the gentle waves easily, barely rising and falling with each swell. I found it soothing. And given that no one seemed to be in hot pursuit, I let myself relax a little.

We passed the south end of East Beach, past the little bluff at the zoo. The gaggle of anchored boats disappeared. The curve of the shore flattened out and the gentle surf picked up speed. I kept the Jet Ski beyond the breaking waves but as close to shore as we could safely stay. We were just passing the beach of the Biltmore Resort when I learned why Chaucer was being so quiet.

First I heard a choking sound. Then a whimper. And then came the unmistakable stench of stomach juices mixed with peanut butter and jelly.

I felt something warm and wet and smelly run down my pants leg. Great. Fresh vomit.

We continued our trek to Fernald Point with Chaucer whimpering and me stinking. We passed Butterfly Beach and rounded the actual point of Fernald Point. I started looking for our safe hideout while racking my memory to remember what the place looked like. Little good it would do me, since I had only seen it from the land. But I did remember the place boasted a hundred feet of waterfront, complete with a beach cabana. And that would make it easy to spot in a neighborhood where twenty-five feet of waterfront is the norm.

I spotted it easily after all. The little cabana was painted in bight orange and lime green. I eased the Jet Ski closer to shore, took advantage of a low set of waves and pulled up onto the beach. I scrambled off with Chaucer in my arms. I didn't bother to secure the Jet Ski. What was I going to do? Return it?

Chapter Twenty-Four

The beach ended at a long stretch of lawn. I've had eyebrow waxes less perfect than that grass. Next to the lawn was the pool, big enough for the *Delirious* to make a U-turn. The pool deck with the lounges for dozens, then the outdoor kitchen. I resisted the urge to check the fridge for stray booze and scooted along the side of the house to the front yard. Chaucer rested his chin on my shoulder like he was watching for bad guys bringing up the rear.

At the front door, I rang the bell. No one home.

I settled Chaucer on the front step and dug around in the backpack. Ginger had prepared well. I found a change of clothes, diapers, toys, and at the very bottom, a juice box and graham crackers. Chaucer pounced on the graham crackers. I watched him devour the snack and tried, yet again, to make sense of it all.

The good news was that Chaucer and I were safely out of Carly's clutches. But I was not exactly free to roam around. If I showed up at a police station with Chaucer in tow, the cops would waste hours booking me for everything I didn't do. And Carly would deliver that damn painting and hit the high seas again.

There was no time to waste explaining things to the cops. It was up to me to stop Carly on my own. I knew where she was headed. And I was willing to bet on who her mysterious client was as well.

I had the whole plan laid out when David showed up and ruined everything.

The gates at the end of the drive swung open. The vehicle that entered was not the maroon van I expected. The car David arrived in was a silver Maserati Quattro Porte. David sat in style in the passenger seat. Jackson Jones drove the car.

David flew out the door before the Maserati came to a stop. He ran toward me, arms outstretched, and then came to a screeching halt. He looked at me like I was wearing white after Labor Day.

"Good grief, darling! What happened to you? We've been *frantic*! Where have you been? Is that *vomit*?"

"I'm fine. I was kidnapped. Did you bring a change of clothes by chance?"

I pulled him away from the Maserati as Jackson Jones emerged.

"What's he doing here?" I whispered in David's ear.

"Oh, darling! Jackson has been just wonderful! Did you know that *awful* Cortez person is his *sister*?"

Jackson came around the Maserati with a look of bemusement on his face.

"What are you laughing at?' I spat the words out.

"Forgive me, Alana. I am not laughing at you. I'm happy to see you alive. Most of my sister's captives are not so lucky."

My turn to be speechless.

"Can you *believe* someone as horrible as that Cortez woman is related to our *darling* Jackson?"

"I can explain, Alana," Jackson said. In much the same tone of voice his sister used to "explain" things to me.

"Why don't you 'explain' who the hell you really are!" I didn't have time for niceties.

David gasped.

Jackson stood with the car keys in one hand, turning them over and over. He looked right at me with an expression I can only describe as puzzled.

I waited for a miracle. Something along the lines of someone telling me the truth for a change.

"Darling, you don't understand!" David pleaded. "Jackson has been just *wonderful*. I don't know *what* Jorjana and I would have done without him!"

"Yeah, I can only imagine." I stood my ground and returned Jackson's gaze. I had my bullshit meter set on high. Or as high as it would go, given the beatings it had taken.

"I am who I said I was, Alana," Jackson began. "I was hired by CiCi DiCarlo to retrieve her stolen painting. She hired me because this is what I do. There is a very lucrative black market for stolen art. Professional art thieves are contracted by unscrupulous collectors to steal from private collections. As I told you, I suspected from the beginning that Carly was behind this."

"You neglected to mention that she was your sister." I just had to point this out.

271

"It was not relevant," he said. "And, until recently, I did not know how you fit into the picture."

I started to protest. Again, for crying out loud. But he held his hand up to stop me.

"Carly is known to recruit locals for her crimes. I realize now that she set you up, but you must admit she was very clever in how she went about it."

True enough. I relaxed a little.

"Carly is my half sister," Jackson said. "She is considerably younger than I am. My sisters and I were at boarding schools when our mother passed away suddenly. After the funeral, Father was alone and an affair fueled by his grief produced Carly. Father did the right thing as far as financially supporting her, but he was a parent *in absentia*. I suspect Carly resented that. At any rate, although her mother raised her on St. Thomas, my family had no contact with her."

"She said you were a thief." Me, tired of beating around the bush.

"Did she now?" That amused him. "She may be inclined to think so. When Father passed away, he left very little to Carly and her mother. I was the executor of the will, and as such had the dubious pleasure of fighting those two in court. Suffice it to say, they left the court…unsatisfied."

"She said you were an *art* thief."

Jackson's eyes widened just a bit at that. He had an explanation, of course.

"I am not a thief, Alana. My family business involves the buying and selling of fine art. That is how I came by my present occupation."

He looked right at me. I knew he felt my skepticism. Which, by the way, I felt was justified, given all I had been through.

"Carly lied to you about everything, Alana. Why would you believe anything she said about me? I have done everything in my power to try to find you. David can vouch for me."

Boy, could David ever. He sprang to Jackson's side and gave the man a huge hug. Jackson winced. David gushed.

"Darling! Jackson has been *tireless* in tracking you down! He's been working the phones day and night! Where have you *been*?"

I told them.

David gasped.

Jackson's face drained of color.

"Did you meet the captain?" Jackson asked quietly. Too quietly.

"No, but she—"

"*She*? Ooh, how delicious!" David was thrilled.

Jackson, not so much. "Was she…" He described the captain of the *Delirious* as clearly as if she were standing by my side.

"Yes! That's her! You know who she is?"

"I'm afraid so. She was the captain of my father's yacht. And Carly's mother."

Chapter Twenty-Five

"Her name is Marguerite Cortez," Jackson said. "She is a native of St. Thomas. She is a very competent captain. Among other talents." He paused. Grimaced. "I heard that she and Carly had a falling out."

"Apparently not. Is the *Delirious* your father's boat?"

"No." Jackson frowned. "I don't know whose boat it is. The name doesn't ring a bell."

It seemed to me this whole fiasco was just one big incestuous family feud. From Mallory's almond orchard grandmother and her contested will to Jackson's bastard sister and her whole twisted set of issues.

And Carly had the nerve to view my lack of family ties as a shortcoming.

"Alana, how did you get off the boat?" Jackson asked, the puzzled look back on his face.

I told him.

David's mouth dropped open enough that I could see he no longer had his tonsils.

"Oh, darling." David came to me with open arms and swallowed me right up in one of his vast hugs. Vomit and all.

"It's all right, David," I said, as I extricated myself from his grip. "I'm not hurt. But I have to stop Carly."

"Of course, darling!" David pulled a cell phone from his pocket. "I'll just ring up Stan right now."

"NO!" I cried. "No cops. Carly is going to deliver CiCi's painting today. I don't have time to waste explaining everything to the cops."

"But, darling, Stan has sirens and guns and..."

Jackson remained quiet through this. Too quiet. He stared hard at the Fernalds' front doorstep. I followed his gaze to see what was so fascinating. All I saw was Chaucer rooting through the backpack for more crackers. I took pity on the kid and went to help him.

David looked at me as if I had sprouted another head.

"I've been a fool," Jackson said, as Chaucer gobbled down his crackers. "It's so obvious. How could I not have seen it?"

"Seen what?" David and me, confused, in unison.

"Seen how I was being manipulated!" Jackson said in disgust. "I trusted him! How could I have been so stupid!"

"Trusted who?" David and me again. Still confused.

"Trusted Stan Sanchez, that's who!" Jackson said. "He convinced me that he and I were working together. I should have suspected something when he refused to follow my lead on Carly."

David and I must have looked like two big question marks because Jackson started over at the beginning.

"CiCi DiCarlo asked Sanchez to cooperate with me in finding the painting. He did at first, but when Kymbyrlee Chapman turned up dead, he seemed less interested in who stole the painting than in who committed the murder. We agreed that I would try to find out what I could from you, Alana."

My turn to grimace. Jackson had the decency to look apologetic.

"After talking to you, I was convinced you were telling the truth. I met with him after we had drinks at the Beach Shack. I told him that I thought you were innocent. And to back it up, I then had my leads on Carly. But he wouldn't listen. He kept saying that there had to be an insider. Which made sense, of course. It just never occurred to me that the insider was Sanchez."

"Stan?" David and me, still on the same page of confusion.

"Yes, Stan. I really did see him in that white van, Alana. And David, think about it. Stan stayed close to you to try to keep the suspicion on Alana. I'll bet anything that 'lead' he had this morning was actually a ruse. He is on his way to meet with Carly."

"But why would he get involved in this?" You would think I had lost all my naiveté by then. But no.

"For the money, most likely," Jackson said. "Carly will make at least seven hundred and fifty thousand dollars once she delivers the painting. Stan's cut will be in the high five figures. That is a lot of money on a cop's salary. We need to figure out where she is taking the painting. Do you have any ideas?"

I did.

"The Disney premiere," I said with confidence. "There is a premiere of the new Disney movie tonight at the old Granita space. It was billed as a costume party. As soon as I saw Carly put on those masks, I knew where she was headed."

"You think Carly is going to crash the party?" Jackson asked.

"No. Carly and Penelope are going to infiltrate the catering staff," I said. "No self-respecting Southern Californian would show up to a movie premiere in costume. The wait staff will be dressed in tuxedos with masks. It's really very clever of Carly. No one pays any attention to the servers."

"No one goes to a costume party in costume?" Jackson, looking at this as an outsider.

"It's an LA thing," I explained.

"Then I won't waste time hunting down a costume," Jackson said. He dug his keys out of his pocket and headed to the car. "Will you two be OK here?"

"I'm coming with you," I said.

"Alana, it is too—"

"No arguments," I said with resolve. "I'm coming with you."

"*Uno momento*, darlings," David said, in a tone of voice that brought the argument to a halt. "Aren't you forgetting something?" David stood at Chaucer's side.

Oh, right. The kid.

"There are clothes and diapers in the backpack, David," I said. "Do you still have the keys to the house?"

"Of course, darling." David hiked Chaucer up on his hip with one arm and shook a set of keys in his other hand. "But you don't honestly expect to get into the premiere dressed like that, do you?"

I looked at Jackson. He was impeccably dressed in a loose silk shirt and linen slacks. He could go anywhere from a tee time to the Oscars. Then I looked down. I wore a T-shirt stained with the dregs of two fistfights, a pair of pants seasoned with vomit, and I was barefoot and desperately in need of a pedicure. David had a point.

"OK, we'll swing by my house and I'll change," I said.

"Your casa is surrounded by police, darling. Come inside. Mrs. Fernald has a wardrobe to die for. You can borrow something and I will explain it to her somehow."

Twenty minutes later, I was showered. David pulled my hair back and secured it with a wildly patterned scarf. Behind the scarf he secured a hairpiece in an unfortunate auburn shade. He ordered me into a strapless sundress. On my feet he put a pair of flat sandals that wrapped up my legs. On my face went a pair of oversized sunglasses and a shade of lipstick not seen in nature. The best I could say for the get-up was that I was clean and I didn't look anything like myself.

Jackson was directed to put on a linen jacket that fit him perfectly. He, of course, looked fabulous. And was finally convinced to take me along with him.

David made a call and arranged for tickets to the premiere to be waiting for his "cousins" at the door. As Jackson and I left, he was busy running a bath for Chaucer and promising him mac and cheese for dinner.

Jackson opened the door to the Maserati for me. No surprise there. He jogged around the front of the car, slid into the driver's seat and turned the key. The engine purred. In no time we merged into the traffic moving south on Highway 101. Just past Summerland, traffic eased. Jackson maneuvered into the fast lane and we were on our way.

"Tell me more about Carly," I said.

"She was raised on St. Thomas. She was educated in Switzerland and France. When she graduated, she asked to work in the family business. Father was reluctant but he gave her a chance." He paused, frowned. "She's smart, I'll give her that. She figured out how to embezzle and it took our accountants nearly two years to catch on. Father did not want a scandal so she was let go quietly. Then Father passed away. I spent two years straightening out the estate, thanks to Carly and Marguerite's intrusion. I thought I had heard the last of them and then the thefts of private art collections started. Our collectors were hit more often than most. I realized that Carly knew enough about our clients to know who collected what pieces. I did a little digging and discovered that she was behind the rash of thefts. I've spent the last three years chasing her. This is the closest I've gotten."

Jackson's jaw was set so tight you could have broken a hammer on it.

"Why is she targeting your clients?"

"To get back at Father, I suppose. A psychologist would tell you that she has 'abandonment' issues. I think she is a common criminal. I can't wait to have her locked up for good."

"No kidding. We need to figure out how to stop her."

"Tell me what we are walking into."

"It's a typical premiere after party. It's a chance for the stars of the movie to get their picture taken on the red carpet and drum up publicity for the opening weekend. It is being held in a building that used to house a restaurant. From the invitation, I gathered there would be a reception on the patio, followed by a dinner."

"How many people will be there?"

"This venue isn't very big. And given how easily David got those tickets, they must not be expecting a full turnout. I'm guessing three hundred, tops."

"You said you think Carly is posing as a waitperson. What do you know about the catering?"

"It will probably be set up in trailers along Malibu Beach Road."

"I thought you said this was a restaurant."

"It used to be. It is empty now, but it gets rented out for events. My guess is they will use the kitchen for a bar setup and do the cooking from the trailers. The kitchen was open to the dining area so it would work well for cocktails."

Jackson was quiet for a moment.

"It would help if I knew who her client is, but none of my sources has any idea. Whoever it is, is new to this kind of thing."

"I think I know who it is," I said quietly. It saddened me to admit it out loud. "I think Carly's client is Donald Wesson."

"You can't be serious!"

"Yeah, I am. Whoever is backing Carly has a lot of money to burn and doesn't mind breaking a few rules along the way. Donald has been in trouble more than once over his business practices."

"Maybe so, but that doesn't mean he is Carly's client."

"There's more. It has bothered me how much Carly knew about my life. Someone filled her in on a lot of details. Donald knows me well enough to give Carly the background she had. And Carly said her clients live above the law. And that her client has a flair for the dramatic. Donald is just childish enough to do that."

Jackson started to argue. My turn to put a hand up to stop him.

"And another thing bothered me about the robbery. Everyone had to turn his or her cell phone in at the gate. Yet Donald's helicopter showed up minutes after the auction tent collapsed. How do you explain that, unless Donald knew ahead of time there would be a need to get out of there in a hurry?"

"Maybe he snuck his phone in?"

"There still wasn't time to make a call and have the helicopter respond. That helicopter was there pretty damn quick."

Jackson pondered that for a while.

"Alright, Alana, I believe you. I think we can pull this off if we work together. Here's what I think we should do."

We spent the rest of the drive discussing our plan.

Across PCH from the Malibu Country Mart is the Malibu Colony Plaza, a strip mall where locals buy their groceries and sundries. At the south end of the mall is the former site of Granita. I loved that place. Best brunch in the world, and I could literally crawl home if I'd had too many usuals. Nevertheless, it went the way of every former hot spot. Now I have my usual at Sunday Brunch at Jorjana's.

Jackson parked well away from the gathering crowd. Tourists, fans, and paparazzi lined a red carpet that rolled out into the parking lot. The Disney people had worked their magic as only they can. The exterior of the restaurant was turned into a vine-covered castle, complete with scampering monkeys and toucans. Wandering performers led live animals—blue camels, orange elephants, and pink horses—in and out of the crowd. A well-trained flock of white-winged somethings swooped in and out of the fake foliage. Music was supplied by a marching troop of musicians heavy on the wind instruments. Jackson surveyed the scene with bemusement.

"How do you suppose they managed to dye the camels blue?" he asked.

"They don't look happy about it, do they?"

We reviewed our plan. We would split up and Jackson would keep an eye out for Donald Wesson and Stan Sanchez.

M.A. Simonetti

We figured there was a good chance ol' Stan would show up for the payday. I was to circle around to the catering trucks and locate Carly. We figured that she would not recognize me in my outfit. Jackson would meet me near the newsstand across from Granita. We would then compare notes.

That was it.

It wasn't much, but I had escaped from the *Delirious* with a lot less.

I had my hand on the door and was about to hop out, when Jackson said, "Just a minute, Alana."

I turned back. He cupped my face with his hands, pulled me toward him, and kissed me so gently on the lips that I almost thought he had missed entirely. Not to worry, he didn't pull away. The next kiss was soft, hot, and not nearly long enough. Just before I lost consciousness, he said, "Be careful."

And then he left.

Left me with a full body blush that took my breath away.

It took me awhile to pull myself together.

Longer than I would have thought.

Longer than I would have liked. It had been a long, long time since a man was in my life.

I summoned my last bit of focus and left in search of Carly Cortez.

I made my way to the north end of the parking lot and ducked down the side alley of Sav-On Drugs. Came out on the service alley running behind the strip mall. Two blocks down, just as I predicted, the catering trailers were parked behind Granita. I snuck around the fence separating the service road from Malibu Road. I adopted the attitude that I was a local just out for a stroll and headed nonchalantly toward the trailers.

Catering trailers come in every size, shape, and color you can think of. From a mobile taco stand to full-fledged commercial kitchens hauled on eighteen wheels. The setup for Granita was somewhere in the middle. Two trailers, an outdoor grill busy with seared meats, and a shaded staging area for the wait staff.

The wait staff was the usual assortment of out-of-work actors. They were dressed from the neck down in tuxedos and from the neck up wore animal masks. I saw pandas, snakes, cats, giraffes, cows, kangaroos, and chickens. Oddly, not a single penguin. To my dismay, there were easily two dozen monkeys—each one an exact copy of the mask I had seen Carly hide the painting under.

Great. Just great.

I walked slowly past the staging area hoping to glimpse a monkey mask on a well-filled-out tuxedo. No such luck. The monkeys were all broad-shouldered and flat-chested. And likely more interested in *Daily Variety* than *Fine Art Connoisseur.*

The street between Granita and the newsstand was blocked to traffic by three Malibu fire trucks. An ambulance stood at the ready. And three LAPD cruisers. I paused on the opposite side of the street to figure out how to get to the newsstand. It was the perfect location to scout out the action.

The firemen were occupied answering the questions of a dozen adoring little boys. The ambulance drivers appeared to be asleep at the wheel. The cops stood around their patrol cars, eyes shaded with dark glasses. They seemed amused by the collection of waiter/animals milling about under the catering canopy. I took a deep breath and moseyed through the blockade, hoping like hell no one recognized me.

I fell into the steady stream of fans moving toward the red carpet. Limousines with dark windows lined up one after another. The crowd outside Granita yelled and clapped as the limos deposited their sequined passengers for the fans' approval. The musicians upped the tempo. An elephant bellowed. One of the camels snorted and flung its head up. The camel handler was lifted off his feet as the beast decided to take a gallop through the parking lot. The crowd let out a collective "uh-oh!" and moved back. The last I saw, the camel was hell-bent on crossing PCH, with five Disney people in hot pursuit.

I managed to slip into the shade of the newsstand. Grabbed a copy of something and pretended to peruse the pages. Looked over the top of my sunglasses for Jackson.

The party at Granita was in full swing. Masked waiters filed out of the staging area with trays of goodies held high over their heads. The limos came and went. The crowd ooh-ed and ah-ed. Over the terrace fence, I spotted carefully coiffed heads moving about. The waiters' trays slipped gracefully between the heads.

Forced laughter. The aroma of grilled steak. No sign of Jackson.

I turned in the direction of the red carpet. The limo line was shorter. Now only minor celebrities piled out and posed and smiled for the cameras and fans. The oohs and ahs grew fainter. Some tourists wandered away. The die-hard fans and paparazzi stayed put. Along with a bunch of barrel-chested young guys with close-cropped hair.

I lowered my sunglasses further to get a better look. Mostly twenty-something. Close-shaved faces, serious looks on them as they scanned the crowd. Not at all interested in the pandemonium around the red carpet. They had to be cops.

And there were a lot of them. In a crowd of eighty or more onlookers, I counted sixteen cops. I looked back to the crowd beyond the terrace wall. Another dozen heads with short cop hair mingled with the coiffed heads.

Twenty-eight cops? What were twenty-eight cops doing at a premiere for a kids' movie? They couldn't all be looking for me. Could they?

What to do? Stay put and risk being arrested between the covers of *Muscle Mania* and *Newsweek*? Walk away and risk being spotted? Or put my trust in the deception of my outfit? I had to find Jackson.

I put my trust in David's talent to disguise me, adjusted my posture to one of confidence and walked right toward the misfits. Just hiding in plain sight, I was. I added a sway to my hips. Kept working the sway until

I passed the cops and felt their backward glances let up. Got two feet on the red carpet before I stopped.

The doors to Granita lay wide open. Just inside, a hostess desk was staffed with a cute young thing collecting tickets. Behind her stood two security guys almost the size of Carly's Broads.

I looked over to the Maserati to see if Jackson was there.

He wasn't.

I walked away from the red carpet and back toward the newsstand. Maybe he was coming around the corner by the roadblock cops.

Nope.

Turned back to the red carpet. And then I spotted him.

I barely recognized him.

Jackson walked out of the doors of Coogie's restaurant. He wore a black T-shirt under a heavy black bomber-style jacket. He wore jeans—the mega-expensive designer kind. His hair was slicked back.

But his clothes weren't the only difference. His walk, his posture, his entire demeanor had changed. He looked like he was trying too hard. Like every loser-on-the-make that lurks around film premieres.

Jackson sauntered in my direction. He was nearly to the red carpet before he recognized me.

The recognition came with a start, then a smile. He put his arms out to greet me.

"There you are, Alana!"

A big hug. Even his after-shave was different. I nearly choked. I swear it was Old Spice. I pulled away to double-check who had his arms around me.

"What is going...?" I didn't get a chance to tell him about all the cops milling around. He pulled me close and whispered, "Just play along, OK?"

Then he draped an arm over my shoulder and we strutted into Granita.

At the hostess desk, Jackson gave David's name. The girl gave Jackson a big giggle and said, "Come on in!"

Jackson gave the girl a wink and said, "Thanks, doll." And gave me a swat on the behind to push me inside.

That was enough. I pushed him aside and said, "What the hell is going on?"

Jackson made a smooth move that put us shoulder to shoulder. He put a hand in his pocket, stood back on one leg and slowly surveyed the crowd. He put his other hand back on my shoulder like I was a possession. I felt a gun holster under his jacket. The holster was as hard as the lump forming in my stomach.

Jackson leaned toward me as if he were whispering sweet nothings in my ear.

"When I walked by here it was obvious I was going to stand out. Look at these people."

I looked. The crowd swarming about was dressed in typical LA upscale casual—the women in a mix of denim, sequins, stilettos, and cleavage; the men in variations on Jackson's T-shirt and leather jacket. Even the cops had a version of the LA cool look going. He was right. His tailored linen slacks and blazer would have stood out like a bride wearing black.

"I had a change of clothes with me," Jackson explained. "Have you seen Carly?"

I turned my head to his ear. Tried hard not to gag on the Old Spice aroma. "Haven't seen her."

"Let's split up here," Jackson said. "I'll look for Carly. You go find Donald and keep him away from Stan Sanchez."

"Jackson, there are a million cops here," I said.

Jackson surveyed the crowd. The cops blended in pretty well if you weren't looking for them. Jackson's jaw tightened. He was not pleased. Which I found confusing. His plan was to bring the cops in sooner or later. Wouldn't sooner be easier? I mean, they were all there. Three or four of them could waste time questioning me and Jackson and the other two dozen cops could find Carly. Or Donald. Or Stan.

"No. Wait until I get my hands on Carly. You go keep on eye on Donald Wesson. We'll meet up after…"

And then he was gone. And I was left not knowing where to meet up "after." After what? After he got his hands on Carly?

My sense that something was amiss turned into a certainty that something was very wrong. I made the mistake of ignoring my better instincts and went to find Donald Wesson.

The place was packed. All the usual premiere amusements were provided. Food and watered-down drinks, of course. But also actors dressed in costumes from the film—which had something to do with the African savanna. Or the Arabian desert, given the camels. Which, by the way, were pressed into service at the photographer's station. Two reasonably calm blue camels stood in front of a backdrop picturing sand dunes and palm trees. Partygoers willing to hazard standing between the camels could have their photos taken and presented in a souvenir frame.

I pushed my way past the bar and popped out of the crowd clogging the doorway and onto the terrace. The guests chatted happily with drinks in their hands. Waiters passed hors d'oeuvres. Actors dressed in colorful costumes weaved in and out of the crowd. Some actors were also magicians who captivated the older children. An artist drew caricatures in one corner. A zebra chewed thoughtfully on a potted palm in another. At the center of the terrace entertainment was a keeper handling a chimpanzee and posing for yet more souvenir pictures.

And standing in line for the chimpanzee photo was Donald Wesson.

As always, Donald towered above the crowd.

As always, Donald looked out of place. Poor Donald was dressed in costume. He wore a white, gauzy garment that looked like it was made out of sheets. On his head was a white turban. On his feet were sandals. At his side was a woman.

I did a double take. A young woman held on to Donald tightly with one hand and with the other she held up a caricature of the two of them. She and Donald giggled at the drawing. She gazed up at Donald and smiled. He gazed down at her with a look that was part goofy admiration and part confident CEO.

Donald had a date.

I recognized her as the one who had checked me in as Kymbyrlee Chapman at Save the Bay. The one with the electric blue eyes. Smart girl. She had checked in the local gazillionaire and ended up dating him. You would have thought she had taken lessons from me.

I looked back at Donald. He was relaxed, happy, enjoying the party. Holding the girl's hand. Not at all interested in anything else going on, like an art thief tracking him down for payment. Even Donald's costume wasn't all that bad, except for it being held up with a brown leather belt.

I looked harder at the belt. Attached to it was the beeper that Donald had dropped at my house. The beeper that had summoned...

Oh no. The beeper that had summoned the two Necks. That was how Donald had contacted the helicopter at Save the Bay. Not because he knew of the robbery ahead of time, but because he had his beeper.

My entire theory was wrong. Donald was not the mysterious client.

I had to tell Jackson.

I shoved my way through the crowd. Where the hell had Jackson gone? And who was Carly's client?

Somewhere inside a bell clanged. It sounded like a dinner bell summoning the partygoers to the buffet line. The motion in the crowd shifted from one of happy milling about to one of a herd of hungry water buffalos trampling a cabbage patch. I waded against the tide to the camels near the back fence.

David's disguise hid me well. I swam right past Donald Wesson, although he wouldn't have noticed anything not plastered on his date's face. I also passed Mia Kaplan arm in arm with none other than Dimitri Greco. Dorothy and Steven Fries followed in their wake, with him somewhat hobbled by the crutches. I sailed past CiCi DiCarlo surrounded by admirers, fresh white bandages on her ears. God forbid she missed a photo op.

As the crowd cleared off the terrace, I got a better look around. Just behind the grazing zebra was a service door leading into Granita. I spotted a man opening the door and ducking inside.

The man was dressed impeccably in LA upscale casual—a local, obviously.

He carried a large leather satchel stuffed to the brim.

It was Sterling Scott, the auctioneer from Save the Bay. And I was willing to bet the satchel contained about seven hundred and fifty grand.

Of course. How stupid could I have been? Sterling Scott knew me just about as well as anyone. We traded info. We attended the same events. He easily could have given Carly all she needed to know to pull the rug out from under my life. And he was just slimy enough to covet a miniature painting worth millions.

Not to mention wealthy enough. Sterling Scott could support himself on an auctioneer's income because he didn't have to. He had made his fortune the old-fashioned way—he married it.

Sterling Scott was Carly's mysterious client. And he was on his way to deliver payment and pick up CiCi's little masterpiece.

But not if I stopped him first. I skirted past the zebra and through the door. It swung closed with a bang. A loud, shattering bang. And then complete darkness. I groped around for a light switch. No such luck.

I slid my hands on the wall and shuffled along.

A door opened at the end of the long hall. Light poured in and I saw Sterling Scott step into Granita. Just before the door slammed shut, I saw Stan Sanchez step up behind Sterling.

Darkness again.

I groped my way to the end of the hall. I found the door. It had one of those push bars across it. I pushed on the bar and cautiously peeked out.

Sterling Scott stared at something to his left. He looked surprised, shocked even.

Stan Sanchez stood off to the other side. He reached under his jacket. He pulled out a gun.

Someone yelled, "NO!"

And then gunshots.

I let the door slam shut and flattened myself against the wall.

Screams. Dishes crashed to the ground.

More gunshots.

It was Save the Bay all over again.

Chapter Twenty-Six

I clung to the wall. Held my breath.

There were more gunshots. BANG! BANG! BANG! They seemed to come from all directions.

There were many more screams. I heard a roar of footsteps—the sound of people fleeing.

Something fell hard against the door. It burst open.

In flooded daylight. Along with Stan Sanchez.

Stan rolled into the hallway, propped himself up against the wall, a gun in his hand. He held his left arm at an odd angle. Blood poured out of his cuff. He caught sight of me just before the door slammed shut.

"What the hell are you doing here?" he yelled into the darkness.

I didn't wait around to explain myself. The one part of Jackson's plan that I was sure of was to steer clear of Stan. Without a word, I raced down the hallway. I heard Stan struggle to his feet. He called out to me to stop. Yeah, right.

I ran in total darkness with one hand stretched out along the wall. I got to the door, pulled it open and raced outside.

A wall of cops stood before me. I swear it was all twenty-eight of them.

All with their guns drawn. All surprised as hell to see me.

Someone grabbed me from behind. An arm went around my neck.

I smelled Old Spice.

It was Jackson. Thank God. Jackson could explain everything.

But then he put something hard and cold against my temple. It was a gun.

"Put your guns down," Jackson said to the wall of cops. "I'll shoot her, I swear it."

Excuse me?

The cops lowered their guns. I was not entirely happy about that.

Jackson took a step back. His grip around my neck tightened. We stepped away from the wall of cops.

Our movement caught the zebra's attention.

One of the cops said, "Let her go, Jones."

We were close enough to the zebra now that its tail switched against my leg.

"Drop your guns," Jackson said.

The cops hesitated. I felt Jackson's muscles tense.

"NOW!" Jackson shouted.

The cops dropped their guns with a collective rattle. The guns made one hell of a racket. Startled the crap out of me.

Startled the zebra, too. It reared up on its hind legs and broke the slim rope tethering it to the potted plant. Its backside slammed into Jackson. He lurched sideways and his arm went slack around my neck. I fell to the ground and rolled away just as Stan Sanchez burst through the service door, gun raised.

Stan took aim at Jackson. BANG! Jackson fell to the ground.

The zebra raced through the wall of cops. The wall parted and then rushed forward to surround Jackson.

Sanchez gave me a hand up and said, "You have some explaining to do, Ms. Fox."

Chapter Twenty-Seven

Emergency vehicles clogged the Malibu Colony Plaza's parking lot, along with ambulances, squad cars, news vans, the SPCA, and a coroner's van. The sky was clogged with the usual flock of helicopters. The cops closed down PCH so the SPCA could round up the spooked zebra, some equally spooked blue camels, and one very ornery orange elephant. Blonde and blow-dried news anchors circled CiCi DiCarlo, who was only too happy to give "exclusive" interviews. And to hold up her retrieved painting for the paparazzi shots.

The cops arrested and hauled away Penelope, the two Broads, and the Hispanic driver.

One ambulance hauled away Jackson Jones, along with the cops assigned to keep him under lock and key. Another took Sterling Scott.

The coroner's van hauled away the body of Carly Cortez.

Turns out Jackson shot his own half sister when she refused to give up that damn painting. Turns out the only thing Carly didn't lie about was her relationship to Jackson. And the fact that he, too, was a thief. The bastard.

Me?

M.A. Simonetti

I sat in the back of an ambulance while a paramedic attended to Stan Sanchez's arm. Stan was bare-chested and his bloody shirt was wadded up next to him. Gauze bandages swathed his left arm. The medic was busy applying a blood pressure cuff to Stan's good right arm. I was busy trying to explain myself. Again.

"Cut the bullshit!" Stan yelled at me. "Where have you been? Is the kid OK?"

"He's fine," I said. "One of your goons went to go get him."

"Those 'goons' have been working their butts off looking for you."

Sanchez winced as the paramedic undid the pressure cuff.

"Go straight to the ER, Stan," the medic said. "Not like the last time."

The guy stepped out of the ambulance before Stan could argue.

"I've had a dozen people working around the clock to find you! You better have a damn good explanation, Ms. Fox!"

"And you will believe me now because—"

"Stop it!" This from that little Gym Rat, Detective Driscoll.

She hopped into the ambulance. Took up about as much room as a butterfly. Had the attitude of one of the blue camels, though.

To me, she said, "We have some questions we need answered." To Stan, she said, "Back off. Who knows what Jones told her?"

Before either of us could talk back, she said, "Ms. Fox, we know you are innocent. Please tell us where you have been and how you ended up here. In return, Stan will be happy to fill you in."

Stan did not look at all happy, but he kept his mouth shut.

I told my story. Stan kept quiet until I got to the part where Jackson accused him of being the insider.

"You thought I was in on it? Are you kidding me?"

"It made sense, at least the way he explained it."

"When did you figure out Jones was lying to you?"

"When he put the gun to my head."

"Boy, you are quick on the uptake, aren't you?"

Driscoll headed that argument off with, "Stan, play nice and tell Ms. Fox what she doesn't know."

The last thing Stan felt like doing was playing nice. That was as obvious as the blood seeping through his bandage. But, to his credit, he gave me his story.

"I was suspicious of Jones from the start," Stan said. "It was just too convenient how quickly he ended up working for CiCi DiCarlo. But I played along to see what he was up to. I never asked him to question you, Ms. Fox. And I don't drive a white van, either. That night at the Beach Shack, I just walked down from my place to have dinner. I was surprised to find you two there. By then we had cleared you of suspicion, so I tried to warn you that there was an insider without tipping off Jones."

"I thought you were threatening me."

He grunted. "I don't have to threaten, Ms. Fox. If I thought you were guilty, I would have arrested you. I was trying to warn you away from that guy."

"I didn't take the hint. Sorry."

Stan looked like he wanted to throttle me. Driscoll finished the story.

"Once we had reason to suspect that Sterling Scott was involved, it didn't take much to get him to confess. He and the wife are getting a divorce and all the money belongs to her. Scott thought he could use his shady contacts in the art world to set up a nest egg for himself. But he really didn't know what he was getting into when he started dealing with the Cortez gang."

Stan winced in pain as he stood up. "I'll say this for her, she was one tough broad."

"Just got word," Driscoll said, as she consulted her cell phone. "The Coast Guard has the boat in custody. Along with eight crew members."

"The captain of the boat is Carly Cortez's mother," I said helpfully.

"Yeah." Driscoll consulted her phone. "One Marguerite Cortez. She was supposed to take the boat up to San Francisco for service."

"Help me with the timing of all this," I said. "When did you learn about Carly and the boat and—"

Stan interrupted. "We didn't know about the boat. We got the confession out of Sterling Scott shortly after I ran into you and Jackson at the Beach Shack. But Scott didn't know where Carly was. We got him to contact Carly and change the plans for delivering the painting. Then you and the kid disappeared. Frankly, we didn't get the connection to Cortez until Jackson showed up and convinced us she was behind it. I'm sure his attorney will use this as leverage at some point." Stan shook his head in disgust. "Anyway, we kept him at bay, so he latched on to David Currie and Jorjana York. So I had to waste time heading him off there." He looked at me as if this were my fault.

"So now what?" I knew better than to assume it was over.

"Now we wait for the courts to work through due process," Stan said. "But we have enough to put Jackson Jones away for a long, long time."

"How long will this all take to prosecute?" I asked.

"Months," Driscoll said.

"Years," Sanchez said. Then he grinned, "You're going to be seeing a lot of me, Ms. Fox."

I was seeing a lot of him already. Naked from the waist up and without his bulletproof vest, Stan was something of a hunk. As he struggled to put his bloodstained shirt back on, I couldn't help but admire the contours of the man's biceps.

I leaned over to help him with his shirt. "Didn't that paramedic say you should get straight to the ER?"

"Yeah, I'll see if one of the guys can give me a ride over," Stan said.

"Not to worry," I said. "I live right down the street. I'll go get my car and take you myself."

"I'm not sure I can trust you, Ms. Fox," Stan said, his mouth twitching the way it did on our first meeting in CiCi's dining room.

"Oh, you can trust me," I said. "Have I ever lied to you?"

Chapter Twenty-Eight

TWO MONTHS LATER...

"Move closer to the children, Alana," Jorjana pleaded.

We were on her Monday outing to the Malibu Country Mart. It was an almost perfect Malibu day. Cloudless and warm, but with the lingering smell of smoke from the most recent Malibu firestorm. The pall of the disaster still hung over the town. Barely three kids romped in the playground.

"This is close enough," I said, as I looked around warily.

In the past few weeks, the police had cleared me of suspicion and my reputation was well on the mend. What with the fire burning down homes right and left, no one gave a damn about me anymore. But Little Miss Tight Buns just had to have a restraining order that prevented me from coming within fifty feet of Chaucer.

Jorjana sensed my unease. She gave a longing look toward the swings but focused her attention on me, where it belonged.

"Have you found a proper office site for your new business, Alana?"

"As a matter of fact, I have," I said. "There is a vacant space in the Town Centre. It's just upstairs from Errands, Etc."

"Lovely. And how is Stan?"

"Stan is fine," I said, willing a blush to stay put. "But he has been stressed to the limit with all the fire emergencies."

"I am very happy that you are going forward with your plans as a consultant. And that you have a man worthy of you," Jorjana said. "When I think of that awful Jones person…"

"Not to worry." I took her hands, cold as ice, and rubbed them gently in my own. "Jackson Jones fooled all of us."

"I cannot believe how gullible we were to a total stranger."

"Remember whom we were dealing with," I said to her. "Jackson Jones did come from a respectable family. But he was the quintessential ne'er-do-well son. He turned his back on his family."

"But he lied about his father passing away, Alana." Jorjana shivered at the thought. "What sort of person lies about the well-being of his parents?"

We had discussed this story a dozen times but she seemed obsessed with rehashing everything. Jackson's falling out with his father. Jackson following Carly into the dark world of art thefts. Jackson befriending David and Jorjana in an effort to find Carly's hideout. And then the sad appearance of Jackson's hale and hearty father at the arraignment.

I kept rubbing her hands. "Yes, he did. He lied about all of it. The only reason he pretended to help me was that he didn't know where Carly was going to deliver the painting. Once he learned that, I was of no use to him."

"That man must be imprisoned forever!" Jorjana said.

"He'll be put away for a long time," I said. "Along with the rest of Carly's gang."

"It is so important to know just whom one associates with," Jorjana mused.

I could tell she was tired. She ended her sentence with a preposition. But, ever the optimist, she looked to the future.

"When do you think it would be appropriate to resume Sunday Brunch?"

The fires had put a temporary halt to Sunday Brunch as everyone in town was too busy dealing with the disaster to socialize. But Jorjana, generous as always, had opened the York estate to weary firefighters and anyone else seeking shelter. David, Franklin, the York staff, and I had run ourselves ragged fetching food, water, and cots.

The best of Malibu comes out in a disaster. There's nothing like a twenty-foot wave of fire racing at you at sixty miles per hour to help you get your priorities straight. Neighbors help neighbors and strangers become friends.

Not that my priorities were ever out of line. A photo of me setting up cots in the York dining hall ran on the front page of the *Malibu Times*. Did wonders to help in the restoration of my good name. Knocked the story of Carly Cortez and Jackson Jones back to the third page. It drove CiCi DiCarlo nuts. What with her planning a big comeback with a movie starring her as the heroine in the Save the Bay robbery. Like she was the one who faced a wall of cops with a gun held to her head.

Then again, if not for a skittish zebra, it all could have turned out horribly wrong.

"Let's go home and have a cocktail and discuss the next Sunday Brunch," I said.

"But it is only two thirty," she protested.

"It's five o'clock somewhere."

THE END

About the Author

M. A. Simonetti is a graduate of the University of Washington's Mystery Writing Program. A former caterer, she divides her time between the Pacific Northwest and Southern California. She is currently working on the next Malibu Mystery featuring Alana Fox. Visit her website at www.masimonetti.com

Made in the USA
Charleston, SC
14 November 2010